Killing by Numbers

An Oxford Murder Mystery

Bridget Hart Book 2

M S MORRIS

This book is a work of fiction and, except in the case
of historical fact, any resemblance to actual persons,
living or dead, is purely coincidental.

M S Morris have asserted their right under the
Copyright, Designs and Patents Act 1988 to be identified
as the author of this work.

Published by Landmark Media, a division of
Landmark Internet Ltd.

Copyright © 2020 Margarita Morris & Steve Morris

msmorrisbooks.com

CHAPTER 1

Gabriel Quinn had spent a lot of time thinking about death. But when it came for him, it didn't happen the way he'd imagined.

In his mind's eye he'd pictured the Four Horsemen on their steeds, brandishing swords and tridents, trampling sinners underfoot. His dreams had featured deadly plagues, fiery pits and seven-headed monsters. He'd spent hours poring over images of Hell and the Apocalypse – elaborate images of exquisite detail and craftsmanship, drawn by an artist with a God-given skill that surpassed all others. His girlfriend said he was obsessed. But Gabriel knew that death could be sudden and violent, and in that respect, at least, he wasn't wrong.

At first he wasn't sure what had happened. He heard a car horn and smelled burning rubber. Not the trumpet of the angel of death. Not the stink of brimstone. When he forced his eyes open, a big man in a checked shirt with a huge camera slung around his neck was leaning over him. Definitely not St Peter.

'Hey, buddy, you all right there?'

American. A tourist.

Gabriel suspected he was far from all right. One minute he'd been cycling along Oxford High Street and now he was lying in the middle of the road with a searing pain in the centre of his chest. Gasping for breath, he squinted at the man's jowly features and tried to figure out what had happened.

He'd just come from Jonathan Wright's art gallery which was displaying some of his paintings along with those of other former students of the Ruskin School of Art. Jonathan was a big supporter of local artists and liked to promote the work of those at the start of their careers. The exhibition had opened just over a week ago, and sales were looking promising. He'd gone to the gallery to discuss substituting some of the sold paintings for new canvases. With any luck his embryonic career was about to take off.

But then Gabriel had seen something that chilled him to the bone. He had left the gallery in a state. It was imperative that he speak to Todd Lee who ran the art supply shop on Broad Street. He had to see Todd straightaway and tell him what he'd found. That was why he'd been cycling along the High Street in such a hurry.

It all started to make sense to him now. For weeks he'd had the feeling he was in danger. Call it a gut reaction, or a sixth sense, whatever you like. A creeping sensation that caused him to look over his shoulder every other minute. Whenever he glanced around there was always someone with a camera or an iPhone pointed in his direction. Spies. That's what they were.

That woman in the red summer coat outside the University Church who'd pointed her lens in his direction while he was unlocking his bicycle. He'd instinctively put up a hand to avoid being photographed. The couple eating ice creams who'd swerved into his path as he wheeled his bike onto the road. The bearded man in the gallery peering at him while he talked to Jonathan. It was impossible to distinguish innocent bystanders from those who were involved.

And now this latest discovery. He had to speak to

Todd. Shaking with nerves, he'd jumped on his bike and pedalled away as fast as he could, overtaking the open-topped sightseeing bus that had stopped to let people on and off.

And then what had happened? He remembered signalling right and pulling into the centre of the road, ready to turn into Turl Street. But then a car had pulled up on his left-hand side. A black car. The driver's window was lowered. Gabriel had looked at the man and noted the close-cropped hair, the two-day-old stubble, the designer sunglasses (Ray-Bans) and the single black stud earring. He had an acute eye for detail and could have drawn the man's likeness in a matter of minutes. It was a gift.

But then he'd seen the barrel of the gun, aimed straight at him. Death was not riding a pale, skeletal horse, but driving a Toyota.

Everything seemed to happen at once. A sudden, sharp pain. The smell of exhaust fumes as the car sped away. The world turning upside down as he lost control of his bike. Landing on the road with an almighty thump. And now a growing crowd of people, following the lead of the American tourist, leaning over him.

'Oh my God, Frank! He's been shot. Look at the blood on his chest.' This from a short, blonde woman who was presumably the American tourist's wife. 'Dial 911. Quick!'

'It's 999 in England, Martha,' said Frank, reaching for his phone.

Numbers. 911. 999. It's important to know the right number, thought Gabriel. If he was going to die – and his chances right now were looking less than fifty-fifty – he had to tell someone what he'd discovered. He tried to speak.

'He's saying something,' said Martha. She knelt down beside him and leaned in close. 'What is it, honey?'

Gabriel didn't know if he was making sense. His mouth was so dry he could hardly talk. His vision was starting to blur and sounds were becoming muffled. It took all his strength to form the words.

'What's that?' asked Martha. 'I couldn't hear you.'

Gabriel tried again. 'L79468235.'

'Hang on, let me write that down.'

He did his best to repeat the number. Then everything went black.

CHAPTER 2

'Did you remember to pack your toothbrush?'

'Yes, Mum. Stop fussing.'

Detective Inspector Bridget Hart pulled off the Wolvercote roundabout onto the Woodstock Road and joined the flow of traffic heading towards the centre of Oxford. Her fifteen-year-old daughter, Chloe, was in the passenger seat clutching her overnight bag on her lap and typing rapidly on her phone with two thumbs.

'And toothpaste?'

'They'll have toothpaste.'

'I guess so.'

It wasn't really the toothbrush, or potential lack thereof, that was making Bridget so anxious. It was the idea of Chloe taking the train to London on her own and staying overnight with Bridget's ex-husband, Ben, and his new girlfriend, Tamsin, who was ten years younger than Bridget and, Bridget imagined, ten pounds lighter.

Rationally, she told herself that Ben was Chloe's father, and if Chloe wanted to have a relationship with him then she shouldn't stand in her daughter's way. It was just that where Ben was concerned, Bridget found it hard to be rational. She harboured a deep-seated, visceral antipathy to her ex-husband, based, not unreasonably, on the fact that he had cheated on her (multiple times) during their brief marriage so that she now found it impossible to trust him, even where Chloe was concerned. She gripped the steering wheel and silently cursed a bus that pulled out in front of her.

'Are you all ready for this evening, Mum?' asked Chloe, interrupting Bridget's uncharitable train of thought. Miraculously her daughter appeared to have put her phone away and was making conversation. Bridget knew she should be delighted by this rare occurrence, but the way Chloe asked the question made her squirm in her seat.

'This evening? You mean going to the opera with Jonathan?'

'I mean your *date* with Jonathan,' said Chloe in an exasperated tone of voice that implied Bridget was a hopeless case where men were concerned. She probably had a point.

'Yes, I'm all ready. But I wouldn't call it a date as such.'

'What is it then?'

'We're just going to see a production of *La Bohème* at the New Theatre, that's all.' She signalled right and turned into Beaumont Street. An elegant couple descended the steps of the Randolph Hotel and climbed into a waiting taxi. A group of foreign schoolchildren were staring at their phones outside the Ashmolean Museum, indifferent to Oxford's antiquities.

'Sounds like a date to me,' said Chloe.

'Yes, well, I suppose so.' Bridget stopped at the red light outside Worcester College.

She had met Jonathan, very briefly, for the first time a couple of weeks ago. Her sister, Vanessa, had invited them both to Sunday lunch in the hope of doing a spot of matchmaking. For the happily-married Vanessa with her doting husband, two perfect children (one of each), adorable dog and comfortable family home, Bridget's single status seemed to be a constant source of anxiety, a problem needing to be fixed. But after dropping Chloe off at Vanessa's that day, Bridget hadn't been able to stay for lunch because she was in the middle of a murder enquiry – a student found dead at Christ Church – so she'd only got as far as saying a quick hello to Jonathan. Afterwards Chloe had told her what a great person he was. Jonathan had then invited her to the opening night of a new exhibition at his art gallery on the High Street. She'd gone along – at Chloe's insistence – and had enjoyed half an hour chatting to him, but then she'd had to leave early after receiving an urgent call from her sergeant. Such was the life of a detective inspector with Thames Valley Police.

'You should go for it, Mum,' said Chloe in the voice of one who seemed to be an expert on affairs of the heart.

Go for what? Bridget wondered. She didn't like to ask. Still, she'd made an effort to tidy her little house in Wolvercote in anticipation of inviting Jonathan back for a nightcap. She'd even put clean sheets on the bed, although that was probably over-anticipating things. This was only a trip to the opera after all. A first date, if you must.

She pulled into the train station car park and skilfully reversed her red Mini into the narrow space left by two much bigger cars. She loved her little car. It was nippy, easy to park and a lot more reliable than her ex-husband. Small is beautiful, she thought. It was something she told herself on a regular basis, in view of the fact that she measured only five foot two at full stretch. Chloe, on the other hand, was already, at fifteen, an impressive five foot six. In this respect, at least, it looked as if she was going to take after her father.

They crossed the footbridge over the Botley Road, and Bridget bought Chloe a return ticket from one of the machines in the station entrance.

'Phone me when you get to Paddington, won't you? Just so I know you've arrived safely.'

'Yes, Mum. And I promise not to talk to any strange men on the train.'

Bridget was about to say something in response when

she saw that Chloe was grinning at her. She hugged her daughter and gave her a kiss. 'Have a lovely time.'

'You too, Mum.'

She watched as Chloe went through the ticket barrier and disappeared from view. She really must try not to turn into one of those tiresomely neurotic mothers, always worrying and nagging about the least little thing. Her own mother had been terrible in that respect, but then that was hardly surprising after what happened to Bridget's younger sister, Abigail.

As Bridget turned to leave, her phone began to vibrate in her bag. She glanced at the screen before answering. Chief Superintendent Grayson. God, that man had a knack of choosing the wrong moment. She was due at the hairdresser's in half an hour, an emergency appointment to touch up a few grey strands that had just started to appear, like unwelcome intruders, in her medium-brown bob. She had stared at them in disbelief in the mirror, wondering how they could have suddenly materialised, just when she was about to go on her first date in years. She wasn't even forty yet.

'Hello?' She stepped outside the station, straight into the path of the smokers congregating there to light up.

'DI Hart, we've got an incident on the High Street.' Grayson always dispensed with pleasantries and got straight to the point.

'What sort of incident?' She waved away the smoke from a nearby cigarette and walked down the steps. The air there was probably even filthier, thanks to the diesel fumes from idling taxis.

'Cyclist killed.'

'Isn't that a job for the traffic cops?' Accidents involving cyclists were an all too common occurrence in a city with hundreds of students riding bikes. Sometimes it was the fault of the car driver, sometimes the fault of the cyclist. Deaths were rare, but not unheard of.

'Reports say he was shot.'

Bridget stopped walking. 'Shot?' Gun crime in the city

of dreaming spires was practically non-existent.

'Uniform from St Aldate's are down there now but this looks like a murder and I need a detective to take charge.'

'Isn't anyone else available?'

'I'd like you to lead the investigation.'

'I see.' She ought to have been pleased that she was his first choice to head up the case. It had been a long, hard slog to get to this point in her career. Having a child at a young age had held her back. Now with Chloe less dependent on her she'd finally started to make a go of things, recently leading her first murder enquiry. That had been touch and go at times, with Grayson wanting to take her off the case and replace her with a more experienced detective when things started to heat up, but she'd fought her corner, kept the case and ultimately solved it. Grayson had even congratulated her and her team in the end, but she still felt as if she needed to prove herself to him, to demonstrate that the last case hadn't been just a lucky fluke.

She took a deep breath. How would the Chief Super react if she told him it was her day off and she had a hair appointment? Somehow she didn't think he would be understanding.

'I'll get down there right away,' she said.

'Keep me updated.' Grayson ended the call.

On the way back to her car, she called the hairdresser's to cancel.

CHAPTER 3

A shooting was such a rare event in Oxford that Bridget wondered what she was going to find when she arrived at the scene. This wasn't a tough inner city. Any guns in this part of the world were typically used for shooting pheasants and partridges. Grayson was demonstrating considerable confidence in her, assigning the case to her instead of one of the more experienced detectives like Davis or Baxter. She hoped she was up to the challenge.

As she turned onto St Aldate's, the dome of Tom Tower loomed up ahead, reminding her of her previous case – the murder of a female student at Christ Church. Her first murder investigation since being promoted to detective inspector. She would never be able to visit the college or the cathedral again without thinking of the beautiful and intelligent young woman who had been battered to death. Such a tragedy.

With Trinity term now over, the undergraduates had left the city, or "gone down" in Oxford-speak, making way for an influx of summer students and conference guests who would stay in rooms overlooking idyllic quadrangles and dine in great halls. At this time of year there was also a huge surge in tourists who flocked to Oxford from all over the world, drawn by the city's renown as home of the oldest university in the English-speaking world, and by its medieval architecture and dreaming spires.

But Oxford wasn't all punting and poetry. The traffic, for one thing, was diabolical. St Aldate's was, as usual, heaving with double decker buses, made worse by the fact that the police had sealed off the top of the road at Carfax so that no one could turn onto the High Street. A hapless traffic cop who looked new to the job was doing her best to re-route buses down Queen Street.

Bridget managed to manoeuvre the Mini around the obstacle course of buses, showed her ID to the officer guarding the crossroads and was granted access to the High Street. A couple of marked police cars were slewed across the road, their blue lights flashing. An ambulance stood with its rear doors open, but no siren sounding. When life had expired there was no urgency to get back to the hospital. She could see that armed police had been called in and were conducting a search of the area, going in and out of the shops and cafés along this stretch of the High Street. They would be concerned that the shooter might still be at large. With the traffic stopped and pedestrians being held at bay, there was an eerie silence to the centre of the city, normally bustling with life.

A bright orange Subaru parked next to the ambulance could mean only one thing. Detective Sergeant Jake Derwent must already be here. She'd worked with him on the last case and appreciated his down-to-earth manner. She pulled up behind his car and soon spotted him standing head and shoulders above everyone else around. At six foot five he made her feel like even more of a midget than usual. He was interviewing a group of bystanders about the incident, scribbling in his notebook.

He spotted her approaching and a welcoming smile spread across his face. 'Morning, ma'am.' He stooped slightly when he spoke to her. 'I was just taking a few witness statements.'

'Good. What's the situation so far?'

Jake frowned at his notebook. 'No one's completely sure what happened. At first people thought that the cyclist had been knocked off his bike but then Mrs Harris over here' – he pointed towards a middle-aged woman who was being comforted by a man, presumably her husband, with a huge camera slung around his neck – 'noticed that he'd been shot. They called the emergency services.'

'Let me speak to them,' said Bridget. She approached the couple, who looked badly shaken but seemed only too happy to co-operate. The man shook her hand with an iron grip and introduced himself as Frank Harris, retired bank manager from Houston, Texas. His wife's name was Martha. She was a small, round woman who made Bridget think of homemade apple pie. Frank explained that they'd been in London and this was their first day in Oxford where they would stay a couple of nights at the Randolph before moving on to Stratford-upon-Avon, then York and Edinburgh. The usual tourist trail.

'We'd just come out of that quaint little street over there,' drawled Frank, pointing towards Turl Street, 'and I was saying to Martha we should go take a look at the University Church and maybe climb the spire to get a good view, when this cyclist topples off his bike and lands on the road like a sack of potatoes. It all happened so quickly, didn't it Martha?'

Martha nodded her head in agreement. 'That poor boy.'

'I went over to him and asked if he was all right,' continued Frank, 'but then Martha noticed the red stain on his chest and said he'd been shot. That's not the kinda thing we expected to see in England, did we Martha?'

'We certainly didn't.' She dabbed her eyes with a handkerchief.

'And did either of you see who fired the shot?' asked Bridget. How could a man be shot in broad daylight in the middle of Oxford High Street without someone seeing or hearing something?'

'I noticed a black car,' said Martha. 'Don't ask me what make it was because I don't know English cars, but it pulled up next to the cyclist right before it happened and then it sped away like a bat out of hell, didn't it Frank?'

'It sure did. It was going that way.' Frank pointed towards Carfax tower. With Cornmarket permanently closed to traffic, and Queen Street open only to buses, Bridget deduced that the car must have gone down St Aldate's, the way she had just come.

'What about the driver?' she asked. 'Did you see who was behind the wheel?'

Both Frank and Martha shook their heads. 'Sorry. We didn't get a proper look.'

'And what time was this?'

Frank thought for a moment. 'Just after eleven o'clock, I think.'

'That's right, honey,' confirmed Martha. 'We'd stopped for a coffee at that nice little café on Turl Street, and you looked at your watch, Frank, and said we should get a move on if we wanted to avoid the crowds at the University Church.'

'Thank you,' said Bridget. 'That's very helpful.'

'Oh, there was one other thing,' said Martha.

'What was that?'

'Well, before he... before he passed away, the poor boy tried to speak.'

'What did he say?'

'Well, that's the strangest thing. It was a number.'

'Can you remember what it was?'

'Sure.' Martha reached into her handbag and pulled out a little pocket diary. 'I wrote it down here so I wouldn't forget.' She put on her reading glasses which were hanging on a gold chain around her neck. 'It was actually a letter followed by a string of numbers. L79468235. He repeated it twice and seemed very keen that someone should know it.'

'He didn't say anything else?'

'No.'

Bridget turned the number over in her mind, but it didn't mean anything to her. It seemed like a very odd thing to utter with your dying breath. It might be significant or it might not; it was too early to tell at this stage of the investigation.

'Make a note of that number,' she told Jake, 'then see if you can find anyone else who saw a black car accelerating away from the scene.'

Bridget thanked the American couple for their help and instructed a uniformed officer to take their statements. Then she braced herself to approach the white screen that had been erected around the victim. A dead body was never an easy thing to look at, especially when the death had been violent.

Dr Sarah Walker, forensic medical examiner, was kneeling by the corpse, doing her final checks. Meanwhile, the head of the scene of crime team, Vikram Vijayaraghavan, better known as Vik, was busy taking photos of the deceased and his injuries.

Bridget kept back so as not to get in the way, and contemplated the dead man. He was young, no more than mid-twenties, with a thin, pallid face, framed by a wispy beard. His clothes – faded jeans, fraying white T-shirt and worn plimsolls – suggested someone who didn't spend a lot of time on his appearance or perhaps couldn't afford to. The overall effect was one of fragility. In the middle of the T-shirt a red stain had bloomed and spread, like one of those ink blot psychological tests. There were other spots of colour on the fabric – blue, green, purple – that might have been paint. The bicycle lay to one side, apparently undamaged. It was a rusty old thing with a bell on the handlebars and threadbare tyres.

On seeing Bridget, Dr Walker rose to her feet. A similar age to Bridget, Sarah Walker was single, and unlike Bridget her career had not been held back by the inconvenience of children. They had worked together briefly before, and Bridget found her polite, serious and above all professional. Bridget would have liked to get to know her better, ideally over a glass or two of wine, but the circumstances of their meetings invariably involved a corpse and little opportunity for small talk.

'Hi,' said Bridget. 'Any conclusions so far?' It was rare for a medical examiner or pathologist to make any firm pronouncement at the scene of the crime, but Bridget was always hopeful.

'A single gunshot wound to the chest at close range,' said Dr Walker gravely. 'The bullet either entered the heart itself or tore one of the coronary arteries resulting in massive haemorrhaging. The victim would have bled out very quickly. We'll know more when Roy Andrews does the post-mortem.'

Dr Roy Andrews was the senior pathologist at the John Radcliffe hospital, a lugubrious Scot with a taste in fancy bow ties.

'A bullet right in the heart?' queried Bridget. 'What are the chances of that happening?'

Dr Walker smiled enigmatically. 'That's not my department. It might have been the victim's unlucky day, or maybe the shooter knew exactly what he was aiming for.'

Vik joined them. 'The victim had a small amount of cash in his back pocket, but no credit cards or any other form of ID.' He held up a couple of plastic evidence bags. 'I bagged up his phone for you. And there's a key, but it doesn't look like a standard house key. It's too small.'

'Thanks,' said Bridget. A phone was always a big help in identifying a victim and finding next of kin.

'Can we move him to the morgue now?' asked Dr Walker.

'Please do,' said Bridget. The sooner they cleared the street and re-opened it to normal business, the better.

'Ma'am?' Jake strode towards her, accompanied by a man in a bus driver's uniform and a young woman with a mobile phone. 'I've been speaking to the driver of the tour bus. He confirms seeing a black car speeding away from the scene. Says it was a Toyota. And this lady' – he indicated the young woman – 'has caught the car on a video she was filming from the top of the bus.' The open-topped double-decker bus was parked to one side, its passengers dispersed.

'It's not a great video,' said the woman. She held her phone out and pressed play. The film showed the view from the top of the bus as it approached Carfax tower. The voice of the tour guide was just audible in the background, explaining how the tower was all that remained of the twelfth-century St Martin's church, and how no new building in the city was allowed to be taller than Carfax tower. About thirty seconds into the video, a black Toyota overtook the bus and pulled up alongside a cyclist. An arm emerged from the car window holding what looked like a gun. It wasn't possible to see any more of the driver from this angle. A sound like a loud click followed and the cyclist toppled from his bike. Then the car accelerated away from the scene at high speed and the video came to an abrupt halt.

'I had to slam my brakes on,' the bus driver was saying, 'or I'd have run over him.'

Bridget thanked the woman who'd taken the video and turned to Jake. 'Get that sent over to Ffion at Kidlington and see if she can enhance it to get the number plate.'

Detective Constable Ffion Hughes was the best person Bridget had in her team when it came to computer skills.

'I'm on it,' said Jake.

'Now, all we need is to identify the victim,' said Bridget, more to herself than anyone in particular. 'Someone must know who he is.'

'I think I might be able to help with that,' said a familiar voice behind her.

Bridget turned in surprise to see Jonathan, her date for the evening, standing there. He must have come from his art gallery which was just down the road opposite the University Church. Her heart did a little somersault at the sight of him. He really was quite a dish in his open-necked shirt and tortoiseshell glasses.

'Did you know him?' she asked, trying to keep her voice level.

Jonathan nodded, looking miserable. 'He was with me at the gallery just before this happened. His name is Gabriel Quinn. He's an artist.'

CHAPTER 4

Jonathan seemed badly shaken by what had happened, and Bridget accompanied him back to his gallery, keen to hear whatever he could tell her about Gabriel Quinn.

She had first visited Jonathan's gallery less than a fortnight earlier, enjoying a glass of wine and chatting to her host on the opening night of his latest exhibition, which was still currently on display. But an unfortunate discovery in the River Thames had put an end to that, calling her away on urgent police business. It seemed that whenever she met Jonathan socially, their encounters were destined to be brief. But today's meeting was strictly business and she felt slightly awkward in her formal capacity as detective inspector in a murder enquiry. Especially when she and Jonathan were supposed to be going to the opera together this evening. She touched the top of her head lightly, hoping he wouldn't notice the grey hairs.

The white walls of the gallery were filled with contemporary oil paintings and some limited edition prints. Jonathan's eclectic tastes matched Bridget's own, and she would have loved to buy one of the really eye-catching works. But with her floor-to-ceiling bookcases and extensive CD collection of mainly opera, there was hardly any room left on the walls of her tiny home. Vanessa, her sister, had a house big enough to take the sort of artwork normally seen only in the National Gallery, but the paintings in Jonathan's gallery were far too bold for her sister's taste. Everything in Vanessa's home had to co-ordinate with the soft furnishings.

Jonathan ushered her inside and bolted the door behind them, turning the sign on the door to closed. The last time Bridget had been here, a crowd of people had filled the space, but today with the High Street cordoned off by the police it was empty apart from a young woman sitting behind the counter.

She had corkscrew curls tied back in a bushy ponytail, and wore a worried expression on her pale, lightly freckled face. 'It wasn't Gabriel in the accident, was it?' she asked, jumping to her feet as they entered the shop.

'I'm afraid so,' said Jonathan. 'Bridget, this is Vicky, my assistant.'

Vicky suppressed a sob and held a handkerchief to her eyes. 'He was such a sweet, gentle person. How could someone run him over like that and then just drive off? Hit and run drivers make me sick.'

Bridget already knew that this was no hit and run incident. More like a shoot and run. But she didn't want to reveal too many details just yet.

'Vicky, this is Detective Inspector Bridget Hart,' said Jonathan. 'She's' – he seemed to hesitate, and Bridget wondered if he was about to introduce her as his date for the evening – 'investigating what happened.'

Vicky smiled at Bridget through her tears. 'Can I get you a cup of tea or a coffee, Inspector?'

The day was hot and Bridget realised she was parched. She was supposed to be at the hairdresser's now, getting her grey strands touched up, browsing a celebrity gossip magazine (she only ever read them at the dentist's or the hair salon) and enjoying a complimentary cappuccino. 'Thanks. Just a glass of water please.'

'There's a bottle of San Pellegrino in the cooler in my office,' said Jonathan. 'Maybe you could bring us all a glass, Vicky?'

'Sure,' said Vicky.

Bridget turned to Jonathan. 'You said Gabriel was an artist. Do you have any of his paintings on display?'

'Actually I do. He's one of half a dozen artists whose work I'm showcasing at the moment. They're all former students of the Ruskin School of Art in Oxford.'

'That's just down the High Street, isn't it?'

'Yes, the Ruskin School is next to the University Examination Schools. This group of artists graduated about five years ago. They're all up and coming, but the art world's a very precarious business. Most people who study Fine Art end up becoming art teachers in schools or else they retrain as accountants.' He gave her a wry smile. 'It's hard for young artists to make a name for themselves, so I try to support any that I think have real talent. Let me show you Gabriel's work.' He led her over to a wall hung with six brightly coloured canvases. 'These pieces are all his.'

Bridget contemplated the paintings and found that they had a strangely mesmerising effect on her. Hypnotic patterns of colour covered the canvases, drawing the viewer in so that it was hard to look away. The patterns were abstract, but seemed to suggest figures or faces that were just out of focus. On closer inspection she saw that the paintings were made up of thousands, if not millions, of tiny dots. They must have taken ages to produce.

'Gabriel was very interested in numbers,' said Jonathan. 'You might say it was something of an obsession. This series of paintings all have numbers in the title.'

Bridget examined the labels next to the canvases. The paintings had titles like *Two million and thirty-six* or *Two to the power of thirty-eight*.

'What do the numbers refer to?' she asked.

'That's part of the paintings' mystique,' said Jonathan. 'Gabriel attached deep significance to his work, but I can't say I really understood the mathematics behind the images.'

Bridget remembered the number that Gabriel had spoken as he lay dying in the middle of the road. She pulled her notebook out of her bag. 'Does he have a painting called L79468235?'

Jonathan shook his head. 'I haven't come across that one, but it's possible it's something new he was working on. Gabriel was a real perfectionist. I imagine he'd hate anyone to see an unfinished work. He'd probably prefer it to be destroyed.'

Oh well, it was worth a try. Bridget put her notebook back in her bag just as Vicky reappeared with three glasses of sparkling water on a tray. Bridget accepted a glass and took a grateful gulp of the refreshing liquid. 'Was Gabriel a successful artist?' she asked. His paintings were all priced between £300 and £500 depending on their size. Two of them had red dots on the accompanying cards to show that they had been sold.

'That depends on your definition of success,' said Jonathan. 'None of the artists here are famous names yet, but if any of them had the potential to make it big, it was Gabriel. As you can see, I'd already sold a couple of his paintings. That's why I invited him round this morning, to speak to him about getting some new ones in to replace them.'

'And how did Gabriel seem this morning? Did you notice anything unusual?'

'Well, he could be a bit of an oddity at the best of times. Perhaps he did seem a little on edge, but he was always rather shy and introverted. He wasn't a great talker, but there were hidden depths in that head of his.'

'I always liked him,' said Vicky, who had resumed her seat behind the counter. 'He was very modest, despite being so talented. One or two of these others' – she indicated the work of the artists on display – 'seem to think they're God's gift and should be worth millions. Gabriel was never like that.'

'Where did he live?' asked Bridget. 'Did he have any family?'

'He never mentioned any family,' said Jonathan. 'He lived alone on a boat on the Oxford Canal. *La Belle Dame*. Let me write the name down for you.'

He wrote the name on the back of a postcard that showed one of Gabriel's paintings. The postcards were stacked on the counter, next to a Sotheby's catalogue. 'I could also give you the phone number of his former tutor at the Ruskin School of Art if that would be helpful. She might be able to tell you more about him.'

'Thanks,' said Bridget.

Jonathan checked on his phone and wrote a number on the back of the postcard. 'Her name is Dr Melissa Price.'

Bridget dropped the postcard into her bag. It was a reproduction of the painting she'd liked best, the one titled *Two to the power of thirty-eight*. She herself was thirty-eight, not such a bad age. Could she justify buying the painting for her tiny house? It was relatively small and would just fill the space above the sofa, not to mention hiding the cracks in the plaster. But this was a murder investigation, not a shopping spree. Her team would be waiting for her at Thames Valley Police headquarters in Kidlington. Not to mention Chief Superintendent Grayson, who would want an update as soon as she entered the building.

She finished the rest of her water. 'Thanks for your help. I'd better get going.'

Jonathan unbolted the door and stepped outside with her. 'Are we still on for this evening?'

Bridget hesitated. She really wanted to go to the opera with Jonathan – *La Bohème* was one of her favourites – but she'd probably be up to her ears in work now. The first twenty-four hours on a case were always crucial.

'I'm not sure,' she said. 'I'll have to let you know. Sorry.'

He nodded understandingly, but she could see the disappointment in his eyes. This would be the second time she had let him down. Her work was developing a habit of coming between the two of them.

'I'll be in touch,' she said.

The High Street had reopened, and her Mini was creating an obstacle for the buses, taxis and cyclists jostling to get past. A bus tooted its horn at her as she returned to the car. She fixed the driver with an angry glare. A carelessly-parked car was hardly a matter of life and death.

CHAPTER 5

Before setting off for HQ, Bridget checked her phone for messages and was alarmed to discover two missed calls from Chloe. She'd been so preoccupied for the last couple of hours that she'd completely forgotten about her daughter. What sort of mother did that make her? She pressed quick dial and waited anxiously for Chloe to pick up. What if she'd been mugged at Paddington? Knife crime was a growing problem in the capital. What if Ben hadn't turned up to collect her and she'd been left on her own? This seemed a more likely scenario.

'Hi, Mum.' The voice on the other end of the line sounded bright and chirpy. Not mugged, then. She really must stop anticipating the worst all the time.

'Is everything all right?' asked Bridget.

'Yes, of course it is. Why wouldn't it be?'

'It's just that you called twice and I didn't pick up because I'm in the middle of a new case. When I saw you'd called I got worried and –'

'Chill, Mum. Everything's good. I was just calling to let you know I'd arrived. Like you asked me to,' Chloe added with only a slight hint of reproach in her voice.

It was supposed to be reassuring, knowing that your offspring were just at the other end of a phone call, but somehow it added to the stress of being a parent, this constant need to stay connected. Part of Bridget wished for a simpler, more innocent age.

'Where are you now?' she asked.

'In a cab heading up to Highgate.'

'Did Dad meet you at the station?'

'No, I got into a car with a strange man.' Ominous pause. 'Of course Dad met me at the station. Stop freaking out, Mum.'

Bridget realised how annoying she was being. She recalled similar exchanges with her own mother, although of course they had taken place without the benefit (or curse) of a mobile phone. Why was she subjecting her daughter to the same treatment? 'Sorry, it's just that I've had quite a stressful morning.'

'I thought you were going to the hairdresser's.'

'Change of plan.'

'Well don't change your plans for this evening. Do you want to speak to Dad?'

Not really, thought Bridget, but she didn't want to spoil Chloe's good mood. 'All right then, put him on.'

She could hear Chloe handing over the phone and then Ben's voice, loud and confident as always. 'Hi, Bridget, how are things?'

Oh, you know, she thought, just dealing with a murder enquiry. And worrying about my teenage daughter. 'Fine,' she said. 'Good.'

'Great. Listen, got to go, we're just arriving at the house. And don't worry. I'll look after her and make sure she's on the right train tomorrow. Enjoy your evening.' And with that Ben ended the call.

For a moment Bridget sat with the phone in her hand, breathing heavily. Speaking to Ben always made her so uptight. Even now he had the power to upset her, just by the casual way he acted, as if his serial infidelities had been nothing more than an oversight on his part. His cheating had dealt Bridget a body blow, leaving her vulnerable, with a young daughter to bring up single-handedly, knocking her career into the slow lane. Of course, it hadn't held Ben's career back one jot. He had moved to London and now held a senior position with the Metropolitan Police. What angered her most was that he had never once apologised for his behaviour. She was still waiting after all these years for him to say the words, 'I'm sorry.'

She put the phone back in her bag and told herself to relax. Ben was far away, and she was a DI now with an important case to solve. Chloe would be fine and she wouldn't thank Bridget for checking up on her every five minutes. And there was still just a chance that she might make the opera with Jonathan this evening.

She looked at her watch. God, it was already gone two. Grayson would be twitching for an update. She was surprised he hadn't already called her. She turned the key in the ignition and set off for Kidlington.

★

Thames Valley Police headquarters was located about three miles north of the Oxford ring road in the sprawling village of Kidlington. It took Bridget half an hour to drive there from the city centre up the Banbury Road, and by the time she arrived she was starving. She had promised herself a healthy salad for lunch in town, but like the rest of her plans for the day, that had come to nothing. She grabbed a coffee, a bag of crisps and a chocolate bar from the vending machine before heading into the main incident room.

She was pleased to see that Jake had got things organised and was working alongside Ffion Hughes, the young Welsh detective constable who had joined the team for the last case, causing heads to turn whenever she strode into the office in her skintight green motorcycle leathers.

A small team of detectives had assembled in the

incident room, starting to gather together the initial witness statements, the scene of crime evidence and the mounds of paperwork that would hopefully lead them to the killer. Bridget recognised Ryan Hooper and Andy Cartwright, two sergeants who had worked with her before. That was good. With a familiar team in place they would be able to hit the ground running. Although Ryan could be a bit of a joker, he was a hard worker and a good police officer, and Andy was always solid and dependable.

'So, what have you got for me so far?' she asked, tearing open the bag of crisps. Salt and vinegar had been the only flavour left in the machine. It was her least favourite, the smell reminding her of a particularly dreary childhood holiday by the sea in Poole, Dorset, spent mostly sheltering from the wind and rain.

'I managed to enhance the number plate of the car in the video,' said Ffion in her singsong Welsh accent. 'And I've got a match from the database.' As well as being enviably slim and stunningly good-looking with her elfin features and pixie haircut, Ffion was rapidly gaining a reputation as the office tech wizard. 'The vehicle is a Toyota Prius, registered to a car-hire company in East Oxford.' Ffion wrote the number plate, make and model on a piece of paper and handed it to Bridget.

'Wow, good work,' said Bridget. 'Jake, can you get over to the car-hire company right away and get the driver's details?'

'Will do.'

'What else do we have?'

'The body's in the morgue,' said Jake, 'and I've arranged for the post-mortem to take place first thing on Monday. Vik and the SOCO team have filed the physical evidence from the scene, and we've interviewed all the witnesses. None of them said anything you haven't already heard.'

'Okay,' said Bridget. 'I've got an ID for the victim. Gabriel Quinn, an artist living on a boat on the Oxford Canal. That key he was carrying is probably the key to the boat. We'll go and check it out next.' She looked around the room. Everyone was busy, staring at screens, typing at their keyboards. She didn't want to interrupt them now, but she would gather everyone together for a briefing after speaking to the Chief. 'Any ideas about the string of numbers that Gabriel uttered before he died?' she asked.

'We've been giving it some thought,' said Jake. 'We have a few ideas.'

'It might be a bank account,' said Ffion. 'Bank accounts have eight digits, although Gabriel's number has a letter before it.'

'What about a telephone number?' asked Ryan, who had come over to join them. Ryan rarely passed up an opportunity to spend time in Ffion's vicinity.

'No. Telephone numbers have ten or eleven digits and start with zero,' said Ffion, batting away Ryan's suggestion like an unwelcome insect.

'What about a driving licence?' he suggested, sounding less hopeful.

'Sixteen alphanumeric characters,' said Ffion dismissively.

'A passport number, then?'

'Nine digits,' said Ffion, shaking her head.

'It could be a company registration number,' suggested Jake. 'They have eight digits.'

'Or the serial number for a boat,' said Ffion, 'or an eight-digit barcode…'

'Okay, I get the picture,' said Bridget. 'A bit of investigation needed, I think. Can I leave that with you, Ffion? Let's get this hire car checked out first.'

'I'm on it,' said Jake, grabbing his jacket and heading for the door.

Bridget made a call to Vik and arranged for a team to go and look over Gabriel's canal boat. She planned to join them and see for herself where Gabriel had lived, but she'd barely replaced the receiver before she heard Chief Superintendent Grayson's stentorious tones summoning her into his office. She gulped down a last mouthful of cold coffee and headed for the glass fishbowl that was the Chief Super's domain.

Grayson sat behind his enormous desk, his back bolt-straight, drumming his fingers impatiently on the polished surface. He was never an easy man to please. Bridget took the chair opposite, hoping that her progress so far would be enough to placate him. Although Grayson had praised her success at solving the case of the murdered student at Christ Church and had even stood the team a round at the pub as a token of his appreciation, Bridget knew she couldn't afford to bask in past glories. All that mattered now was how quickly she could get on top of this new murder.

'Give me the essentials,' he said.

'Well,' said Bridget, 'the victim was a young man, mid-twenties, by the name of Gabriel Quinn. He appears to have been shot at point blank range from a car on the High Street. We've identified the vehicle as a Toyota Prius belonging to a car-hire company in East Oxford. Sergeant Jake Derwent is on his way there now to get details of the driver.'

'Hmm,' said Grayson. 'Any idea what kind of weapon was used?'

'Not yet. Hopefully ballistics will be able to tell us more. But one thing strikes me as odd.'

'Yes?'

'No one reported hearing a gun being fired. I know that it was a busy location, but I've seen a video of the incident, and all I could hear was a noise something like a loud click, not the deafening crack you'd expect from a normal firearm. I'm thinking that the shooter may have used a silencer.'

'Sounds like a gangland execution,' said Grayson, furrowing his brow.

'A professional hit?'

'Not your usual Oxford crime, at any rate. Who was this Gabriel Quinn? What do we know about him?'

'He was an artist.'

'An artist?' Grayson's tone suggested that he classed artists along with other social misfits, subversives and generally worthless individuals. Bridget suspected that his politics were not very liberal. 'What on earth is an *artist* doing getting himself shot? What sort of artist was he anyway?'

Bridget reached into her bag, pulled out the postcard of Gabriel's painting, and passed it across the desk.

Grayson grunted unenthusiastically.

The Chief Super was evidently not a big fan of modern art, or perhaps art of any kind. The only pictures on display in his office were photographs of himself on various golf courses and one of him and his wife at an official function in the Town Hall with the city's mayor.

'It's called *Two to the power of thirty-eight*,' she told him.

'What in God's name is that supposed to mean?'

'The title is part of the work's mystique,' she said, quoting Jonathan. She felt strangely compelled to defend the artist's work, whether because she'd felt drawn to it herself, or because Jonathan was clearly a fan, she wasn't sure. 'Jonathan told me that Gabriel was very interested in mathematics, and in numbers in particular.'

'Jonathan?'

Bridget felt her cheeks growing hot. 'The gallery owner who identified the victim.'

Grayson studied her for a moment before pushing the postcard back across the desk. Bridget quickly tucked it away in her bag.

'If you say so,' said Grayson. 'Can't say art galleries are my thing. The wife likes them' – he glanced at the photograph of Mrs Grayson on his desk – 'but I prefer golf courses myself.'

'Yes, sir.' Bridget paused, wondering if she should mention the other fact relevant to the case. Would Grayson even consider it to be relevant? 'There was one other thing.'

'Yes?'

'Just before he died, Gabriel communicated an eight

digit number to a witness on the scene.'

Grayson looked as if this latest piece of information confirmed all his worst suspicions about artists and their ilk. 'What does the number refer to?'

'We don't know yet,' admitted Bridget. 'But it's one line of enquiry.'

'I hope you've got others.'

'Certainly. Like I said, Sergeant Derwent is on his way to the car-hire company, and I'm about to go down to Gabriel's canal boat. SOCO should be there already. The post-mortem is scheduled for the first available slot.'

'Good. You didn't have any plans for the weekend, did you?'

Bridget thought with longing of the opera which she was almost certainly not going to see after all. 'No, sir. Nothing important.'

CHAPTER 6

Bridget would have liked to take Jake to accompany her to the canal boat. She appreciated his calm and level-headed nature. But with Jake out at the car-hire company, she chose Ffion instead. It was always good to have two pairs of eyes when visiting a site that might hold clues to a crime, and Ffion's emerald green eyes were as sharp as they came.

The young detective constable slid effortlessly into the passenger seat of the Mini, like a cat folding itself into its basket. Clad in skintight black trousers and a leather jacket, she seemed so lithe and supple, Bridget wondered if it was natural or if she practised yoga in her spare time. Bridget had tried a yoga class once and had barely been able to walk for a week afterwards. But it wasn't hard to imagine Ffion sitting for hours in the lotus position at a mountain-top retreat. There was something aloof and detached about the Welsh woman. Despite working closely together on her previous murder case, Bridget still felt she hardly knew Ffion at all.

'How are you settling in to Kidlington?' she asked as they drove down the Banbury Road into Oxford. Ffion had transferred from the Reading office just a couple of months ago. It wasn't always easy settling in to a new work environment, especially as a woman, and Bridget wanted to be the sort of boss who supported other women at the start of their careers.

'It's fine,' said Ffion brightly.

'Getting on all right with the rest of the team?' By that, Bridget primarily meant Jake and Ryan. Despite the equality and diversity training they all underwent these days, office banter could still be very male-orientated, and if left to themselves the guys could easily lapse into a discussion focusing largely on football, beer and girls. Bridget guessed that the subject of DC Ffion Hughes, as one of the few female detectives on the team, might sometimes enter into their debate.

'I think I can handle the boys,' said Ffion, a distinct note of amusement in her voice.

I'm sure you can, thought Bridget, smiling to herself. She had no doubt that Ffion would put them in their place if they ever stepped out of line.

She turned the car into Beaumont Street, following the same route she'd taken that morning with Chloe. What was Chloe doing now? Out with Ben in London, no doubt. And with Tamsin too. What kind of impression would Ben's new girlfriend be making on Chloe? Tamsin was so much closer in age to Chloe, they might have a lot in common. Bridget sincerely hoped not. She wanted to keep Chloe all to herself. The girl was growing up so fast, she only had three more years left at school and then she'd be off to university. Or maybe she would want to go backpacking around the world instead. Either way, she'd be gone. Bridget's heart lurched at the thought.

She parked in Worcester Street public car park, slotting the Mini into a tight corner that had been avoided by other drivers. From there they headed down to the nearby canal, picking up the towpath by the bridge over Castle Mill Stream, an offshoot of the River Thames. This was where the canal started, or ended, depending on how you looked at it. With the gently flowing stream on one side and the tree-lined canal on the other, a feeling of tranquillity descended as soon as they left the bridge behind, even though they were still just a stone's throw from Oxford's traffic-laden streets. Bridget quite fancied the idea of living on a canal boat herself, being able to sail away to a new location whenever she felt like it.

La Belle Dame was moored a few hundred yards from the bridge, next to another boat called *Dragonfly*. Unfortunately *La Belle Dame* was no longer very belle. The red paintwork was peeling, and the hull revealed distinct patches of rust. The grime on the windows was so thick in places that it was impossible to see inside. *Dragonfly*, on the other hand, was in pristine condition and looked like a contender for the Britain in Bloom competition. The deck and roof were a riot of flowering pot plants of every shape and colour, from vivid violets to summery yellows and strident reds. Their fragrance wafted over Bridget as she walked along the tow path. The green-fingered owner of the boat, a middle-aged woman with silver hair, was sitting on a deck chair amongst her horticultural charges, anxiously watching proceedings on *La Belle Dame* as the SOCO team went about their business, searching for any clues as to why someone would have shot dead its owner.

'Hello,' called Bridget. 'You must be Gabriel Quinn's neighbour.' She introduced herself and Ffion.

The woman got to her feet and stepped nimbly off the boat onto the bank. Dressed in faded pink dungarees over a man's checked shirt, and with a large straw hat perched lopsidedly on her head, she was every inch the true English eccentric. Bridget wondered what Superintendent Grayson would make of her. The woman extended a cautious hand. 'I'm Harriet Watson, but everyone calls me Hat.' Her accent was local, with a strong rural flavour. She drew out the "a" in Hat, adding a hint of an "r" to the vowel sound.

Bridget shook her hand, which was hard and calloused. Bridget supposed it was a tough life living on a canal boat.

Hat was probably in her late forties or early fifties but her weathered face made her look older. 'I let the police have a key to Gabriel's boat when they turned up and told me what had happened. I can't believe it. Is it true?' Harriet seemed flustered and on the brink of tears.

'I'm sorry,' said Bridget, 'but I'm afraid it is.'

'Oh dear.' Harriet pulled an enormous handkerchief from the pocket of her dungarees and dabbed at her eyes. 'The poor boy.'

'How long had you known Gabriel?'

'We'd been neighbours on the canal for five years, ever since he first started living on the boat,' said Harriet. 'We kept an eye out for each other. When you live afloat, it's special you see. Not like living in an ordinary house.'

'Did Gabriel have any relatives?'

Harriet shook her head. 'I don't think so. He inherited the boat from an elderly uncle, but he never mentioned any other family. I got the impression his parents were dead.'

'What about friends?'

'Well, we're all friends here on the canal. You have to be, when you live on board a narrowboat. You could say we're a tribe. We all help each other as much as we can. But Gabriel was shy. He didn't talk much to the other boaters.'

'Any special friends?' asked Ffion, who was busy inspecting Hat's pot plants.

'There was a girlfriend who used to come round now and again. Gabriel was besotted with her, but to be honest, I had my doubts. I used to say to him, Gabriel go carefully with that one. But he was in love. Anyone could see that.'

'She didn't live with him, this girlfriend?'

'No, she said the boat was too cramped for her. Life on board a narrowboat's a lot harder than people think. It doesn't suit everyone.' Harriet sniffed to show her disapproval.

'And what is the girlfriend's name?'

'Amber. I don't know her surname. She does a bit of modelling for the art school. You know, life drawing, that sort of thing. I suppose that's how Gabriel met her. He was such a talented artist. He could paint or draw anything. Have you seen any of his work?'

'Yes, I have,' said Bridget. 'You're right. He was very talented. And he was starting to make a name for himself, I understand.'

Harriet nodded. 'Not that he wanted to be famous. Gabriel wasn't like that. He was dedicated to his art. You never met anyone with so much talent who was so modest. And he wasn't a bit materialistic, either. Well you can't be, if you live on a narrowboat.'

Bridget guessed that was true. And on a day like today, with the sunlight dappling the water, and the narrowboat bobbing lazily up and down, she could easily see herself fitting into the lifestyle of a boater, free of the clutter that weighed down most people's lives.

Vik, the head of the SOCO team, emerged from the interior of *La Belle Dame* and Bridget took the opportunity to finish her conversation with Harriet. 'Here's my card. If you think of anything that might be relevant, do please give me a ring.'

Harriet tucked the card inside the top front pocket of her dungarees. 'Of course, Inspector.'

Bridget could feel Harriet's eyes following her as she walked the short distance along the bank to *La Belle Dame*. The narrowboat shifted gently under her weight as she boarded it.

Vik was on deck, removing the white gloves from his hands. 'All done here,' he said. 'Feel free to take a look inside. We've swept the place for fingerprints and DNA.'

'Find anything interesting?' Bridget asked. She was glad his team had finished their work. She always looked ridiculous if she had to don a white, plastic SOCO suit.

'Well, I would say so,' he said wryly. 'The guy who lived here was clearly a bit on the weird side, if you ask me.'

'In what way?'

'Go and see for yourself.' He grinned, and Bridget descended the steps into the dimly-lit cabin of the boat, closely followed by Ffion.

'What on earth?' Whatever Bridget had expected to find inside the boat, it wasn't this.

She had never been inside a canal boat before, but now she saw why they were called narrowboats. The cabin space was extremely cramped, with barely enough room for her to pass the other members of the SOCO team, who were filing out one by one. Even for Bridget, who normally didn't mind small spaces and never had a problem with leg room when flying economy, the interior of the boat made her feel slightly claustrophobic. But that wasn't what had surprised her.

Every available inch of wall space – and some of the window glass too – was stuck with pieces of paper covered in numbers, symbols, equations and diagrams, all in tiny handwriting. No wonder Amber hadn't wanted to move in.

'It looks as if our murder victim had something of a mania for maths,' said Ffion, examining the strange collage of paper sheets.

Bridget peered closely at some of the crazy scribblings, but she could barely decipher any of them.

Ffion on the other hand, seemed to be able to make some sense of Gabriel's writing. She pointed at some sheets pinned up in the narrow galley kitchen. 'Look at this. He's written down the Fibonacci sequence, and drawn a spiral to show how it works in geometry. I once saw something like this superimposed on the *Mona Lisa*, indicating how Leonardo da Vinci used geometric principles to plan his portraits.'

'Remind me what the Fibonacci sequence is,' said Bridget.

'It's a sequence of numbers where each number is the sum of the two preceding ones. So you get 0, 1, 1, 2, 3, 5, 8, and so on.'

'Thanks. I think.' Ffion really was a fount of interesting facts, and Bridget was very glad she'd brought the DC with her. 'Talking of paintings, there aren't any here. Gabriel must have done all his art somewhere else.' The canvases she'd seen in Jonathan's gallery that morning would have filled the tiny living space in the boat with no room to spare.

'There is this,' said Ffion, indicating a postcard fixed above the table in the main seating area.

Bridget leaned in to examine it. The image was nothing like the brightly-coloured canvases from the gallery. Instead, the postcard showed a black-and-white drawing of a disgruntled-looking female figure surrounded by an assortment of seemingly random objects.

With gloved hands, Ffion unpinned the postcard from the wall and turned it over. '*Melencolia I* by Albrecht Dürer,' she read from the back.

'Does that mean anything to you?' Bridget asked her.

'He was a German artist from the Renaissance period, but that's all I know about him.'

Apart from the papers covering every surface, there was little else to see. Gabriel seemed to have owned very few material possessions. The tiny kitchen cupboards contained only a few rudimentary cooking utensils, a couple of chipped plates, mugs and a handful of mismatched cutlery. The sleeping quarters were poky to say the least, and the sitting area was upholstered in an old tartan fabric that gave the place a dismal air. Bridget was quickly coming to the conclusion that life on a canal boat might not be so romantic after all.

A fold-out table was stacked with a pile of books. Bridget sifted through them, glancing at the titles. They all appeared to be about art and mathematics, a strange combination in her view. Yet judging from the number of books in the pile, not everyone shared her opinion.

'You studied Mathematics at university, didn't you?' she said to Ffion.

'Computer Science. But there's a lot of overlap between the two subjects. Everything that happens inside a computer is just binary arithmetic and logic.'

It was remarks like that, mused Bridget, that turned her

off the subject. The language of mathematics had always felt dry and cold to her, not to mention largely incomprehensible, whereas the arts were all about feeling and emotion. Deep down, she craved the passion of opera; the highs and lows of human experience.

She moved aside the last book in the collection to reveal a small poster advertising a public lecture at the maths institute in Oxford. *Numbers in art and nature* with Professor Michael Henderson. The date and time of the talk had been circled in red ink. Today at five o'clock. Presumably Gabriel had been planning to attend.

Bridget knew there and then that she wasn't going to make *La Bohème*. There would be no passion for her tonight, of either the operatic or the romantic kind. She would be going to a maths lecture instead.

CHAPTER 7

Life was good. Detective Sergeant Jake Derwent drove his Subaru Impreza round the Oxford ring road, munching on a Snickers bar, the latest album from The Killers blasting from the car's souped-up speakers.

When he'd taken this job six months back, he'd been reeling after the break-up with his long-term girlfriend who he'd followed south when she got a job in Oxford. He'd been in half a mind to return north to his native Leeds in West Yorkshire. He wasn't sure he belonged in Oxford, with its medieval colleges, dusty libraries and black-gowned academics, some of whom seemed to speak Latin as a first language.

But something had held him here and made him stick at the job. Pride probably, if he was honest – not wanting to return home admitting defeat. And Oxford hadn't beaten him yet. His mates up north could tease him all they liked about becoming a soft southerner, but Jake knew differently. Even with his detective sergeant's salary, he could only afford to rent a one-bed flat above a launderette on the Cowley Road, sandwiched between an Indian restaurant and a Chinese takeaway. Some of his former school mates had actually managed to get themselves on the housing ladder, buying Victorian terraced houses in Leeds which would cost three to four times as much in Oxford. But he wasn't complaining. At least his flat was convenient for getting his washing done and he didn't have to go far for a tasty meal.

Right now he was riding high on the success of the last case, a high-profile murder which had hit the national headlines. Chief Superintendent Grayson had personally commended his bravery in what had been a hair-raising situation. Even the sharp-tongued Ffion Hughes, not known for her words of praise, had said he'd done all right. He'd seen a real hint of admiration in those stunning green eyes of hers and it had sent a shiver down his spine. If he could impress Ffion, he could impress anyone. And DI Hart was a good boss, always giving credit where it was due, and never afraid to get stuck in herself. Yes, on the whole, Jake thought he'd made the right decision to stay in Oxford.

He turned off the eastern by-pass and drove into a bland industrial estate comprising warehouses, builders' merchants and self-storage units. Yeah, Oxford wasn't all dreaming spires, by any means. He located the anonymous-looking car-hire company situated next to a fencing and decking specialist. A high-end global brand, this company wasn't. He parked on the forecourt and went into the single-storey building where a girl on the reception desk was flicking through a magazine with a bored expression on her face.

She glanced up when Jake appeared and hid the magazine under the counter. 'Can I help you?' She gave him a bright smile which showed the braces on her teeth. She didn't look much older than sixteen.

'Detective Sergeant Jake Derwent from Thames Valley Police.' Jake held out his warrant card. 'I'm looking for some information about one of your customers.'

At the sight of the warrant card the smile slid off the

girl's face, and her heavily mascaraed eyes opened so wide they made Jake think of spiders.

'What do you want to know?' she asked.

'I'd like you to tell me who hired this car.' He produced a piece of paper with the Toyota's number plate, and slid it across the counter.

She stared at it glumly without touching it. 'I'm not sure. We're not supposed to give out customer information. Data protection, you know?'

'This is a police matter.'

'I'll have to ask my manager,' she said, sliding off her seat. 'Can you wait here?'

She vanished into a room at the back of the office and reappeared a minute later, half-hidden behind a man in rolled-up shirt sleeves and a loose tie.

'Thank you, Millie,' said the new arrival. He strode over and placed his hands on the counter. 'Now, what's this all about then? I'm Jason Spooner. I'm the managing director here.'

Jake introduced himself and showed his warrant card again. 'Mr Spooner, we'd like you to provide us with some information about one of your vehicles.' He indicated the sheet of paper on the counter. 'It appears that the vehicle in question was used to carry out a serious crime, and we need to trace the driver urgently.'

Spooner frowned. 'What sort of crime?'

'I'm afraid I can't tell you that, sir, however we have video footage of the car in question being driven away at high speed from the scene.'

The manager digested the news with obvious scepticism but instructed the receptionist to find the details on the computer.

Millie did as she was told. 'The car was hired yesterday,' she said, looking up from her computer screen. 'It hasn't been returned yet.'

'Do you have the driver's details?' asked Jake.

'Yes,' said Millie. 'Shall I print them off?' She looked for confirmation to her manager, who nodded, his hairy arms folded across his chest. 'I've got a copy of his driving licence too,' she said, volunteering some assistance for the first time.

'Thanks.' Jake gave her a quick smile and took the printouts from her.

The manager walked Jake to the door as if determined to make sure he left the premises. 'Listen, mate,' he said as Jake was leaving, 'we run a legit business here, and we don't want any trouble. Whatever this guy's gone and done with one of our cars, it's got nothing to do with us. Understand?'

Jake nodded politely. He wondered if it would be worth tipping off the local Trading Standards office to take a close look at the company's operations. They would be sure to find something dodgy. But that wasn't really Jake's concern. 'Thank you for your assistance, Mr Spooner. I'm sure you have nothing to hide.'

Back outside, he studied the information Millie had printed for him. The car had been hired by a Mr Edward Davies, with an address in Headington in East Oxford. Jake couldn't believe it had been so easy to track down the driver. Now he just had to get back to the station and report his news.

It looked like he was going to be the hero of this case too. Luck was with him today. He wondered if he might push it a little further and ask Ffion if she was doing anything this evening. They could go for a drink or catch a film. Who knew how far things might go?

He jumped back in the Subaru, pushed the start button and grinned as the car flashed eagerly to life.

CHAPTER 8

'I'm really sorry,' said Bridget, calling Jonathan to explain that the investigation had ruled out all possibility of going to the opera that evening. Jonathan was always very understanding, but even he must be starting to have doubts about the wisdom of dating a police detective.

That word again, dating. Fat chance of the two of them ever going out on a proper date. All she'd managed today was to interview him as part of a police investigation. She could imagine how horrified Chloe would be at the news, and what her sister, Vanessa, would say. *You'll never get a man if you don't make the effort.*

But how much effort was Bridget willing to make to get a man, even one as sweet as Jonathan? It took all her energy just being a single mum with a demanding career. And after the way Ben had let her down she still wasn't sure that she would ever truly be able to trust another man.

But then Jonathan's calm voice came over the line, interrupting her thoughts. 'Just make sure you catch the person responsible for Gabriel's death. He was such a lovely young man, and a very talented artist. Vicky and I are very upset about what's happened.'

'I'll do my best,' she said.

The lecture was in the Mathematical Institute, a new building on the Woodstock Road next to the eighteenth-century Radcliffe Observatory. The huge foyer, empty apart from an abstract sculpture in the middle of the floor, resembled an airport lounge without the seats or perfume counters. The woman on reception directed Bridget down the stairs where the feeling of being in an airport was only enhanced by the open-plan café, tables and chairs, and expanses of glass and steel. The doors to the lecture theatre were just closing as Bridget rushed to take her place in the auditorium.

She found one of the last remaining seats at the back of the large, semi-circular lecture theatre, surprised at how full it was. She herself had studied History at Oxford and hadn't done maths since she was sixteen. She doubted she'd be able to solve a quadratic equation anymore. In fact she could barely remember what they were. No doubt Chloe would be able to tell her. Or Ffion. She'd dropped Ffion back at the office before coming to the lecture but maybe she ought to have brought her along. Too late now, the lecture was about to start.

The title of the lecture was *Numbers in art and nature*. Professor Michael Henderson, tutorial fellow in pure mathematics at St John's College took to the stage to a polite smattering of applause.

A greying man in his mid-fifties, Professor Henderson had the unmistakable air of an Oxford academic, wearing the obligatory tweed jacket with leather patches on the elbows so beloved by his kind. He crept onto the stage and stood behind the lectern with the dusty air of someone who had spent too much time in libraries. Yet despite his unprepossessing appearance, the professor proved to be an enthusiastic speaker who communicated his subject with passion.

An opening slide appeared on the large screen, bearing a single question: *What do numbers have to do with art and nature?*

'At first glance, the answer to this question may not be obvious,' began the professor. 'You might think these subjects have little in common, or perhaps nothing.'

You read my mind, thought Bridget, intrigued.

'By the end of this lecture, I hope to convince you that the answer is everything, or at least, that they are strongly connected. For what is art, other than the exploration of space, form, volume and pattern? And what is my own subject, mathematics, except precisely that?'

Henderson paused, giving the audience a moment to reflect on his words.

'Does anyone here know what the Golden Ratio is?'

A few hands in the audience went up. Professor Henderson nodded appreciatively.

'The Golden Ratio was first discovered by Pythagoras in the sixth century BC, and has inspired great thinkers from the astronomer Kepler, to the artist Leonardo da Vinci, to the architect Le Corbusier. It has been called the Golden Section and the Divine Proportion. It is a number that appears naturally in geometric studies of two-dimensional shapes and Platonic solids, and is regarded by many artists and architects as the most pleasing proportion to the human eye.'

Images of various ancient buildings appeared on the screen, including the Great Pyramid of Giza and finishing with the Parthenon of Athens. A rectangle was superimposed on the outline of the Greek temple.

'No prizes for guessing that the ratio of the breadth to the height of many classical buildings is the Golden Ratio,' remarked the professor.

Bridget found her interest piqued. The professor's enthusiasm was quite infectious.

The next image to appear was Leonardo's famous drawing of the Vitruvian Man, his arms outstretched and legs apart so that his fingers and toes just touched an inscribed circle and square. 'Here we see that the Golden Ratio is also linked to the ideal human form.' Images from nature followed on screen, including a sunflower and leaves growing on a plant stem. 'Look here, and here,' intoned Henderson, pointing at various parts of the images. 'In each case, nature itself is conforming to the rule of the Golden Ratio.'

The professor went on to talk about the Fibonacci sequence, which Ffion had found a reference to in Gabriel's boat. Bridget soon began to lose track of the details, but even she joined in the laughter at the discussion of Fibonacci's rabbits, and their out-of-control procreation, illustrated by an animated slide showing one pair of rabbits, joined by successively more offspring until rabbits filled the entire screen.

'Now let's look at an example of how a Renaissance artist incorporated mathematical concepts into a work of art,' said the professor.

After what Ffion had said about the *Mona Lisa*, Bridget was expecting the next slide to be a painting by Leonardo da Vinci. Instead she was surprised to see the same image that she had found on the postcard in Gabriel's canal boat.

The curious picture seemed to defy any simple interpretation. The main figure in the scene was a gloomy winged woman who sat with her head leaning on her fist, glowering darkly into the distance. The rest of the image was cluttered with a bizarre assortment of creatures and objects including a cherub busily writing, an emaciated dog asleep at the woman's feet, a ladder, a rainbow, an hourglass, a lethal looking knife with a serrated edge, and what looked like a block of marble cut into an odd three-dimensional shape with the hint of a ghostly image on its front face.

The professor smiled mischievously, as if he knew the reaction the strange image would evoke in his audience.

'Here we have *Melencolia I* by the German artist Albrecht Dürer. Dürer was a painter and printmaker from Nuremberg in the late fifteenth and early sixteenth centuries with connections to Raphael, Bellini and Leonardo. He was famous for his exceptionally detailed woodcut prints and engravings. He was also very interested in mathematics and wrote a book on geometry and another on human proportions. *Melencolia* is his most widely studied and debated work.'

Bridget felt a sense of awe at the skill and craftsmanship that had produced this engraving, but the message it was intended to convey was a mystery to her.

'Let's look at some of the references to maths and geometry that Dürer incorporated into this work,' said the professor, his enthusiasm reaching new heights. 'As you can see, the figure personifying melancholy is holding a pair of compasses in her right hand. And this sphere' – he pointed his laser at a sphere positioned in front of the sleeping dog – 'has a radius equal to the distance marked by the compass.' He paused a moment while the audience digested what he was saying. 'Now, look at the top right of the image. Does anyone know what that is?'

He pointed his laser at a grid of numbers that Bridget hadn't noticed at first, so cluttered was the image.

'It's a magic square,' called a voice from the audience.

'Correct,' said the professor. 'Full marks. This is a four by four magic square where every row, column and diagonal adds up to thirty-four.' Bridget did a couple of quick calculations in her head and found it to be true. The numbers, which appeared at first glance to be random, did indeed add up to thirty-four, whichever column or row you looked at. 'And not only that,' continued the professor, 'but the corners of each quadrant total thirty-four, and any number added to its symmetric opposite equals seventeen.'

Fascinating, thought Bridget, but what does it all mean?

'And now we come to the most hotly-contested part of the image,' said the professor, aiming his laser at the three-dimensional geometric shape that looked strangely out of place next to the cherub, hourglass and old-fashioned weighing scales, like a twenty-first century sculpture that had intruded on a sixteenth-century work of art. 'This is a truncated rhombohedron which has become known as

Dürer's solid. Some of the greatest minds in mathematics have tried to determine its geometric properties, but no one seems to be able to agree on the ratio between the long and short diagonals of the rhombi, which just goes to show that sometimes even mathematics can be controversial.'

A titter of laughter passed through the hall. Bridget glanced at her watch. She was definitely starting to lose the thread of the lecture now.

'But how are we to interpret this image?' asked the professor. 'Dürer himself said that the keys and purse hanging from the belt of the figure's dress represent power and wealth, so I think we can say that he was an artist who understood business and the need to put food on the table, but there seems to be more to it than that. Some argue that the personification of melancholy represents the Muse who is fearful that inspiration will not return. All around her are the tools needed to craft a work of art, but instead of applying herself she sits slumped in a slough of despond. But on the other hand, maybe Dürer is telling us that melancholy is a normal, even necessary, part of the creative process. Dürer was influenced by the humanist thinkers Agrippa and Ficino, who associated melancholy with genius. And whatever interpretation we may put on this enigmatic image, I think we can all agree that it is, indeed, a work of genius. Thank you.'

The audience broke into appreciative applause which Professor Henderson acknowledged with a slight bow. After it had subsided, Bridget made her way down to the front of the lecture theatre, battling against the tide of people heading towards the exits in the opposite direction. It had been an interesting talk, but she was really here to see what the professor knew, if anything, about Gabriel Quinn. She waited while a trio of bespectacled teenagers quizzed the professor on the more esoteric parts of his lecture.

When everyone had finally left, Bridget approached the professor, holding out her warrant card. 'Detective Inspector Bridget Hart. I wonder if I could have a word,

Professor?'

Professor Henderson appeared startled by the sight of her ID, as if he half-expected her to arrest him and drag him off in handcuffs. His confident manner quickly drained away and he once again became a shy, retiring academic. He tugged nervously at the sleeves of his tweed jacket. Up close Bridget noticed that one of the sleeves was badly frayed.

She hastily put her card away. 'Nothing to be alarmed about. I just wanted to ask you a few questions.'

Henderson didn't look very reassured. 'I'm not used to police officers asking me questions after my talks. I don't suppose you're here to ask about the Golden Ratio?'

She guessed he was trying to make a joke. 'No, I'm afraid not. Some of the mathematics was a bit beyond me, I have to admit.'

'Oh.' The professor seemed disappointed by her response. 'It's not always easy to pitch these public lectures at the right level. Some members of the audience are quite knowledgeable, others… less so.'

A certain disdain had crept into the professor's voice. It was obvious which category he thought Bridget fell into. He stuffed his notes into an old briefcase. 'So, what did you want to talk to me about?'

'Do you know a young artist by the name of Gabriel Quinn?'

A look of concern crept across the professor's face. 'I do, as a matter of fact. Why, what about him?'

'I'm sorry to have to tell you that he was killed this morning in Oxford. We believe that he was killed deliberately.'

'Killed? You mean murdered?' The Professor's face blanched and his shoulders slumped. 'I wondered what had happened to him. I was expecting him to be here this evening. Gabriel usually attends all my lectures without exception.'

'I'm sorry to bring you such bad news. Is there somewhere we can talk?'

'Yes, of course. Come up to my office. We can talk there.'

She followed him through the public parts of the building, through a maze of corridors to a tiny room on the second floor.

The desk in the office was piled high with books and papers, but Bridget's attention was caught by a canvas hanging on the wall behind. It was smaller than the ones she'd seen in Jonathan's gallery but was unmistakably one of Gabriel's works – colourful, mysterious and mesmerising.

'Please have a seat, Inspector.' Professor Henderson removed a stack of books from a chair, taking the seat behind the desk himself. 'Gabriel killed, you say. Can you tell me how it happened?'

Bridget didn't see any harm in telling the professor the bare facts of the case. They would be in the public domain very soon anyway. 'He was shot while cycling along the High Street.'

'Shot? By a gun? Sorry, that's a stupid thing to say. Obviously with a gun – and yet, this is Oxford; Gabriel was a painter. Why would anyone shoot him?' Henderson stopped. 'That's what you're investigating, of course. Sorry, I'm talking too much. It's just the shock of hearing the news. Please, go ahead and ask your questions.'

Bridget nodded at the painting on the wall. 'I see you're a fan of Gabriel's. How did you know him?'

The professor leaned back in his chair. Now that he was behind his desk, he seemed to be recovering some of the ease and self-confidence he had displayed while giving his lecture. 'You might say that Gabriel was a fan of mine. An admirer, perhaps. That painting was a gift from him. Gabriel was very interested in mathematics, you see. His paintings often have hidden meanings based on numbers. This one is called *In Search of the Missing Numbers*. If you look closely, you'll see that the painting contains the integers from one to a thousand, but with a handful of them missing. As well as posing a challenge to the viewer to identify which numbers are missing, one is encouraged to speculate on what might have happened to them.' He smiled awkwardly. 'That's what Gabriel told me, anyway. It rather brightens the place up, don't you think?'

Bridget agreed that it did. 'So tell me, Professor, how did you and Gabriel first meet?'

Henderson steepled his fingertips under his chin. 'Let me see, it must have been around eighteen months ago. Yes, that was it, he came to a public lecture I gave, and afterwards he came up to speak to me. He wasn't a mathematician but it was immediately apparent that he had an affinity with numbers, an instinctive gift for mathematical language, if you like. And he was bursting with questions. He intrigued me, and so I invited him to join me for a coffee. He told me about his paintings, and about the principles underlying his quest to express beauty. One does sometimes meet such characters – people with no formal schooling in the subject, but who study by themselves. They can be quite exhilarating to talk to, but also very obsessive, with peculiar ideas. Gabriel struck me as odd, certainly, but also as an exciting, young man with so much natural talent. I have to say he made a refreshing change from some of my own students. Formal education can sometimes dampen intellectual curiosity, unfortunately.'

The professor fell into a quiet, pensive mood. 'Gabriel, dead,' he muttered. 'I really can't take it in.'

'Did you meet him again?' prompted Bridget.

'Yes, several times. We would go out for coffee, and sometimes he would email me – at all times of the night – with questions about numbers and whatever theory he was currently working on. I was always happy to help.'

'That painting you showed during the lecture – the one with the strange woman surrounded by all the objects –'

'You mean Dürer's *Melencolia I*? It's technically an engraving, of course, not a painting.'

'Right. Gabriel had a copy of it on the wall in his boat.'

'Ah yes,' said Henderson. 'That doesn't surprise me at

all. In fact it was Gabriel who first introduced me to *Melencolia I*. He was a big fan of Dürer, for obvious reasons.'

'Because of Dürer's interest in numbers?'

'Not so much an interest, more like an obsession.'

Bridget retrieved the mysterious number from her bag.

'In the moments before his death, Gabriel was very concerned to communicate a number. Does this mean anything to you?' She read out the number – L79468235 – and Professor Henderson wrote it down on a piece of graph paper he had to hand.

'Hmm,' he said, jiggling his pen between the first and second fingers of his right hand while frowning at the number. 'Well, technically this is a numeral, not a number.'

'Meaning?'

'Sorry,' said Henderson. 'Just a pedantic point. There's a difference between a string of digits and the number they represent. For example, a one and a zero would be interpreted by most people as ten, but in binary those two digits have the value of two. So this is a numeral, denoting a number.'

'Right,' said Bridget, feeling lost. 'And is it significant in any way?'

'Every number is significant in some way,' continued Henderson. He began to jot down scribbles on his paper. 'I can tell you straight off that this isn't a prime number and it isn't part of the Fibonacci sequence. However, all eight of the digits are unique. That is, they occur only once in the sequence.'

'Is that important?'

'It could be,' said Henderson, 'and then again, it could be a complete red herring.'

'I see.'

'And of course, there's the letter at the start. That might indicate that this isn't really a number at all, but some kind of code or reference.'

'Do you have any idea what it might be?'

'Not immediately. I'll tell you what, why don't you leave it with me and I'll have a think about it. If I come up with any ideas I'll let you know.'

Bridget gave him her card. 'One last thing. Can you think of any reason why someone would want to kill Gabriel Quinn?'

Henderson spread his hands across his desk. 'No idea at all. Human behaviour is an unpredictable mystery. Give me the certainty of mathematics any day.'

'Thank you for your time, Professor.' She rose to her feet. 'I'll leave you in peace now.'

'Far from it, Inspector Hart. You've just set me a mathematical challenge to solve. I assure you that I shall be thinking about your mysterious number all evening.'

*

Back at Kidlington, Detective Constable Ffion Hughes was busy running searches on her computer. Bank accounts, payment card numbers, company registration numbers, all kinds of numbers with eight digits. She would have liked to accompany Bridget to the maths lecture, but hadn't been asked. Never mind. She already had plenty of work to do, and was in her comfort zone investigating Gabriel's mysterious number and pondering his notes from the canal boat. Fibonacci's sequence, the Golden Ratio, theories of linear perspective and Euclidean geometry. Not the usual sort of thing you encountered in police work, and a refreshing change for someone with an interest in the subject, like Ffion.

The guys in the office were engaged in their usual adolescent behaviour, with Ryan Hooper in particular trying to attract her attention. She took no notice. She'd already given Ryan a brutal putdown when he'd asked her out on a date a week or two ago, but some guys just didn't seem to get the message. If he asked her again, she might simply tell him he wasn't her type. On the other hand, maybe she wouldn't. With men like Ryan, there was no point giving them a reason. You simply had to say no.

The door to the incident room crashed open and she looked up. Jake Derwent rushed in, brandishing a sheet of paper like it was a winning lottery ticket. He bounded over to her desk, holding the paper out for her to see.

'Found something?' she asked casually, suppressing a smile and dropping her eyes back to her computer screen, her fingers flying over the keyboard at breakneck speed.

'Look!' He slapped his trophy down on her desk.

She couldn't help but like Jake Derwent. Unlike Ryan, who was always adopting a pose and doing his best to look cool, Jake was quite charmingly guileless. He was like his car – eager, unsophisticated, and straight-talking. He reminded her of her first and only boyfriend, who she'd dated at school for a short while before deciding she liked girls too.

She glanced back up at him and was rewarded with an ear-to-ear grin.

'I just got back from the car-hire company,' he announced breathlessly. 'These are the driver's details. I managed to get a copy of his driving licence, complete with his address.'

On the other side of the office, Ryan's face turned to thunder.

'Nice work,' she told Jake. She tapped in the details from the ID and executed a search with a few deft clicks of the mouse. 'Okay, Sherlock,' she said. 'Do you want the good news or the bad?'

'Good news first,' said Jake, starting to look less sure of himself.

'Well, the good news is that the driver's licence checks out. Mr Edward Davies is registered on the system with an address in Headington.'

'And?'

'And the bad news is that he died in 2002.'

'2002? Oh. I guess it wasn't him driving the car, then.'

'No, probably not.'

The sound of Ryan's sniggering was loud enough to

carry across the office.

'So perhaps Mr Davies isn't our shooter, after all.' Ffion thrust the photocopied licence back at Jake. 'Nice try though.'

'Never mind, mate,' said Ryan, standing up. 'Harry and I were just about to head out for a beer. We're meeting some of the lads at the King's Head to watch the match. Want to join us?'

Jake sighed, his eyes no longer able to meet Ffion's. 'Yeah, go on then. I think it's time to call it a day.'

Ffion watched them go. Beer and football. It was no less than she had expected from them. She pulled on her green leather motorcycle jacket and headed for home.

*

By the time Bridget returned to the station after the maths lecture it was already getting late. What had she achieved today? She'd spoken to an eccentric woman who lived on a canal boat surrounded by her pot plants, and a helpful, if annoyingly erudite, professor of mathematics. Jake had called her from a noisy pub to say that the driver had used a fake ID, effectively shutting down their best lead. And Ffion had sent her an email reporting no progress on the mysterious eight digit number.

A talented young artist was dead, but nobody seemed to have the faintest idea why anyone would want to kill him.

She entered her notes for the day into the Holmes database and left work feeling downbeat. Even listening to *La Bohème* in her car on the way home did little to raise her mood. It just reminded her that she'd missed her date at the opera with Jonathan. Her first real date in years. Since she'd divorced Ben in fact. It hadn't been the opera she'd been looking forward to so much as Jonathan's company. She'd let him down twice now. Maybe he wouldn't bother asking her again.

Returning home to Wolvercote along the Godstow

Road she drove over the Oxford Canal. It was still just light enough to make out the colourful shapes of narrowboats moored along the canal bank for the night. She carried on to the village green and parked the Mini outside her little terraced cottage, turning off the opera and the car's headlights. Twilight settled silently around her, and with it came a sense of peace.

She liked living here. Tucked inside the north-west corner of the Oxford ring road, Wolvercote still had the feel of a village, set apart from the bustle of the city centre. The children's swings in the centre of the green were quiet at this time of night, but sounds of weekend revelry drifted through the open doors of the pub opposite. A man walking a dog ambled past, probably on his way back from Port Meadow. Bridget let herself into the house and shut the door.

It was way too quiet without Chloe at home and the house felt strangely empty. There had been no more texts or calls, so Bridget assumed Chloe was too busy enjoying herself to bother getting in touch with her mum.

A red light blinking on the home phone indicated that someone had left a message for her. She pressed play and listened as her sister's voice addressed her. 'Bridget. Hi, it's Vanessa here. I don't want to interrupt your visit to the opera with Jonathan this evening' – Vanessa could barely suppress her breathless excitement – 'but I just wanted to check that you're on for lunch at our place tomorrow. Such a shame Chloe can't come, but I expect she's having a super time in London.' The message ended with a long beep that echoed around the empty house.

Bridget dropped her bag in the hallway and went through to the kitchen where the unwashed breakfast things still waited for her in the sink. She'd intended to see to them after her trip to the hairdresser's, something else that she had failed to achieve today.

Turning her back on the washing up, she pulled open the fridge door and started hunting for something that wasn't too far past its use-by date. She found some leftover takeaway chicken tikka masala that didn't smell off and shoved it in the microwave to reheat. She was always meaning to cook homemade food with fresh, wholesome ingredients and had even asked for, and received from Vanessa, an Italian cookery book for Christmas. 'Even you'll be able to manage these recipes,' Vanessa had said. So far she hadn't got past reading about calorie-laden pasta sauces and dreaming of sun-drenched Tuscan hillsides. The book was starting to gather dust on the top shelf in the kitchen.

The microwave pinged and Bridget retrieved her reheated meal. She poured herself a large glass of Pinot Noir from a bottle she'd started the night before and took her supper-for-one into the lounge where she put on a CD of Pavarotti singing popular Italian arias, a birthday present from Chloe. Comfort music to go with the comfort food. She turned it up to full volume and let the tenor's rich tones embrace her. At midnight, with the bottle of wine empty and the soaring cry of 'Vincerò! Vincerò! Vincerò!' finally lifting her spirits, she climbed into her freshly laundered bed alone. 'I will win!' she thought to herself. 'I will win!'

CHAPTER 9

Bridget woke early on Sunday morning, unable to sleep with the summer sun streaming through the curtains and the tweeting of birds right outside her window. Her head thumped, reminding her of the bottle of wine she had rashly finished off, and her stomach growled, raising doubts about whether the chicken tikka masala had been a wise choice after all. But mostly it was the new case on her mind that had given her such a restless night and then woken her at the crack of dawn.

Standing in the shower, she tried to work out what was bothering her the most. She decided it was the cold-blooded ruthlessness with which the killing had been carried out. It couldn't simply be a random attack or a case of road rage. The murder showed every sign of being meticulously planned. There had to be a good reason why someone had targeted a young and – from what she'd seen of his lifestyle on the canal – impoverished artist. Who and what had Gabriel become entangled with?

Over breakfast – a quick slice of toast with a low-calorie spread that really didn't compare with the acacia honey she craved – she thought about calling Chloe to see how she was getting on, but then realised it was far too early for her teenage daughter to be up and about. Anyway, she'd be collecting her this evening from the station, assuming Ben got her to Paddington on time. She'd find out all about the trip then. She considered texting Jonathan instead, but what would she say? Hope you enjoyed the opera last night? No, he deserved better than that. She'd give it more thought later. Right now she needed to concentrate on the case.

She drove to the office, hoping that one of her team would have come up with an idea overnight. She could use some fresh inspiration.

'Morning, ma'am,' said the desk sergeant as she entered the building. 'I was told to pass this on to you.' He handed her a report.

'What's this?'

'That car involved in the shooting yesterday morning, it's been found torched in a farmer's field near Abingdon.'

'Terrific,' said Bridget, pulling a face. 'There goes all our forensic data up in flames. I don't suppose the farmer saw anything useful?'

'It happened overnight, early hours of the morning. No one was around.'

'Of course.'

She hoped this wasn't a sign of how the rest of the day was going to go. Arriving at her desk, she swallowed a couple of paracetamol to quench her mounting headache.

When everyone was in, she called the team together for a briefing. Jake sat slumped in his chair, breakfasting on a chocolate bar. Ryan and Andy were rubbing at bloodshot eyes, looking just as hungover as Bridget felt. Only Ffion seemed to be wide awake and alert, drinking a herbal concoction from her mug with the Welsh dragon on it.

'Right,' said Bridget. 'Let's go over what we've got.' She stood in front of the incident room noticeboard which, so far, was looking decidedly sparse. 'Gabriel Quinn, aged twenty-six, an artist, was shot from a passing car yesterday morning at approximately ten fifteen. He had just come from Wright's art gallery on the High Street where a number of his paintings are up for sale with a group of artists, all former students of the Ruskin School of Art. We don't know where he was going when he left the gallery, but witnesses say it looked as if he was about to turn right into Turl Street just before he was shot.'

Ffion raised a hand. 'There's an art supply shop on Broad Street, near the other end of Turl Street. They sell paints, brushes, canvases, that sort of thing. He might have been going there.'

'That's a possibility,' acknowledged Bridget, grateful that at least one member of her team was alert and coming up with ideas. 'Now, the vehicle used by the killer was a black Toyota hire car, but we've established that the driver used a false ID' – Jake squirmed in his seat and his ears turned pink – 'and I've just received a report that the car has been found torched in a farmer's field.'

'It's looking more and more like a professional hit job,' said Ryan. 'Organised crime if you ask me.'

'Maybe,' said Bridget. The idea of the streets of Oxford being overrun by gangs of organised criminals was a terrifying prospect. 'The only clue we have so far is the number that Gabriel uttered before he died. Have we made any progress on that?'

Again, it was Ffion who spoke up. 'I've been working on it. There are several types of registration numbers or ID numbers that have eight digits, but the letter 'L' at the start rules most of them out. It might be a bank account, with the letter 'L' referring to the name of the bank.'

'I can only think of one bank beginning with "L",' said Jake, cramming the last of the chocolate into his mouth. 'Lloyds.'

'That's the most obvious one, of course,' said Ffion, her green eyes twinkling. 'But there's also the Bank of London and the Middle East. And if you include building societies, there's Leeds, Leek, Loughborough, Leicester, London and Lambeth.' She ticked the names off on her long fingers.

Jake seemed to shrink with each name she listed.

'Yeah, everyone knew that,' said Ryan drolly. 'Apart from Jake.'

'I've already submitted disclosure requests to all the banks on my list,' said Ffion, ignoring Ryan's witticism.

'Excellent,' said Bridget, who couldn't fault Ffion for her efficiency. 'While you're waiting to hear back from the banks, maybe you can go through Gabriel's phone and laptop.'

'Will do,' said Ffion brightly.

Bridget turned to Ryan and Andy. 'Can you two try and find out the identity of this mysterious driver? Ryan, check out traffic cameras along the roads between Oxford and Abingdon. Andy, I'd like you to liaise with other police forces and look for recent cases that follow a similar pattern.'

'Yes, ma'am,' said Ryan without much enthusiasm. He probably knew it was a job unlikely to yield results, but still they had to try.

'And Jake,' said Bridget, turning to her sergeant. 'Come with me to the Ruskin School of Art. I've arranged to go and see Dr Melissa Price, Gabriel's former tutor. I'm hoping she can shed some light on his character and who he had dealings with.'

Jake jumped to his feet, scrunching up his chocolate bar wrapper. He looked pleased to be getting out of the office.

*

The Ruskin School of Art was a small stone building on the High Street finished in the neo-Gothic nineteenth-century style. It stood next to the university's Examination Schools where Bridget had sat her History Finals more years ago now than she cared to remember. She could never walk past the grandiose building without recalling that frantic, stressful time, the culmination of three years' hard work. Her entire degree had rested on her performance in those gruelling examinations. None of the exams she'd sat in the police force compared in any way to Oxford Finals.

Dr Melissa Price met them in the entrance hall. In her early fifties and with almond-shaped eyes, Gabriel's former art tutor cut a striking figure, due in large part to the colourful kaftan dress which billowed as she walked, the chunky bead necklace that hung around her long neck, and the African-style wooden bracelets that adorned her arms. She wore her long, silvery-grey hair loose.

Going grey gracefully was supposed to be liberating and on-trend, according to an article Bridget had read in a women's magazine the last time she'd visited the hairdresser's. Bridget remained unconvinced. Why go grey when you could pursue a comforting lie with a little help from your stylist? Still, she had to admit, the fashion suited Melissa Price well enough.

'Thank you for agreeing to meet us, Dr Price.' Bridget held out her hand.

'Not at all, and please call me Melissa.' She took Bridget's hand in her long, slim fingers with a studied casualness, and Bridget had the sense that the art tutor's Bohemianism was carefully crafted, as if she knew the precise image she wanted to create. A living work of art. 'Shall we go up to my office?'

'That would be good. Thanks.'

'I've just come from Modern Art Oxford,' said Melissa as they walked along the corridor. 'Do you know it?'

'The gallery on Pembroke Street?'

'Yes. My recent crop of students have an exhibition there over the summer. It's well worth a visit. *Such* an impressive array of work. *So* much talent.'

Bridget got the impression that Melissa wanted to take credit for the exhibition herself. 'Maybe when we've completed the investigation,' she said.

They followed her up the stairs, past walls adorned with students' paintings and drawings, quite a lot of it challenging or disturbing in a dystopian kind of way. The works seemed notably at odds with the Victorian architecture of the building itself.

'The School was founded by John Ruskin,' remarked Melissa. When Jake looked blank, she explained further. 'A Victorian art critic and, like so many of his male contemporaries, a professional bore. He was very influential though, in his time. He was a driving force behind the Pre-Raphaelite movement.'

At the top of the staircase, several pieces of junk had apparently been dumped in the corridor. 'Be careful with that,' warned Melissa. 'It's one of my final year student's examination pieces.'

Bridget was no great fan of conceptual art, and she regarded the random assortment of objects with a degree of bafflement.

Jake, it seemed, was also not an admirer of the work. He struggled to suppress a snigger, and Melissa rounded on him angrily.

'Do you have something to say, Sergeant?' She didn't wait to find out if he did. 'I expect you think you know what art is: nice pictures of pretty landscapes. Well, real art should be difficult and challenging. It should open us up to new ways of thinking about ourselves and the world. Otherwise, what's the point?'

Bridget could see the confusion on Jake's face. As far as the pieces of junk in the corridor were concerned, she had to agree with him. What, indeed, was the point?

Melissa opened a door at the end of the corridor and ushered them inside. They were greeted by a huge canvas of a female nude, dominating the centre of the room. The naked woman in the painting lay on a chaise longue, one arm draped over the arm rest, the other resting languidly on her hips, the direction of the fingers guiding the viewer's eyes inexorably towards the patch of hair between her legs. The doleful eyes that stared out of an alabaster face and the mane of wavy, red hair that tumbled over her shoulders, revealing rounded breasts and pink nipples, reminded Bridget of Lizzie Siddal, the Pre-Raphaelite model who had lain for hours in a bath of water so that

Millais could paint her as the drowned Ophelia. Lizzie had died young from an overdose of laudanum, if Bridget remembered correctly.

But this painting was no Pre-Raphaelite masterpiece. The paint was daubed on clumsily in dollops, and the woman's proportions all seemed wrong. Maybe that was deliberate. Or maybe not.

'Quite a stunner, don't you think?' said Melissa.

Bridget was unsure whether she was referring to the woman in the painting, or to the artwork itself.

Jake coughed and busied himself with taking out his notebook.

'What's the matter, Sergeant?' asked Melissa sharply. 'Does the female body cause you embarrassment or disgust? You wouldn't be the first. John Ruskin himself was a pompous oaf where women were concerned. He failed to consummate his marriage because his beautiful young wife, Effie, wasn't as smooth down there' – she pointed to her own crotch – 'as the marble statues he was familiar with.' She twisted a lock of her long grey hair around a finger and studied Jake, waiting for his reaction.

Jake cleared his throat and looked away, his ears turning red.

'Maybe we can make a start with some questions about Gabriel,' said Bridget, rescuing Jake before his ears could turn an even brighter shade.

'Of course,' said Melissa. 'Please, take a seat.'

She sat down on a stool in front of the canvas, inviting Bridget and Jake to take the sofa opposite. From here, it was impossible to look at Melissa without looking at the painting behind her. Bridget wondered if she'd positioned it there deliberately to distract her audience.

'I simply can't believe what happened to Gabriel,' said Melissa. 'And in broad daylight in the middle of Oxford, too.'

'Quite,' said Bridget. 'I understand you were Gabriel's tutor here at Oxford?'

'I was indeed,' said Melissa, tossing her hair over her

shoulder and crossing one leg over the other. Turquoise-painted toenails peeped out from beneath the embroidered hem of her kaftan. 'The intake that year was particularly good, but even so, Gabriel caught my attention from the start.'

'In what way?' asked Bridget.

'Oh, you know.' Melissa waved a hand in the air. 'He had an eye,' she said enigmatically.

'For anything in particular?'

'For detail. Art is all about seeing and then conveying what you see through your chosen medium.'

'And Gabriel's medium was oil painting?'

'Yes, but he also did drawing and engraving. He was quite old-fashioned in that respect. He wasn't interested in installation art or experimental media like video. He admired the old masters, particularly artists of the Renaissance, and wanted to learn all he could from them. If he'd been born five hundred years ago he'd have been apprenticed to someone like Michelangelo.'

'So he was talented.'

'Very talented in some ways,' said Melissa, crossing her legs the other way, 'but not particularly astute. His works were too obscure to attract a wide audience. He was too shy to promote himself effectively. I used to tell him that he needed to woo the buyers, to cultivate his own image, but he was too naive to take my advice. The idea of the artist eking out an existence in a garret is a very romantic one, Inspector, but even artists have to eat and pay the bills.'

'You didn't like him much?' suggested Bridget.

'I was his tutor, not his friend. My job was not to like him, but to develop his potential.'

'And yet he seemed to be making a career for himself, despite your reservations.'

Melissa shrugged.

'What about his interest in numbers?' asked Bridget.

'Ah, yes, that was one of Gabriel's particularly unusual traits.' Melissa's almond eyes narrowed with disdain. 'He was obsessed by concepts such as the Golden Ratio and the Fibonacci sequence. I assume you know what they are?'

Bridget acknowledged her familiarity, and felt relieved that she'd attended the lecture yesterday. Not that any of her newly-acquired mathematical knowledge was helping her to crack the case. If only there were an equation for solving murders.

'I told him to forget all that,' said Melissa. 'No one cares. To succeed in art you have to be original, not revisit ideas that were explored hundreds of years ago.'

'There was one number that was apparently very important to Gabriel,' said Bridget, 'because he repeated it a couple of times before he died.'

Jake read out the mysterious eight-digit number from his notebook.

Melissa shook her head. 'I've no idea what that could refer to.'

'Gabriel was displaying some of his paintings at Wright's art gallery on the High Street,' said Bridget. 'Do you know anything about that?'

'Ah, yes, Jonathan Wright is a great supporter of our students,' said Melissa. 'Although I always tell them that they really need to be exhibiting their work in London, not Oxford.' She smiled at Bridget in a patronising way. 'Mind you, I expect that the value of Gabriel's work will soar now that he's dead. No doubt Jonathan is secretly delighted.'

Bridget was about to jump to Jonathan's defence when Jake interrupted. 'Are you suggesting that Gabriel's death may have been motivated by financial gain?'

Melissa brushed her silver hair with her long fingernails. 'Well, who can say? That's your job to find out, isn't it?'

Bridget decided to change the subject. 'I met Gabriel's neighbour on the canal yesterday and she mentioned a girlfriend called Amber. Do you know her, by any chance?'

'Well, yes I do.' A slow lascivious smile spread across Melissa's face. 'You're looking at her, in fact.' She swivelled on her stool to admire the canvas behind her. 'Amber Morgan is something of a muse to our artists.'

Bridget looked more closely at the girl depicted on the canvas. She really was quite beautiful, a "stunner" as Melissa had said. Emerald eyes, huge pouting lips and a sultry expression. But there was also something fragile about her, as if she might shatter at any moment. Did she mind taking her clothes off for classes of students? Presumably not. But what about Gabriel? How had he felt about it all?

'Where can we find Amber now?' asked Jake.

'On a Sunday? I'm not sure,' said Melissa. 'When she's not modelling for our life-drawing classes, she sometimes works at the art supply shop on Broad Street.'

'Do you have a contact number for her?' asked Jake.

'Yes, I do.' Melissa scrolled through the contacts on her iPhone. 'Here it is.' She passed the phone to Jake to make a note of the number.

'The other artists on display at the art gallery, they were all students of yours?' asked Bridget.

'Yes,' said Melissa. 'A very gifted group. So much talent, you know?'

'Do they all live in Oxford?'

'Yes, mostly, or hereabouts.'

'And did Gabriel have a particularly close connection to any of them?'

'Oh,' said Melissa, a faintly mocking smile playing on her lips. 'Gabriel didn't find it easy to make friends. He was something of a recluse. But now you mention it, Amber did have a relationship with one of the other artists in that group. Hunter Reed. The love life of these young artists and their muses really can be rather complicated.'

'Complicated in what way?' asked Bridget.

'I'll say no more, Inspector. Just speak to Hunter. I'm sure you'll find him interesting.'

★

It was already almost lunchtime when Bridget and Jake emerged from the Ruskin School of Art back onto the High Street. Bridget wasn't sure they were any further forward but at least they had the girlfriend's name and phone number, and knew where she worked. Bridget asked Jake to give Amber a call, and see if he could interview her. Meanwhile, Bridget had family matters to attend to.

There was an unwritten rule that she would always go to her sister's for Sunday lunch, but her recent workload had made her an unreliable guest. She didn't think it would hurt if she took a couple of hours off and made an appearance now, and so ten minutes later her tyres were crunching on the gravel driveway in front of Vanessa's house on Charlbury Road in leafy North Oxford.

The Large Edwardian detached house behind its perfectly-clipped hedges always felt reassuringly solid and permanent, especially at times like this when Bridget was conscious of how fragile human life could be. She would have loved to have Chloe here with her, and wondered again what her daughter was doing right now.

It was James, her brother-in-law, who opened the door to her. He was dressed for the summer in a pair of baggy khaki shorts and a short-sleeved linen shirt.

'Bridget,' he said, kissing her on the cheek, 'how lovely to see you. We hoped you'd make it this weekend.' Rufus, the family's Golden Labrador bounded down the hallway to greet her, his tail wagging. 'Chloe not with you?'

'She's in London, visiting Ben,' said Bridget, unable to stop herself from grimacing.

'Ah, I see,' said James with a smile. 'Well, I'm sure she'll be fine. Come through to the lounge. Vanessa's just making the gravy.'

The house was filled with the aroma of roast lamb and rosemary. 'It smells lovely,' said Bridget, envying her sister's culinary abilities. Vanessa prided herself on making every meal from scratch with fresh ingredients. Not for her a two-day-old takeaway, re-heated in the microwave in a desperate attempt to resuscitate it. Vanessa would have been appalled if she knew the truth of what went on in Bridget's kitchen.

'Hello Auntie Bridget,' chimed her niece and nephew as she entered the lounge, which to Bridget's eye always resembled a show home, despite the presence of two young children and a dog. Eight-year-old Florence and six-year-old Toby were sitting in front of the hearth, playing a game of *Guess Who*. Rufus flopped down beside them and rested his head on his front paws. It was a scene of domestic bliss such that Bridget herself had never known in her life with Ben and Chloe. How did Vanessa manage to achieve it?

But Bridget knew the answer to that question. Hard work, relentless planning, and obsessive attention to detail. Behavioural patterns that could be traced directly back to the murder of their sister, Abigail. Beneath the surface perfection of Vanessa's life lurked ugly coping mechanisms that would keep a psychiatrist occupied for a long time.

'Lunch is ready,' called Vanessa, walking into the room. 'Bridget, I'm so glad you could come.' Vanessa took her hand and drew her into an embrace. 'After dessert you'll have to tell me all about your visit to the opera,' she whispered loudly into Bridget's ear.

Bridget's heart sank. Vanessa had been the one to introduce her to Jonathan, going to considerable lengths to bring them together. She'd be furious when she learned that Bridget had cried off because of work.

'Toby, Florence, go and wash your hands, then come and sit down.' The children trotted off to the bathroom obediently while Bridget took her place at the dining table. The French windows to the back garden were open, letting in a heady scent of honeysuckle.

James carved the joint while Vanessa passed around tureens of steamed vegetables and roast potatoes. Bridget poured a generous portion of gravy over her meat and tucked in. She wished she could eat this sort of food every day but her job just didn't allow it, and nor would her waistline. Regretfully she declined the offer of wine, knowing that she'd have to get back to the office just as soon as she could politely leave.

'Isn't Chloe coming?' asked Florence, looking expectantly at Bridget. The two young children doted on their older cousin.

'Not today,' said Bridget. 'She's in London visiting her dad.'

'And his girlfriend?' asked Vanessa in a hushed voice. She never missed an opportunity to dig for gossip about the fabled Tamsin.

'I expect so,' said Bridget curtly.

'And you said she's what, ten years younger than you?' Vanessa couldn't hide the incredulity in her voice.

'More potatoes, anyone?' asked James, jumping to his feet and picking up the tureen of perfectly roasted spuds.

'Me, me!' chimed the children. Bridget gave her brother-in-law a grateful smile for changing the conversation.

Over dessert of homemade apple crumble and custard the conversation turned to the children's achievements in school – Toby had won an award for writing a story about an anteater, and Florence had just passed her grade one piano with distinction – and James's business which, according to Vanessa, was on the brink of closing a big deal with another Oxford-based company.

'It's about to go through any day now,' she said, her voice brimming with pride. 'It will be a big step up for James.'

Bridget congratulated him, wondering privately just how much further up the ladder James needed to climb. He already seemed very rich and successful to her.

'Don't get too excited,' said James, taking a sip of his wine. 'The deal's not done until it's signed.'

'And which company is the deal with?' asked Bridget politely.

'Sorry, can't say anything more just yet,' said James, tapping his nose and giving her a wink. 'Confidentiality, you know how it is.'

After the meal, when the children had been excused to

go and play in the garden and James was in the kitchen making coffee, Vanessa leaned across the table. 'So tell me all about your date. How was it? I want to know *everything*. Did you invite him back to your place afterwards?'

Bridget groaned inwardly, but it was impossible to avoid the inevitable. 'I had to cancel at the last minute. I'm working on a new case.'

Vanessa's face fell. 'Oh, Bridget. What are we going to do with you?'

'I know. I'm hopeless. Chloe keeps telling me the same thing.'

'But you'll never find a man if you keep letting work get in the way.'

'I do try. But something urgent came up. Did you hear about the shooting on the High Street?'

'Don't tell me you're involved in that,' said Vanessa, wrinkling her nose in distaste, as if Bridget were responsible for committing the crime, rather than investigating it.

'Involved in what?' asked James, reappearing with three coffees on a tray.

'The High Street shooting,' said Bridget. 'And yes, I am involved. I'm in charge of the investigation.'

'Congratulations,' said James, passing round the coffee cups. 'So, any leads yet?'

'Not many,' admitted Bridget. 'All we really know so far is that the victim was an artist. Some of his paintings are for sale in Jonathan's gallery at the moment, as it happens.'

'Jonathan?' asked Vanessa, her eyes wide. 'You don't think this has anything to do with him, do you?'

'No, of course not,' said Bridget. And yet Vanessa was the second person that day to mention Jonathan in relation to Gabriel's murder. Dr Melissa Price had implied that Jonathan stood to gain financially from the artist's death. The thought made her distinctly uncomfortable.

She was glad when the conversation turned again to safer topics. When her sister wasn't lecturing her about her love life, she could be very good company, and Bridget would happily have whiled away the rest of the afternoon chatting to Vanessa and James and watching the children play. After consuming such a large lunch, she would have been glad to catch up with a little sleep in the dappled shade of the huge magnolia tree in the garden too. But she couldn't abandon her team any longer. She made her excuses.

'But you can't go already,' scolded Vanessa.

'Sorry, work,' said Bridget.

'On a Sunday? Well, just promise me that you'll get back in touch with Jonathan.'

CHAPTER 10

Jake was relieved to have made his escape from the sexually-aggressive Dr Melissa Price with nothing worse than a little embarrassment. What was that woman's problem? He wondered if she hated all men on sight, or if she simply relished making them squirm. She had deliberately gone out of her way to taunt him with her provocative comments, and he still wasn't sure if she'd invented that story about John Ruskin just for his benefit. She clearly had no respect for the founder of her own art school.

Anyway, Jake was no prude. Of course he wasn't embarrassed by a painting of a female nude. He just didn't appreciate having to sit staring at one in the presence of his boss. Especially when, in his humble opinion, the painting wasn't even very good.

Glad to be back in the open air, away from the smell of oil paints and the attentions of the man-eating middle-aged art tutor, he called the number Melissa had given him for Gabriel's girlfriend. He had to admit, he was intrigued by the prospect of meeting Amber Morgan in the flesh, so to speak. From what he knew about Gabriel Quinn, it was difficult to reconcile the shy, retiring artist with this stunningly attractive girl, confident enough to pose nude in a life class. As the phone rang, he found it impossible to push aside the life-size image of the red-headed young woman reclining fully naked on a couch, her red curly hair exposed for all the world to see. Her pale breasts and pink nipples...

The call was answered on the sixth ring, interrupting his waking dream. 'Hello? Who is it?'

'Is that Amber Morgan speaking?'

'Yeah.' The voice on the other end of the line sounded hesitant and nervous. 'Who's calling?'

'Detective Sergeant Jake Derwent from Thames Valley Police. I got your number from Dr Melissa Price at the Ruskin School of Art. I was wondering if we could meet for a chat?' *Chat* was one of Jake's favourite words for speaking to witnesses. Ffion would probably have said *interview*, and put Amber even more on edge than she already was.

'Is it about... is it about Gabriel?' The voice was almost breaking now.

'Yes, it's regarding Gabriel Quinn.'

Jake could hear noises in the background – footsteps and shuffling as if someone were moving around, and a hushed conversation with a man.

Eventually Amber came back on the line. 'I suppose you could come here.' She didn't sound at all keen.

'And where would that be?'

She gave him an address in Jericho, an area just north of the city centre, known for its art-house cinema, independent bookshop, trendy cafés and alternative vibe. It wasn't a part of the city that Jake tended to frequent.

'I'll be there in twenty minutes.'

Oxford was a fairly compact city – not like Leeds – and he set off on foot. He popped into a Tesco Metro on the way, feeling in need of emergency carbs, and grabbed a cheese sandwich and a Mars bar. He took a large bite out of each as he strode up St Giles' towards Jericho.

What a morning. When Bridget had asked him to accompany her to the Ruskin School, he'd been glad to get out of the office and take a break from Ffion's casual put-downs and Ryan's relentless banter. But Dr Melissa Price had been far worse than anything he'd endured at the office. With luck he would never have to see that woman again.

As for Ffion, he was confused. He thought they made a good team. They'd worked well together on the last case. Sometimes she could be quite nice to him. At other times she was decidedly prickly and had a way of saying things that made him feel stupid. His plan to ask her out when he returned from the car-hire company with the driver's ID had been rapidly brought to a halt by her barbed comments. He wasn't sure if she did it on purpose, or was simply oblivious to the effect her words had. But boy, was she a looker. He couldn't be blamed for showing a healthy male interest in her.

Since the bust-up with his long-term girlfriend, Jake had been afraid of asking another girl out. He'd been scared of being turned down, or worse, cheated on again. But he couldn't put if off forever. Besides, if not Ffion, who else was there? He couldn't see how he was going to meet someone doing this job with its unpredictable hours. He'd wondered about trying a dating app, but if Ryan or one of the other blokes at work ever found his profile on a dating website he'd never hear the end of it.

He turned off St Giles' and soon found himself on a wide road, which the map on his phone informed him was Great Clarendon Street. He passed the Oxford University Press building, which looked something like a Roman temple, and entered a maze of narrow streets in the heart of Jericho. The tiny redbrick terraces had probably been built for Victorian railway workers and weren't much to look at, but even they were beyond his price range. He wondered who lived there now. At the end of the street stood the church of St Barnabas, an imposing building with a tall, square bell tower that looked like it had been plucked from an Italian piazza and dropped into the middle of Victorian England. That was Oxford for you. You never knew what strange architectural flight of fancy might be waiting round the next corner.

The address Amber had given him was for a smart new apartment block located right on the bank of the canal. Jake pressed the buzzer on the door and, when it clicked open, let himself into the building. The development still had a pristine newness about it, as if the builders had only recently packed up their tools and left. He dreaded to think how much an apartment here would cost, and wondered how a girl who worked part-time in an art supply shop and did a spot of life drawing modelling on the side managed to live in such a trendy place.

The door to the apartment was yanked open. A young man stood in the doorway, regarding Jake menacingly. He was lean and muscular, with a few days' worth of stubble on his chin. Barefoot, he wore a pair of loose jogging pants and a tight-fitting T-shirt. There was no sign of Amber.

Jake held up his warrant card. 'I'm here to see Amber Morgan.'

The guy peered at it suspiciously before stepping aside. 'Yeah. Okay.'

He offered no further introduction and Jake followed him through to the living area where Amber was sitting on a sofa, her legs tucked under her. Jake recognised her immediately from Melissa's painting, even though this time she was wearing clothes – a strappy top and cropped jeans. Her creamy skin, luxuriant red hair, and that nervous, haunted look in her eyes were unmistakable.

Jake sniffed. Unless he was very much mistaken, the air contained a faint but lingering smell of cannabis, which was not masked by the vanilla-scented candles burning on the coffee table.

He took a look around the large open-plan space. The apartment had bright, natural lighting, and the living room window directly overlooked the canal, where a blue and yellow narrowboat was slowly drifting past. Views like that didn't come cheap, and yet the place was a dump. The coffee table was littered with half-empty fast-food packaging, crushed beer cans and an overflowing ashtray. It seemed like it didn't take much effort to turn a nice new apartment into a pigsty.

Amber studied him through misty eyes. 'You're the policeman who phoned.'

'That's right. DS Jake Derwent.'

The surly guy took a seat next to her on the sofa, wrapping a protective arm around her. 'I hope you're not going to upset her,' he said.

'And you are?'

'Hunter. Hunter Reed.'

The art tutor had mentioned his name. Hunter belonged to the group of artists exhibiting alongside Gabriel at Wright's art gallery. Melissa Price had said that Amber used to go out with Hunter. She'd also hinted that Amber's love life was complicated. Well, from where Jake was standing it didn't look that complicated to him.

Amber curled up in Hunter's arms. 'Hunter's been looking after me, after what happened to Gabriel,' she said.

He was looking after her very attentively, it seemed to Jake. 'Is this your apartment?' Jake asked him.

'Yeah.' A note of pride crept into the monosyllable. Hunter swept his gaze around, nodding his head with a self-satisfied air. He lit up a cigarette, passed it to Amber and lit one for himself.

'You're an artist too, right?' asked Jake.

Hunter took a long drag of his cigarette and blew the smoke toward the ceiling. 'Yeah.'

The wall behind him was almost entirely covered by a huge canvas that looked like it had been produced by a group of two-year-olds let loose in a paint shop. 'Is that one of yours?' Jake asked.

'Yeah, not bad is it?'

Jake didn't answer the question directly. Instead he indicated the apartment with a wave of his hand. 'You seem to be doing all right for yourself.'

A hint of jealousy must have entered his voice, because Hunter narrowed his eyes at the statement. 'You have a problem with that, Mr Policeman?'

'No,' said Jake, although if he was honest, it rankled with him that a guy who seemed to have no talent or charm, who stole his mate's girlfriend the day after he'd been murdered, and who treated his possessions like dirt could afford to live in a place that Jake had no hope of moving into.

'It's not easy to make a living as an artist,' said Hunter. 'No one gives me a big fat pay cheque at the end of each month. To succeed in this game you need a lucky break, or else to be exceptionally talented.'

'And are you exceptionally talented?' asked Jake, letting his gaze drift again to the mess of paint hanging on the wall.

Hunter's thin mouth cracked into a smile. 'I got spotted early on. A collector noticed my talents and took a strong interest in my work. He commissioned a series of pieces for his offices.'

'I see. And what about this latest exhibition? How is that going for you?'

The smile disappeared. 'I thought you were here to talk to Amber.'

'Yes, I am.' Jake turned his attention to the girl. She looked so much like her painting, it took an effort not to picture her with her clothes off. He cleared his throat and sat down in a chair opposite the sofa. 'How long had you been Gabriel's girlfriend?'

'I guess about five or six years, on and off.'

Jake raised his eyebrows, surprised that Amber and Gabriel had been together for so long. For some reason he had imagined the relationship beginning much more recently. It was because of something that Melissa had said. He studied his notes. 'I understand that you were Hunter's girlfriend before you met Gabriel?'

'No,' said Amber. 'I was with Hunter at the same time as Gabriel.'

Jake looked at her, confused. 'At the same time?'

Amber met his eyes. 'It's not like I belonged to Gabriel. I wasn't his property. Or Hunter's. I'm not an object to be possessed.'

'We don't believe in ownership,' cut in Hunter. 'Ownership leads to exploitation. Relationships should be open and based on trust and mutual respect.'

'Is that so?' said Jake. He noted that Hunter was happy for other people to take ownership of his paintings in return for a sufficiently-large payment, and that Hunter seemed unduly pleased with himself for owning the apartment. 'And was Gabriel cool with this… open relationship?'

Amber shrugged. 'We had an understanding, you know?'

Jake didn't, really. What he did know is that when he eventually found the right person, he just wanted to settle down with them. Was he old-fashioned? Probably.

'Can you tell me a little more about Gabriel?' he asked.

Amber started to relax as she spoke about her dead boyfriend. 'Gabriel was just the sweetest person. He was kind, considerate, gentle.' She looked up into Hunter's face. 'I can't imagine why anyone would want to kill him.'

'Was Gabriel successful as an artist?' asked Jake. 'He didn't live in a nice apartment like this.'

'Gabriel didn't care about money. He just wanted to make art.'

'And would you say he was good at what he did?'

'Oh, yeah. Gabriel had tons of talent. He was going to make a big name for himself one day, wasn't he, Hunter?'

Hunter nodded noncommittally.

Amber tucked a loose strand of hair behind her ear. 'He used to say that I was his muse.'

Jake's pen hovered over his notebook. 'His muse?'

She nodded her head enthusiastically. 'An artist like Gabriel doesn't just want a model, he needs someone to unlock his creativity and inspire real passion. A muse and an artist have a special relationship that outsiders can't understand. They feed off each other organically. An artist without a muse is nothing, really.' Her green eyes glistened with unshed tears. 'Gabriel used to say that I was like the women who modelled for the Pre-Raphaelite artists. You know? Jane Morris posed for her husband as Queen Guinevere, and then for her lover, Dante Gabriel Rossetti, as the goddess Venus. Lizzie Siddal modelled as the drowned Ophelia for John Everett Millais before marrying Rossetti. And then there was Effie Gray, who married John Ruskin and then later Millais.'

Jake made no attempt to make sense of the various models and their merry-go-round of husbands and lovers. Instead he let Amber carry on talking.

'The Pre-Raphaelites called their muses stunners,' she continued, 'To them, they represented the ideal female form. And Gabriel always said I was his stunner.' Tears began to fall from her eyes and stream down her cheeks.

Hunter's lip curled up in dislike and he stubbed his cigarette out angrily. He really wasn't very good at concealing his true feelings about his dead rival. 'You are a stunner,' he said to Amber, brushing his fingers through her lustrous hair. 'You're my stunner now.'

So much for not believing in ownership, thought Jake. 'Did Gabriel have any wealthy collectors wanting to buy his paintings?' he asked.

It was Hunter who answered his question. 'Lawrence bought works from all the artists in the Ruskin group, not just me.'

'Lawrence?'

'That's Lawrence Taylor, a local businessman. He runs his own financial company in Oxford.'

Jake jotted the name down. 'This is the collector who commissioned work from you?'

'Yeah. Lawrence has an eye for talent,' continued Hunter, 'but he's an investor at heart.' He chuckled to himself.

'What's so funny?'

'Lawrence stands to make a killing now, out of Gabriel's paintings.'

'That's an unfortunate turn of phrase, sir.'

'A fortune, then, if you prefer. There's nothing like the death of an artist to push the value of their work sky-high.'

'Could that be a motive for murder?' Jake asked.

Hunter snorted with derision. 'Lawrence is already a wealthy man. And there are easier ways of making money than shooting artists.'

The flickering candles had almost burnt out, and Amber stared at them, her eyes filling again with tears.

'Then can either of you think of anyone who might want to do Gabriel harm?' asked Jake. 'Had he upset anyone recently? Did he have any enemies?'

Amber shifted her position on the sofa, bringing her knees up to her chin and hugging them tight. 'I can't imagine why anyone would want to hurt Gabriel. But...'

'But what?'

'He'd been acting a bit paranoid recently.'

'In what way?'

'He kept saying that someone was following him.'

'Who?'

'He didn't say. But he told me someone had broken into his boat.'

Jake began to scribble in his notebook. 'When was this?'

'About a week ago. Ten days maybe.'

'And did he report the break-in to the police?'

'The police? No.' Amber shook her head. 'He said nothing was taken, anyway.'

A thought occurred to Jake. 'So where did Gabriel do his painting? We didn't find any painting stuff on his canal boat.'

'He used a room at the art shop as his studio,' said Amber. 'Todd let him use the space.'

'Todd?'

'Todd Lee. He's the owner of the shop on Broad Street. My boss,' she added. 'I work at the shop part-time.'

'I see,' said Jake. Ffion had mentioned an art shop on Broad Street as a possibility for where Gabriel was cycling when he was shot. 'Is the shop near the end of Turl Street?'

'Yeah, that's the one.'

'Were you there yesterday morning?'

'No, I was here. With Hunter.'

'I see,' said Jake, noting it down. 'Is that correct?' he asked Hunter.

Hunter glared at him malevolently. 'Are you suggesting either of us had anything to do with Gabriel's death?'

'Calm down, mate. I'm just asking a routine question, that's all.'

'I was here, all right? Like Amber said.'

'Between nine and eleven?'

Hunter stood suddenly, anger blazing in his eyes. 'We've answered your questions. You should leave now.'

Jake stood too. 'Thanks for your help,' he said to Amber. 'I'll see myself out,' he told Hunter.

*

Ffion ran over the bridge that spanned the canal, her long legs picking up speed as she left Jericho behind and crossed over into Port Meadow, the grassy flood plain that stretched to the west of Oxford. She ran most days, in the early morning or after work. Her favourite route was from her house in Jericho, which she shared with a group of post-graduate students, to the northernmost part of Port Meadow at Wolvercote, a distance of five miles there and back. Sunday was usually her day off and she'd only called into the office this morning to catch up with the latest developments on the new case. Now she was where she wanted to be – out running, across country in the open air – and she could think.

As her feet pounded over the grass, her mind worked, trying to figure out the significance of the eight digits Gabriel had spoken before he died. The number wasn't anything obvious like a prime, a perfect number, a triangular number or any of the other types of numbers that she'd encountered when poring over the pieces of paper recovered from Gabriel's canal boat. The letter that preceded the numerals was baffling too, suggesting not a number but a code of some kind. It might be a bank account, but after examining Gabriel's obsessively scribbled numbers, drawings and equations, that idea seemed too mundane.

The running conditions were good today. There was hardly anyone about, which was just how she liked it. She hated the idea of running competitively in a marathon or half-marathon, part of a herd with other people getting in her way. For her, running had to be a solo activity. She loved the sense of freedom that came from running across the huge open space, the wind on her face, the fresh air filling her lungs. In the winter the meadow was often flooded, and she would suddenly find herself splashing through icy water, which only added to the challenge. Today the ground was baked dry, the grass turning yellow, and she ran at a brisk pace, hoping to match or even beat her personal best.

As she ran, her mind continued to turn over the mysterious code.

A string of eight digits, preceded by a letter. It was an odd legacy. Gabriel must have known he was dying, and of all the things he felt the need to communicate, it was this that he had chosen. It made Ffion wonder what her own last words would be. Surely not a mysterious number spoken to a stranger. Although, come to think of it, that might be quite cool. She wondered briefly if Gabriel had left the clue simply as a mystery intended to baffle people after his death. But no, it had to be significant in some way.

Maths had been her strongest subject in school, and it irritated her that she couldn't make headway with the mysterious code. She pushed herself to run faster, passing Godstow Lock and the crumbling walls of Godstow Abbey on the other side of the river. Grazing horses regarded her nonchalantly as she flew past. A flock of geese took flight and swooped into the air, screeching noisily.

She wasn't having any better luck at cracking the password to Gabriel's laptop or phone, something else she was normally good at. Most people used obvious passwords that were easy to guess. She'd once gained access to a computer used by a criminal gang, whose password was "secret". Duh. Even when people chose something less straightforward, it was often a birthday, or the name of a family member or pet. Knowing the way Gabriel was obsessed by numbers, his password was probably something mathematical – the Fibonacci sequence or the Golden Ratio, or the first few digits of pi. Perhaps even the mysterious nine-character code he had whispered as he died. But nothing Ffion had tried so far had worked.

She reached the car park at Wolvercote and stopped to take a short rest and have a quick drink of water. Usually, running gave her the spark of inspiration she needed to solve whatever problem she was working on, but all today's run had given her was a stitch in her side. She leaned against the stone wall of the car park, breathless, and angry with herself at her defeat.

She'd first taken up running at the age of fourteen in an effort to outrun and, ultimately, defeat the bullies at her school. The small Welsh mining village where she had grown up held traditional values and didn't welcome diversity. A girl like Ffion, who studied hard at school, was attracted to girls as well as boys, and wore her hair short, hadn't fitted in. Running had given her the courage and strength to escape the Rhondda Valley and to study Computer Science at Oxford.

She swallowed another mouthful of water and waited until the pain in her side faded. She had never been able to resist a hard challenge, and she wouldn't allow herself to be beaten so easily. It would be good to show Bridget what she was capable of. And even though she was loathe to admit it, she didn't want to fail in front of the rest of the team. No, to be totally honest, she didn't want to fail in front of Jake.

She'd sensed his interest in her like a dog senses the smell of a rabbit. It was the reason she used barbed comments to keep him in his place. It wasn't that she didn't like him. In fact he had a certain charm and had earned her admiration on the previous case by proving himself to be a man of considerable courage. But she was wary of their relationship going any further. She didn't rule out the possibility of having an intimate relationship with a man. After all, there had been the one boyfriend in the past, but she was more comfortable with girls. Would someone like Jake understand that? She honestly didn't know. He seemed very conventional in his outlook.

A group of elderly ramblers appeared suddenly, marching along the path with their walking poles, disturbing the peace and tranquillity of the morning. Ffion took a deep breath and began the long run back to Jericho.

★

The train from Paddington was running forty minutes late because of engineering works at Slough. Bridget waited by the ticket barriers in Oxford station, clutching her phone anxiously. At least Chloe had texted to say she was on the train, the first text she'd sent since arriving in London yesterday morning.

Of course, Bridget hadn't even had a mobile phone when she was Chloe's age. No one had, back then. She wondered how her own parents had coped when she and her two sisters, Vanessa and Abigail, had started leading independent lives, going out with friends and staying out late. Vanessa and Bridget had always been sensible, but Abigail, the youngest sister, had been something of a rebel. She must have driven their parents mad with worry. And look how that had ended. Abigail had been murdered at the age of sixteen; her killer never caught. It didn't need a psychologist to understand why Bridget had become a police detective, or why Vanessa worked so hard to build a perfect life for herself and insulate her own children from danger.

Bridget could hardly be blamed for wanting to keep

track of Chloe's whereabouts. Ben should have understood that, even if Chloe didn't. He should have made sure that Chloe kept her posted at all times.

She lifted her phone to send yet another text when a voice over the loudspeaker announced that the next train would be terminating at Oxford. Bridget quickly put the phone away to avoid looking like she'd been waiting anxiously for news.

The passengers started to stream through the ticket barriers and Bridget scanned the faces, not wanting to miss Chloe in the rush. Dozens of people streamed past – young, old, singly, in couples, and in groups. She searched the faces with steadily mounting agitation. Her daughter was not among them. Finally, only one or two stragglers were emerging into the station concourse. Bridget looked around desperately, wondering if she could somehow have missed Chloe in the crowds. Panicky thoughts fluttered through her mind.

Then, almost the very last passenger to appear from the train, Chloe pushed her way through the barriers nonchalantly, her gaze fixed on the screen of her phone, her ear buds in her ears.

Bridget rushed forward and hugged her tight.

'Mum! What are you doing?' Chloe plucked the ear buds from her ears.

Bridget pulled away. 'Where were you?'

Chloe rolled her eyes in self-conscious imitation of an embarrassed teenager. 'On the train. Where else?'

'Well, I knew that.' Bridget stopped herself from launching into a full-scale rebuke and allowed herself a moment of relief that her daughter was safe. 'How was the journey?'

'Slow. The train kept stopping.'

'Well, you're here now.' Even to her own ears, the words made it sound like the train delay was Chloe's fault. She tried again, searching for a more conciliatory tone. 'I thought we could collect pizzas on the way home. How does that sound?'

Inevitably Bridget hadn't had time to go shopping and prepare a meal. She hoped that pizza and maybe some TV together would allow time for a bit of mother-daughter bonding.

'Yeah, sure,' said Chloe without any obvious enthusiasm.

'So what did you have to eat last night?' Bridget asked as they crossed the footbridge to the car park. She hoped that Ben's new girlfriend wouldn't turn out to be a Cordon Bleu cook in addition to her other charms.

Chloe brightened. 'We went out to a Lebanese restaurant in the West End. It was amazing.'

'Right. That sounds nice.'

'Why do you say it like that?' said Chloe with a scowl on her face.

'Like what?'

'Like it wasn't nice at all. You're always doing that.'

'I'm sorry. It's just been a long day, that's all. I'm glad you enjoyed going out to eat, really I am.' Maybe the girlfriend wasn't a cook after all, thought Bridget uncharitably.

They got into the Mini, which had grown hot and stuffy in the late afternoon heat. It was a good opportunity to put the roof down and enjoy the sunshine, a chance that didn't often occur with the British weather. If only Bridget could have been born Italian...

'I hope you're wearing sun cream,' said Chloe.

'What?'

'Sun cream. You shouldn't drive around with the roof down if you're not wearing sun cream. You'll get wrinkles. That's what Tamsin says, anyway.'

Bridget gripped the steering wheel with clenched fists as she turned right into Frideswide Square. So now she had wrinkles to worry about, as well as grey hairs. Well, wasn't life just full of nice surprises.

'So what's Tamsin like?' she enquired, taking care to keep her voice free from any hint of scorn.

'She's really nice,' said Chloe enthusiastically. 'She's

younger than you and Dad, of course' – Bridget felt herself wincing at the reminder – 'and a lot of fun. We went shopping together in Oxford Street and I spent some money Dad gave me. Tamsin's got really good style. She gave me some great fashion advice.'

'And what advice did she give you?' asked Bridget through gritted teeth.

'She says I suit vibrant shades and need to show off my best assets such as my collar bone and waist.'

'Maybe she could help me with my wardrobe,' said Bridget. She had more black trousers than she knew what to do with, most of which were too tight. She imagined Tamsin as a svelte blonde with perfect skin and not a grey hair in sight. 'And how is your father?' she asked, determined not to let her resentment show.

'Dad's fine. But never mind him, how was your date?' asked Chloe, twisting in her seat to look at Bridget.

'My date?' Bridget felt her face begin to redden, and it wasn't the sun that was responsible.

'You did go on it, didn't you?' asked Chloe.

'Well, actually something came up at work, and I had to cancel. It was a shame because I was really looking forward to it.'

'Oh, Mum!' The disappointment in Chloe's voice mirrored Vanessa's from earlier in the day. If anything, it was worse coming from her own daughter. 'You're not getting any younger. Don't let him slip past.'

CHAPTER 11

Bridget pressed send on the text before she could change her mind yet again.

Having been thoroughly chastised yesterday by her sister and her daughter – it felt as if they were ganging up on her – she had decided to invite Jonathan out for dinner. It would be her treat, to make up for the fact that she'd had to bail out of going to the opera. It seemed that every time he invited her anywhere, she had to leave early or cancel. Maybe if she made the arrangements herself, the date (or whatever you wanted to call it) would be more likely to go ahead.

Feeling pleased that she'd done the right thing for once, she put her phone on silent and called her team together for the Monday morning meeting, inviting them to update her on progress. Jake was the first to volunteer, towering over her as he took the floor. He flicked to the right page in his notebook and spent a moment or two squinting at his notes, deciphering the spidery scrawl that passed for handwriting.

'I tracked the girlfriend down yesterday. Amber Morgan. She was really upset by Gabriel's death. At any rate there were lots of tears on display. But she seems to be finding comfort in the arms of one of the other artists in the exhibition, Hunter Reed, her former boyfriend. He's got a flash apartment in the new canal-side development in Jericho, and Amber appears to have moved in with him.'

'That didn't take long,' said Ryan with a snigger. 'The other bloke hasn't been dead forty-eight hours and she's gone and shacked up with his mate.'

'She said that she and Gabriel had an "open relationship"' – Jake mimed inverted commas with the first two fingers of each hand – 'whatever that means. Hunter was certainly all over her and she seemed pretty attached to him. She talked about being a "muse", whatever that is.' His fingers were at work again as he said the word.

'Sounds very Pre-Raphaelite to me,' said Ffion. 'Sharing the female muse.'

Jake pulled a face. 'Hunter didn't strike me as the sharing type, to be honest.'

'You think he might have been jealous of Gabriel, and wanted Amber all to himself?' asked Bridget. 'Is this a crime of passion?'

'It's certainly one possible angle,' said Jake. 'The guy came across as very aggressive. The way he answered my questions he acted like I was accusing him. He was certainly jumpy about something, but that might just have been because of the strong smell of cannabis in his apartment...'

'Does he have an alibi for the time of the shooting?'

'He says he was at home all day Saturday, but the only person who can confirm that is Amber.'

'I bet she can,' said Ryan with a smirk.

Bridget unscrewed the top of her pen and wrote the heading "suspects" on the noticeboard. Hunter's name was the first to join the list. 'Did you learn anything else about Gabriel from talking to his girlfriend, or whatever she was?'

Jake consulted his notes. 'According to Amber, Gabriel believed he was being followed by someone. He thought his boat had been broken into about ten days ago, but he didn't report it because nothing was taken. Amber seemed to think he was being paranoid. I also found out where he did his painting. He used a spare room at the art shop on Broad Street where Amber works. The owner of the shop is called Todd Lee. Perhaps Ffion was right about Gabriel being on his way to the art shop when he was killed.' Jake looked across to Ffion, who acknowledged him with a trace of a smile.

'Good, that's all useful. Anything else?'

'Just to say that Hunter's doing all right for himself, even though his paintings look like the work of a toddler having a tantrum. His genius was recognised early on, apparently, by an art collector. The bloke must be blind or something. But this guy supports all the artists in the group, so he probably owns some of Gabriel's paintings too.'

'Although Gabriel didn't live in an expensive apartment,' pointed out Ryan.

'Did you get the name of the collector?' asked Bridget.

'Yes, Lawrence Taylor. I checked him out this morning. He runs a company called Taylor Financial Technology here in Oxford.'

'Okay,' said Bridget, 'let's see what else we can find out about him. Anyone else got anything for me?'

Jake sat down, but no one came forward to take his place.

Bridget turned to Ffion. 'How are you getting on with the eight-digit number?'

'Still waiting to hear back from the banks,' said Ffion with uncharacteristic glumness. 'And I'm having trouble getting into Gabriel's phone and laptop,' she added.

'Well, keep trying.' It wasn't like Ffion to admit defeat on something.

'Ryan, Andy, have you made any progress tracing the driver of the car?'

'I contacted other forces,' said Andy, 'but without a description of the driver, and with no forensic data from the car, it's pretty hopeless. The shooting has all the hallmarks of a gangland killing, but we don't have any leads to work with.'

Ryan shook his head. 'Nothing useful from CCTV either.'

Bridget nodded gloomily. 'Well, he can't have vanished into thin air,' she said in exasperation.

She was only too aware that they were no further forward solving the case. Chief Superintendent Grayson would be wanting an update before too long. They needed to get out of the office and talk to more people.

'Jake, Ffion, I'd like you two to go to the art shop and find out what you can from this Todd Lee. I'm going to visit Taylor Financial Technology and speak to the art collector. Ryan, Andy, just keep trying.'

As she left the office her phone buzzed in her pocket with an incoming text. It was from Jonathan, saying he'd love to do dinner this evening. She smiled to herself. At least today wasn't going to be a complete write-off.

*

The Science Park on the edge of Oxford, close to the Kassam football stadium, was an area of well-groomed hedges, uniform trees planted at regular intervals, and large, modern buildings constructed mainly of glass and metal. Bridget left her Mini in the car park in front of Taylor Financial Technology and entered the building through revolving glass doors. The interior space was big and airy; all bright, reflective surfaces.

A receptionist sat behind a gleaming curved desk, looking like she'd had her hair and make-up done for a photo shoot on a glossy magazine. She tapped busily at the keys of a computer whose sleek, metal screen made the desktops at Kidlington look like something out of a museum.

The receptionist's name was Kerry, according to a badge pinned to her jacket. She looked up as Bridget approached, flashing her a warm smile. 'Good morning. How may I help you?'

Bridget presented her warrant card for inspection. 'I'd like to speak to Lawrence Taylor, please.'

Kerry's smile didn't waver at the sight of the warrant card, although Bridget detected a moment's hesitation before she replied. 'Just one moment, please. I'll see if Mr Taylor is free. Would you like to take a seat while you wait?'

While Kerry put a call through to Lawrence Taylor's personal assistant, Bridget seated herself on one of the black leather sofas arranged around a low table to the side of the desk. The copies of the *Financial Times* and *The Economist* that were laid out neatly on the table didn't interest her, nor did a stunning purple orchid in its stylish ceramic pot, but the huge canvas on the wall above them did. From the style of the painting, Bridget guessed that it was one of Gabriel Quinn's creations. It was a bold splash of colour in this otherwise white, chrome and glass environment.

She stood up again and went to study the painting more closely.

'Mr Taylor will be down shortly,' said Kerry brightly. 'Would you like a coffee?'

'No, thank you.'

A small card fixed to the wall beneath the painting confirmed that the work was Gabriel's and had been painted two years previously. The title of the piece was *Exponential Growth*. Bridget didn't really understand how that applied to the painting, but she supposed it was something that would appeal to the director of a financial technology company.

The lift doors on the opposite side of the lobby pinged open and she turned to see a tall man in a well-cut suit walking briskly towards her. Lawrence Taylor was perhaps in his mid-fifties but looking good for his age. His silvery hair was clipped short to disguise his creeping baldness and he sported a thick, carefully-trimmed beard that Bridget associated with men half his age. His skin was smooth and bronzed, and the gleaming gold watch that adorned his wrist was either a Rolex or a very good imitation. Bridget had the odd feeling that she'd seen him before, but she couldn't think where.

A mobile phone was glued to Lawrence's ear. 'Tell him we can't wait any longer,' he snapped as he strode across the floor. 'We must have that contract signed by close of play today. I don't care how busy he is.' He ended the call and pocketed his phone, holding out a hand to Bridget, and instantly swapping the look of anger on his face for a broad, welcoming smile. 'Sorry about that. Crazy busy time at the moment. Just on the brink of closing one of the most important deals in the history of the company. But I'm sure you didn't come here to talk business. How can I help you, Inspector?'

'I'm here regarding the death of Gabriel Quinn. I'm sure you're aware of it?' The shooting had been all over the news, both local and national.

Lawrence nodded dolefully. 'Ah, yes, poor Gabriel. What a terrible business.'

'I understand that you're a big supporter of some of the artists from the Ruskin School of Art. In fact, I see you have one of Gabriel's paintings right here.'

Lawrence cast an admiring gaze over the canvas. 'Indeed, I acquired *Exponential Growth* a couple of years back, when Gabriel was just beginning to get himself established. A bargain. I paid £100 for it. Of course, it's increased significantly in value since then. And now that Gabriel's gone and got himself murdered, the value could well be into the tens of thousands.' Any trace of sadness on Lawrence's face had been quickly erased by the thought of profit. Bridget was already taking a strong dislike to the man.

'I suppose that's what's meant by *Exponential Growth*,' she said curtly.

Lawrence beamed at her. 'It's the only kind of growth that interests me.'

'Is there somewhere more private we could go to talk?' Bridget asked, aware that behind her desk, Kerry was doing a poor job of pretending not to listen to every word.

'Of course, let's go to my office.'

They took the lift to the third floor and walked through a busy, open-plan area where employees sat at desks in front of hi-tech computer monitors. Taylor asked his PA not to put any calls through for the next ten minutes, then invited Bridget into his office, the walls of which were decorated with more paintings.

'Beauties aren't they?' said Lawrence, noticing Bridget's interest in the pictures.

Bridget wasn't sure that was the word she would have used. 'These don't look like Gabriel's work.'

'No. These were painted by Hunter Reed, one of my protégés. I can honestly say that I discovered Hunter's work when he was completely unknown. I bought them for a song and now they're worth thousands. What do you think of them?'

Bridget examined the large canvases. Like Jake had said, Hunter's painting style seemed to consist of pouring primary-coloured paints onto the canvas and smearing the resulting mess around with his hands, quite possibly with his eyes shut. 'What are they supposed to be?'

'They're abstract, Inspector,' said Lawrence, unable to conceal his irritation at her response. 'Don't ask me to explain any of this stuff, that's my wife's department. She understands the meaning of art far better than I do. I just recognise an investment opportunity when I see one.'

'Your wife?'

'Dr Melissa Price. She's an art tutor at the Ruskin School in Oxford. She first introduced me to the work of her students.'

'I see,' said Bridget. It was a curious coincidence for Melissa Price's name to come up again, and also somewhat surprising that a woman so desperate to cultivate a Bohemian image would be married to a business executive like Lawrence Taylor. Despite his hipster-style beard, he was no rock star or poet.

Bridget took a seat in front of Taylor's desk. 'I met your wife yesterday.'

'You did? Melissa's a wonderful woman, isn't she? She recognised the talent of this particular group of artists and brought them to my attention. As soon as I saw their early work, I knew they had the potential to go far. But you have to invest in the right artist at the right time, Inspector. Buy before the crowds and you can make a fortune. Did you hear that a Monet sold last year at auction for over eighty million pounds? Eighty million! It was a picture of a haystack. Just goes to show.'

'What exactly does it show?'

'Scarcity value,' said Taylor, tapping the desk in front of him. 'Mark Twain wrote that to make a man covet a thing, it is only necessary to make the thing difficult to attain. The reason Monet's haystack is so valuable isn't because of its intrinsic value, but because Claude Monet is dead and can't paint any more like it. Now Gabriel Quinn is dead too. Overnight, the value of his work must have risen ten-fold. Getting himself murdered was a smart career move, if you ask me.'

'But Gabriel will hardly benefit from being dead, will he?' said Bridget coldly. 'The only people who stand to benefit from his death are those who already own his paintings.'

'Yes, well,' said Lawrence, 'I see the point you're making. But if you're suggesting that I might have something to do with Gabriel's death, then you've got the wrong idea completely. I'm a very wealthy man, Inspector. I don't need to kill anyone to make more money. Not that I haven't been tempted once or twice.' His grin was firmly back again. 'That's just a joke!'

'Who else collected Gabriel's paintings?' asked Bridget.

Lawrence shrugged. 'No idea. You should ask the owner of the gallery that sells his work.'

'Jonathan Wright?'

'That's him. You know the guy?'

Bridget ignored the question and asked one of her own. 'How well did you know Gabriel? Did you meet him personally?'

'A few times. Obviously Melissa knew him much better than me. She was his tutor. But I spoke to him at exhibition openings, that kind of thing. Quiet guy. A bit weird, you know.'

'No. Tell me.'

'Introspective. Thoughtful. Something of a hermit, by all accounts. That's always good for an artist's reputation. And there was this whole obsession with numbers. Melissa's always stressing the importance of originality in art. Gabriel certainly had a unique angle, and that made his work attractive. To be honest, it's the only reason I bought his paintings.'

Bridget stared at him. 'That was the only reason?'

Lawrence smiled. 'I told you I don't know much about art.'

She glanced up at Hunter's paintings on the wall of the office. 'Why did you buy Hunter's paintings?'

Lawrence's smile took on a mischievous air. 'I can hardly remember now. They seemed fun at the time. But to tell you the truth, although Hunter showed initial promise, he hasn't produced anything notable for some while. Gabriel was very much the rising star. I'm so glad I bought *Exponential Growth* when I did.'

'There are a few more questions that I have to ask you,' said Bridget. 'When did you last see Gabriel?'

'I suppose it must have been at the opening of the latest exhibition. All of the artists were there at the gallery. I went with Melissa to view the paintings and to buy a few that I was interested in.'

So that's where Bridget had seen him. She had briefly been at the exhibition opening herself, before being called away on police business. So she must very briefly have crossed paths with Gabriel herself. A shiver ran down her spine at the thought, but she had no recollection of the young artist. As everyone said, he was too shy and retiring to make a memorable impact. She wondered what she might have said to him if she'd known then that he would be dead in just a few short weeks. But if we could see the future, no doubt we'd do so many things differently.

'Can you account for your movements on Saturday morning?' she asked Lawrence.

His face froze for a second before his grin reappeared. 'You think I shot Gabriel, Inspector? I can reassure you on that score. I was here in my office. My personal secretary can vouch for that, as well as the client I was discussing business with. Would you like me to give you his details?'

'I'm sure that won't be necessary. For now, at least.'

'I can tell you one thing, Inspector. If I wanted someone dead, I wouldn't do it myself. I don't even know how to use a gun. Besides, there's one thing I've learnt in business. When you don't know how to do something well, don't try to do it yourself. Outsource it.'

'A contract killing?'

'That's how I would do it,' said Lawrence. 'No question about it. So you needn't concern yourself with my whereabouts at the time of the murder. Instead, ask yourself who had the means and the motive.'

'And who do you think did, Mr Taylor?'

'Ah, now that's your job, I think, Inspector. So, if you don't have any more questions, I have a meeting to attend in five minutes.'

'I'll see myself out,' said Bridget. 'Thank you for your time.'

She left the building unsettled by the interview. She wasn't sure that her visit to Taylor Financial Technology had taught her much that she hadn't already known about Gabriel Quinn. But she had learned a lot about Lawrence Taylor and his enigmatic wife, Melissa Price. One thing that was very clear to her was that despite his protestations, Taylor had not only the means to hire a contract killer, but also the motive.

CHAPTER 12

Jake and Ffion drove to the centre of Oxford in near silence. Jake tried to make conversation by asking her about her weekend, but received only curt answers. She'd gone for a run. That was it. He asked her if she'd like any help figuring out the meaning of the eight-digit number, but she snapped at him, saying she had it under control.

Suit yourself, he thought. Honestly, sometimes he couldn't make Ffion out. She often seemed to treat her colleagues as the enemy. He guessed she didn't like to admit she was stuck with something. He could understand that, but there was no point being pig-headed about things. They were supposed to be a team.

He parked the Subaru in St Giles' outside St John's college and they walked the short distance to Broad Street, cutting down the side of St Mary Magdalen with its tiny but overgrown graveyard. A *Big Issue* magazine seller standing outside the Oxfam shop caught his eye. Jake recognised him as Stu, the guy he and Ffion had spoken to on the previous case when they'd been searching for a homeless girl.

'How are you doing, Stu?' he asked.

'Not too bad.' Stu pointed a finger at the sun. 'Can't complain in this weather.' He held out a magazine expectantly.

Jake rummaged in his pocket for some spare change and handed it over.

'Cheers, mate,' said Stu with a toothless grin, giving him the copy.

'Look after yourself,' said Jake as they walked off.

'You're generous today,' said Ffion.

Jake shrugged. He might be struggling to afford to buy himself a place of his own in Oxford's over-heated housing market, but he wasn't struggling in the way guys like Stu were. The homeless problem in Oxford had shocked him the first time he'd gone out for a few beers in the city centre. Besides, it was a good idea to keep on the right side of guys like Stu. Their eyes and ears might be useful one day.

The art shop was located in an old Georgian building near the corner of Turl Street. An old-fashioned bell tinkled as Jake pushed open the door. Arranged over two floors, every inch of available space in the building was packed with art supplies, from paper, paints and pastels to chisels, palette knives and bottles of stripper for cleaning brushes. Art had never really been Jake's thing at school and the sight of all those brushes and paints brought back unpleasant memories of Mrs King's art lessons where most of the kids had just messed around. Including himself.

Amber was behind the counter. When she saw Jake, a look of alarm spread across her pale features. 'What is it now?' she asked. 'Have you found something?'

'Nothing to worry about,' said Jake quickly. He introduced Ffion and asked if they could speak to Todd, the owner.

'I'll go and see if he's free,' said Amber. 'Can you watch the till for me, please?'

She vanished up the stairs, reappearing a few minutes later followed by a shifty-looking character with black hair and a goatee beard.

'Todd Lee?' asked Jake.

The man had a wiry build and wore a loose-fitting T-shirt. A distinctive octopus tattoo adorned his right arm. He gave Jake and Ffion a cagey nod.

'I wonder if we could have a chat about Gabriel Quinn?' said Jake. 'We understand that he used a room in your shop as his art studio.'

'Who told you that?'

'Is it true?'

Todd rubbed his hands together. 'Er, sure, the room's upstairs.'

'Perhaps we could take a look at it?'

Todd didn't seem very keen on the suggestion. 'It's not very big. Maybe we could go to a café or something if you want to talk about Gabriel?'

'I think we'd like to see his studio, if you don't mind,' said Ffion, making her way towards the stairs.

'If that's all right with you, sir?' said Jake.

Ffion was already climbing the rickety staircase.

'Er, yes, well I suppose we could go up there,' said Todd, watching her go. 'It's just that it's a bit of a mess at the moment.'

'I'm sure that won't be a problem, sir,' said Jake.

The studio was at the top of the shop and looked out over a small yard onto the backs of the old terraced houses on Ship Street. Todd had not been lying when he'd described the room as a bit of a mess. It was unfurnished, with bare plaster walls, and floorboards covered in splashes of dried paint. A large easel stood in the centre of the room with a half-finished canvas propped on it. Presumably Gabriel's last work-in-progress, thought Jake, sadly never to be completed. Dozens more canvases in various states of completion leaned against the walls. A wooden palette covered in thick oozy swirls of oil paint was lying on the floor, along with hundreds of tubes of paint. Brushes standing in jam jars of white spirit were lined up in rows along the skirting boards. Jake felt a childish urge to stick his finger in the paint on the palette. Maybe that was why he'd never done well in art at school. He just couldn't take it seriously.

There was barely enough room for one person to stand amid the clutter, certainly not enough for all three of them to enter the studio at once. Jake stood in the doorway while Ffion picked her way around the contents of the room. Todd lingered at the top of the staircase, wringing his hands anxiously.

'How long had Gabriel been making use of this room?' asked Jake.

'About three or four years, I guess,' said Todd, dragging his eyes away from Ffion.

'Did anyone else use the studio?'

'No. Just Gabriel.'

'So he did all his painting here?'

'Yeah, it suited him well enough. I mean, he didn't have any space on his boat, did he? Canvases take up a lot of room.'

'I'm sure they do,' agreed Jake.

'Gabriel paid a small rent for this space,' continued Todd, his gaze drifting back to Ffion, who was lifting canvases and looking at each one. 'Not much,' he added hastily, as if Jake had accused him of profiteering. 'He couldn't afford a lot. And we had an arrangement.'

'What kind of arrangement?'

'Nothing against the law,' said Todd. 'I mean, I gave him special rates on art supplies and he bought all his stuff from me.'

'When was Gabriel last here?'

'Friday, I think,' said Todd. 'He was supposed to be coming in on Saturday, and then...' He trailed off miserably.

'Somebody shot him dead,' concluded Jake.

Todd shuddered visibly. 'Gabriel was a good bloke, you know? He didn't say much, but he always paid his rent on time. Well, mostly. And he kept the place neat and tidy.' He turned to look again at the room full of paints and brushes. 'Apart from all the mess, of course. But that's artists for you. That's normal.'

Ffion stepped carefully between the paint tubes to a stack of large canvases propped up next to the door. She moved the stack aside and retrieved a sketchpad from behind them. She started to turn the pages. 'What are these?'

'Nothing,' blurted Todd. 'I expect. Just rubbish.'

'They don't look like rubbish.'

'Sketches for a painting, then.'

'They're not in Gabriel's usual style.'

'Well, like I said, they're probably just doodles.' Todd reached out to take the sketchpad from her. 'You shouldn't look at them. Gabriel hated it when people looked at his work in progress. He was a very private man.'

'Actually,' said Ffion, holding the sketchpad close to her chest. 'I think I might take this with me as evidence.'

Jake didn't miss the look of alarm that crossed Todd's face. 'Evidence of what? They're just worthless scribbles,' he protested, but a hard stare from Ffion shut him up.

'So what will happen to all Gabriel's things now he's dead?' asked Jake.

'Landfill, I expect,' said Todd. 'It's no good to anyone else.'

'You don't think that this might be worth something, now that he's dead? Gabriel Quinn's final uncompleted work?'

A light bulb seemed to switch on in Todd's head. 'I never thought of that. Maybe I could flog it.'

'Except that it doesn't belong to you, does it?' said Ffion. 'This is Gabriel's property.'

'But he's snuffed it,' said Todd.

'Right now this is evidence in a criminal investigation,' said Jake. 'But when that's concluded, all of Gabriel's possessions will go into his estate. His canal boat, his unfinished paintings, and any money he had. Do you know if he had any family?'

'Nah. All dead, I reckon. But I bet he'd have wanted it

to go to Amber. Although' – he turned and checked that Amber was still downstairs before continuing – 'if you ask me, he deserved better than her. She was always sleeping with other men behind his back.'

'Do you mean Hunter Reed?' queried Jake.

'Well, Hunter, yeah. But there have been others. Too many for me to remember. That was the trouble with Gabriel – he was naive, he let other people take advantage of him.'

'Like who?'

Todd immediately looked like he wished he'd never said anything. 'Well... like Lawrence Taylor, the art collector. He spotted Gabriel's talent, but he never paid him a fair price for his work, just bought a bunch of his paintings on the cheap. And Gabriel's art tutor at the Ruskin, Melissa Price, she was the one who first introduced Gabriel to Lawrence. Sharks, the pair of them.'

'That's interesting,' said Jake, 'I've got two more questions for you before we leave. First of all, can you think of any reason why anyone would want to harm Gabriel? Did he have any enemies? Had anyone made threats against him?'

Todd's hand moved to the tip of his beard and began to tug it nervously. 'Enemies? A man like Gabriel? No, of course not. He was just a painter. Kept himself to himself. Never did anyone any harm.'

'In the days before he died, he told Amber that he thought he was being followed,' said Ffion. 'Someone broke into his boat.'

Todd's beard looked ready to snap under the strain of the repeated tugging. 'Followed? That's crazy talk. Who would want to do that?'

'That's what we'd like to know,' said Ffion. 'We'd also like to know if the code L79468235 means anything to you.'

Todd looked blank. 'No, nothing.' He turned back to Jake. 'Are you done now? Is that all your questions?'

'Just one more. Where were you on Saturday morning?'

A look of relief flooded Todd's face. 'I was here, running the shop. I have loads of people who can vouch for me. Saturday morning is the busiest time for us.'

'All right,' said Jake. 'Thanks for your help.'

They made their way back down the narrow staircase and out into Broad Street.

'What was he hiding?' asked Ffion as they started to walk back to St Giles'.

'Not just a pile of old canvases,' said Jake, pleased that Ffion seemed to be talking to him again.

'And what do you think Amber was so frightened about?' asked Ffion.

'Frightened?'

'Didn't you see her face when we first entered the shop?'

'Yes, but maybe she was just worried we were bringing her more bad news.'

'Worse than the news that her boyfriend had been shot dead?'

'Well, I don't know. I think she just has a nervous disposition.'

'Is that what you call it?' said Ffion with a smile on her lips. 'You don't think it's strange that she's back at work just two days after Gabriel was murdered?'

For some reason, Jake felt a compulsion to defend Amber from Ffion's suspicions. 'Some people find work therapeutic. Perhaps it's better than moping at home alone.'

'Maybe. You didn't tell me she was so stunning.'

A familiar burning at the tips of his ears told Jake that they must have turned pink. 'Do you think she is?'

'Don't you think so?'

The warmth in Jake's ears was starting to spread to his cheeks. 'I hadn't really noticed.'

Ffion regarded him coolly with her emerald eyes. 'I did. It was the very first thing I noticed.'

He tried to think of an answer to that, but she was already striding ahead of him, back to the car. He jogged to catch up.

★

Todd Lee stood outside his shop, in the tiny yard at the back. With a trembling hand he drew a packet of tobacco from his inside coat pocket, extracted a roll of paper, and folded it clumsily between thumb and fingers. He tapped loose leaves into the crease of the paper then rolled it until the tobacco was enclosed in a smooth, stubby cylinder. His hands began to shake less as the familiar ritual soothed him. They said that smoking was bad for your health, that every smoke was another nail in your coffin, but to Todd's way of thinking it was a bloody life saver. He couldn't imagine how he'd ever be able to calm his nerves without it.

He pinched stray tobacco from the ends of the cigarette and narrowed the tip between thumb and forefinger. Todd never used filters. He twisted the ends of the paper so that no tobacco could fall out, then jammed the completed cigarette in his mouth while he reached inside his pocket to pull out a box of matches.

His fingers were still shaking and he fumbled the first match. The second one caught, and he lit the cigarette. There was no breeze in the yard, but he cupped one hand around the cigarette out of habit, sucking at it until the flame caught. He inhaled deeply, then coughed pleasantly as cool smoke filled his lungs.

Clamping the soothing cigarette between his teeth for a second time, he pulled out his phone and dialled a number. The call was answered quickly. Todd spoke quietly into the phone, outlining what had just happened.

The person at the end of the line showed little sympathy for his plight.

'Don't call me a bloody idiot!' protested Todd. 'I nearly got arrested. They looked in the studio. They took one of Gabriel's sketchpads with them. Gabriel had dumped it behind some canvases, probably forgot it was there.'

He listened carefully, then spoke again: 'Yeah, yeah, of course not. What do you take me for, a fool?'

His brows furrowed in consternation as he listened to the reply.

'I know what happened to Gabriel. You don't need to remind me about that.'

The line went dead and he slipped the phone back into his jeans. Slowly he lifted his hands and held them before his face. Bloody hell. They were shaking again now, even more than before.

CHAPTER 13

The pathologist's report was waiting on Bridget's desk when she arrived back at the office. Efficient as ever, Dr Roy Andrews must have done the post-mortem that morning and sent his results over straight away. She tore open the envelope and pulled out the report.

There were no surprises as to the cause of death. A single gunshot wound to the chest. The bullet had entered the left ventricle of the heart, tearing through the left coronary artery as it went, resulting in massive and immediate internal haemorrhaging. The victim had probably taken less than a minute to die.

Roy informed her in a handwritten note paper-clipped to the main report that he had retrieved the bullet – 9mm calibre – and sent it off to ballistics for further examination. 9mm was a common calibre, used mainly in handguns and military-grade assault rifles. Firearm laws in the UK outlawed the ownership of both handguns and assault rifles, so even the possession of a weapon like this was illegal. Roy's best guess was that the weapon was likely to be the kind of handgun issued to soldiers in the British army, or else a similar imported firearm. The ballistics experts might be able to glean some more useful information from it.

Roy had added a post-script to say that given the position of the shot in the middle of the chest, the gunman had either been extremely lucky or was a trained professional, probably ex-military. He would put money on the latter. Bridget was inclined to agree with him, especially given the nature of the weapon used. She went back to the main post-mortem report and read on.

Gabriel hadn't been suffering from any diseases, but toxicology tests had detected both cannabinoids and psilocin in his body. The high level of cannabinoids in Gabriel's liver strongly suggested that he was a regular user of cannabis, and the presence of psilocin indicated that he had consumed magic mushrooms very recently, probably within the previous twenty-four hours. Interesting. Both cannabis and magic mushrooms could cause paranoia. Bridget wondered if Gabriel's fear of being followed was nothing more than a side effect of consuming mushrooms. And where did he get his drugs from? She made a note to investigate further.

She made a copy of the report and went to see how Ryan and Andy were getting on. They were both sitting at their desks, idly tapping at their keyboards, looking bored out of their skulls.

'Any progress with tracing the driver?' she asked.

'Nope,' said Ryan, shaking his head. 'Nothing. The guy seems to have teleported the car to the field before setting it alight. And then vanished into thin air.'

'Nothing here either, ma'am,' said Andy. 'We just don't have enough info to work with.'

'Then try this.' Bridget dropped the copy of the post-mortem report onto Andy's desk. 'The bullet was 9mm calibre, probably from a handgun. Ballistics are looking into it as a matter of urgency, and hopefully they'll be able to tell us more soon, but for the moment our best guess is that we're looking for a veteran with military training, possibly using an ex-army weapon.'

Andy sat up with obvious enthusiasm. 'Well, that certainly helps to narrow things down.' He opened the report and started reading. 'I'll get onto it right away, ma'am.'

'Got anything new for me?' asked Ryan. 'CCTV's proved to be a dead end.'

'I have, actually. I'd like you to take a close look at the art collector, Lawrence Taylor, and see if you can dig up anything interesting on Taylor Financial Technology – any criminal connections, suspicious financial transactions, dirt of any kind.'

'With pleasure.' Ryan shot her a wicked grin. 'You think our friend might have something to hide?'

'You mean apart from greed, narcissism and shockingly bad taste in art? Let's see.'

She looked up as Jake and Ffion returned to the office. She'd sent them off to the art shop hoping that a little time spent working together would help them to bond. If she was going to get the best from her team, she needed everyone to co-operate without any friction. She'd hoped that Jake might be able to soften Ffion's prickly exterior, and that Ffion's eagle eye would spot anything that Jake missed. She was disappointed to see from their body language that the mysterious tension between them hadn't completely dissipated.

Ffion entered the room first, striding purposely as if trying to keep as much distance between herself and Jake as possible. Jake followed with a hangdog look, his earlobes a tell-tale shade of pink. Something had happened between them, but Bridget had no desire to unearth it now.

'How did you get on at the art shop?' she asked. 'Did you get to meet the owner?'

'Yeah,' said Jake. 'We met Todd Lee. He's a bit of a dodgy character actually.'

'In what way?'

'Just generally untrustworthy. He really didn't want to answer any of our questions. In fact, he didn't like us being in the shop at all. Gabriel rented a studio from him on the top floor, but Todd was very reluctant to let us go up and look at it. Ffion practically had to push past him to get up the stairs.'

'What was he hiding?'

'Mostly a terrible mess, but I don't suppose we can arrest him for that.'

Bridget shook her head. If making a mess were a crime, then Jake would be behind bars himself, the state he kept his car in. 'Then why the evasiveness?'

Jake looked to Ffion.

'I found this,' she said, pulling a sketchpad out of her bag. 'The drawings are Gabriel's but they're not his usual style. Todd did his best to stop me from looking at them. He looked horrified when we told him we were taking them away as evidence.'

'Can I see?' asked Bridget.

Ffion turned the pages of the sketchpad. The pictures were religious scenes, possibly from the Book of Revelation. Angels swooping down from the sky; the Four Horsemen of the Apocalypse; the damned burning in sulphurous lakes while demons tormented them.

'Interesting,' commented Bridget. 'They're not quite the kind of picture you'd hang above your mantelpiece, but I'm not sure why Todd wanted to hide them.'

'And another thing,' said Jake. 'Todd claimed that Amber often cheated on Gabriel, and not just with Hunter, but with other men too.'

'And he didn't think much of Lawrence Taylor or Melissa Price either,' added Ffion. 'He said they took advantage of Gabriel, paying him a pittance for his work.'

'Well that figures,' agreed Bridget. 'Lawrence openly boasted about underpaying all the artists he buys paintings from. It seemed to be a badge of honour for him.'

'So what next?' asked Jake.

Bridget filled them in on the latest from the pathologist's report.

'Cannabis and magic mushrooms?' said Ffion. 'Well

that may well explain the mysterious break-in on Gabriel's boat. Perhaps he imagined the whole episode.'

'Possibly,' said Bridget.

'And I definitely smelled cannabis when I was at Hunter's place,' said Jake.

'I wonder if they used the same supplier?' said Bridget. 'I'd like to find out.'

Jake looked sceptical. 'Do you think it's related to Gabriel's shooting? Smoking weed is hardly organised crime.'

'Even so, it's a lead, and we need to follow up every one, especially with so little to work with. I'd like you to go and talk to Amber again, and see what you can find out. Do you know where she is?'

'She's working in the art shop right now,' said Jake. 'We spoke to her just half an hour ago.'

Bridget looked at her watch. 'Well, if you go back now, you should be able to catch her before the shop closes.'

'All right,' sighed Jake, turning to leave again. 'I'll get my skates on.'

*

It didn't take Ryan very long to complete his background checks on Lawrence Taylor. The company director might well be avaricious and self-absorbed, but he was completely clean as far as criminal behaviour was concerned. Either clean, or very good at cleaning up afterwards. Though after what, Ryan had no idea. As far as he could tell, the boss of Taylor Financial Technology hadn't even fiddled his taxes, let alone got caught up in any serious financial irregularities. His company had never been investigated by the Serious Fraud Office. Even the Financial Conduct Authority had shown no particular interest in his affairs.

Frustrated by his lack of results, Ryan helped himself to Andy's copy of the post-mortem report and proceeded to read it cover to cover, tossing it back onto Andy's desk when finished. 'That's a very interesting read, Andy. Very interesting indeed, don't you think?'

From the desk opposite, the older sergeant grunted and continued to tap away earnestly on his keyboard, keeping his eyes on his screen. Andy was a solid worker, you couldn't deny that, even if it made him desperately dull to work with.

But Ryan wasn't so easily deflected. 'Reading between the lines, I'd say that our young Gabriel Quinn was off his head on drugs the morning he was killed. It's not surprising his last words were complete and utter gibberish. It's a wonder he could still cycle straight. It's a miracle he didn't imagine he was being followed by a pink elephant.' He waited to see if this pronouncement would elicit a response from his colleague.

Andy frowned, and Ryan watched his face as he processed the comment. Andy was never the quickest thinker in the office. You could ask him a question, nip out to the bathroom, and he'd still be preparing his reply when you got back. 'Traces of cannabis and magic mushrooms in his system,' said Andy at last. 'That's all the report says.'

'Mushrooms don't stay in the body for long,' persisted Ryan. 'If traces were detectable, he must have taken them very recently. He was probably still under their influence.'

'That may be true,' said Andy. 'But he didn't hallucinate the gunman who shot him.'

'You don't reckon drugs might be involved in this case somehow?'

'I don't know. It's a possibility, I suppose.'

'It seems plausible to me. A contract killing sounds much more like the work of a drugs gang than a bunch of artists. What do artists know about guns? They'd probably just stick one in a glass case and put it on display in a gallery.'

'We'll know more once the ballistics boys have filed their report,' said Andy.

'Yeah, sure. But what do you think right now?'

'I'm not sure, really.'

Ryan sighed. There was more chance of the delectable DC Ffion Hughes having a sudden change of mind and begging him to go out on a date than getting Andy to show any imagination.

Speaking of Ffion, he'd noticed Jake paying her rather a lot of attention recently. Why was it always Jake and Ffion who got to go out investigating together? It ought to be Jake who stayed in the office and did the boring desk jobs. But in any case, Jake surely didn't stand a chance with the deadly Welsh woman. She'd break his bloody balls.

Andy looked up from his desk. 'Time for a coffee break, mate?'

'Yeah, go on,' said Ryan. 'If Bridget asks, I'll tell her you forced me into it.' He leaned back in his chair. 'Harry!' he called, summoning the junior detective constable over to his desk. 'It's time for a coffee.'

Harry approached with trepidation. 'Not me again. Why do I always have to fetch the coffees?'

Ryan rolled his eyes in mock affront. 'We've talked about this before, young Harry. Hierarchy. Andy and I are your superior officers, and that means you have to do whatever we tell you.' He winked at Andy. Harry was too credulous by far, much too easy for Ryan to manipulate. 'Junior staff these days have no respect for their elders, eh, Andy?'

The older sergeant chuckled. 'You're still just a kid yourself, Ryan.'

'Too right, mate. I'm not an old fart like you, at any rate.' Andy was well into his thirties already – married with two kids, a mortgage, and a liking for early nights in front of the telly. He was also a plodder, likely to remain a sergeant until he retired. That wasn't how Ryan saw his own future. He had plans, ambitions. 'By the time I'm your age, Andy, I expect to be a DI at least. Probably DCI. I'll probably be your boss.'

'Good luck with that, mate. By the time you get to my age, you're more likely to have been dismissed for gross misconduct.'

Harry was still hovering nervously, waiting for the banter to come to an end. 'What shall I get you, then?' he asked. 'Black, white, sugar or no sugar?' Those were the only options available at the police canteen.

'A double full-fat latte with two sugars for me,' replied Ryan, stretching back lazily in his chair. 'And for my colleague DS Cartwright here, a vanilla iced espresso.'

'Seriously?' moaned Harry. 'That means I have to go all the way to Starbucks. They don't do that in the canteen.'

'An excellent deduction,' said Ryan with a grin. 'You'll make a first-rate detective one day. Just remember to call me "boss" when you address me.'

'Unless the real boss is within earshot,' said Andy.

Harry looked puzzled. 'You mean Bridget?'

'Detective Inspector Hart to you. Show some respect, lad.'

Harry looked thoroughly fed up. 'Do I really have to do this? I have other jobs to do.'

'Nothing is as important as keeping your superiors fully topped-up with their addictions of choice. In Andy's case, that's actually a twenty-pack of Marlboro, except he's given up smoking now.'

'I don't miss it,' said Andy. 'All that standing outside in winter, freezing your balls off. It was horrible.'

'Caffeine is a much more sensible choice,' agreed Ryan. 'What about you, Harry? What's your addiction?'

'I don't really have one.'

'Everyone has something. Go on, tell us. We promise not to tell anyone.'

'Seriously, I like to stay clean. I'm into healthy eating and exercise.'

'Very commendable, I'm sure. So what if I told you that this case is really all about drugs?'

Harry's eyes widened at the word. 'You think it is?'

'Reckon so. All this stuff about artists and numbers is bullshit, if you ask me. This is serious organised crime we're looking at. Trust me, I know these things.'

Andy leaned across the desk and punched his shoulder playfully. 'Ryan, you don't know a thing. Stop winding Harry up.'

Ryan yawned. 'Yeah, all right. Off you go, then, Harry. And be quick about it. I like my coffee nice and hot.'

*

By the time Jake had negotiated his way back through Oxford's medieval city centre and found a parking space for the Subaru it was already five o'clock. Stu, the *Big Issue* seller, was long gone. Jake ran to the shop on Broad Street and found it already closed.

'Damn it!' He banged on the door of the shop, peering in at its darkened interior, but no answer came. Instead, he scanned the street, hoping for a glimpse of flowing red hair among the swarming crowds of tourists and locals.

He spotted her in an instant, head down and with a bag slung over her shoulder. She was lighting a cigarette at the corner of Turl Street and Market Street. He called out her name, but she scurried away in the direction of Cornmarket.

He sprinted off in pursuit, catching up with her at the back of the covered market. 'Amber, hang on,' he called, breathlessly.

She turned and scowled at him. 'You again. What is it this time?'

'I just wanted to ask you a few questions.'

She took a drag on her cigarette and blew the smoke in his face. 'What about? You already spoke to me once this afternoon. Have you found out who killed Gabriel?'

Jake waved the cloud of smoke away with his hand. 'Look, why don't we go and sit down somewhere? Would you like a coffee? A bite to eat?'

She still seemed suspicious, but eventually nodded her consent. 'Yeah, all right then. If you're buying. I've been on my feet all day. I'm starving.'

They went to a café inside the covered market and Jake

ordered coffee and chocolate muffins for both of them while Amber found a place to sit. She chose a table by the window, looking out over a butcher's shop that had a whole pig's carcass hanging outside from a hook. The sight of the dead animal, its belly slit wide open from head to hind legs, made Jake feel queasy, but Amber didn't seem bothered. She sat hunched over the table, a thin, pale figure in her denim jacket and summer dress, picking greedily at her muffin with slender fingers and cramming the pieces into her mouth. It didn't take long for her to put it away. For such a skinny waif, she had a surprisingly big appetite.

'So what is it?' she asked, her mouth still full of cake. 'What questions do you want to ask?' There was no hiding the hostility in her voice.

Jake wondered how best to proceed. Mentioning that the pathologist had carried out his post-mortem examination of Gabriel's body didn't seem like the best dinner-table conversation. 'We found traces of cannabis and magic mushrooms in Gabriel's system,' he began.

Amber took a sip of her coffee. 'So?'

'You don't seem surprised.'

She gazed sullenly at him. 'Weed? Shrooms? What were you expecting me to say?'

'I was hoping you could shed some light on Gabriel's drug habit.'

'Drug habit? You make it sound like he was some kind of heroin junkie.'

'Psilocin is a class A drug. The maximum sentence for its possession is seven years. If you supply it you can go to prison for life.'

'Gabriel wasn't a dealer.'

'Then who was? Where did he get it from?'

Amber shot a meaningful glance at the untouched chocolate muffin on Jake's plate. 'Are you going to eat that?'

Outside, the deceased pig gazed dolefully in Jake's direction, making his stomach churn. 'No,' he said, sliding the plate across the table, 'You can have it.'

Her fingers began to dissect the cake, pulling off portions to stuff into her mouth. 'Don't tell me you've never smoked dope at a party.'

Jake hadn't, as it happened, but he had a curious feeling that admitting it would somehow lessen him in Amber's eyes. 'I know that you and Hunter smoke cannabis too.'

Amber stopped eating and raised her voice in anger. 'What if we do? Are you seriously telling me that you're here to arrest me and Hunter for using some weed? What's wrong with you? Why aren't you looking for Gabriel's killer?'

Aware that everyone in the café had turned to stare, Jake tried to calm her down. 'I'm not here to arrest you. I'm simply following up a possible lead. To find out who murdered Gabriel, we need to ask a lot of questions, even if some of them may seem irrelevant or distressing to you. So if you can tell me who supplied Gabriel, it will be a big help in our investigation. We're not looking to prosecute anyone for minor drugs offences, we're trying to catch a cold-blooded murderer.'

Tears were beginning to well up in Amber's eyes. Beneath the façade of defiance lurked a frightened and vulnerable child. It didn't take much to break down her thin armour. 'I just want you to catch him,' she said, sobbing. 'Find the bastard who killed my Gabriel.'

'Then help me,' said Jake. 'Tell me where he got his drugs from.'

Amber shook her head, sending tears streaming down her cheeks. 'I can't.' She stood up suddenly and ran from the café in a flurry of bright hair and cotton dress.

Jake let her go. She would come to him if she felt able to talk again, he was sure of it. He already felt bad about pushing her so hard. The girl seemed so fragile, he feared that under any more pressure she might simply break.

The second muffin lay half eaten on the plate, and after a moment's hesitation he reached for it. The carcass hanging from the butcher's hook outside wasn't quite enough to kill his appetite, and he took a large bite. *Greedy pig*, he thought, and began to chew.

★

Ffion's opponent regarded her with a look of gritty determination. The bearded man, older than her, and much heavier built, stood sideways on, in the stance of a fighter, his hands raised in fists before his face. He yelled out a cry and jabbed at her at shoulder height with a closed fist. Ffion ducked to the left, avoiding the blow easily. The man struck again, this time with a swinging backfist that came directly at her face. She dodged back just in time, and moved for a counter strike. Lifting her knee off the ground she swung her hips, pivoted on her left foot and snapped her right leg out at ninety degrees. The ball of her foot connected with her opponent's shoulder and he staggered back, knocked off balance.

'All right!' he cried. 'Enough!'

He bowed low to her and she returned his bow before leaving the mat. In Taekwondo, bowing was a sign of respect between two sparring partners, acknowledging the skill of the opponent. Martial arts were as much about mental discipline as physical fitness and strength, and it was important even for a master to show humility in order to develop and improve.

This evening her mental discipline was sorely wanting, despite the ease with which she had defeated her opponent. She'd hoped that by coming here to train, she might find clarity, but she had too much on her mind, and left the dojang with her thoughts less focused than normal.

It was hard to concentrate with the mystery of the eight-digit number tantalisingly out of reach. And she was getting nowhere trying to crack the passwords to Gabriel's laptop and phone.

And then there was the problem of Jake. This was a very different kind of problem, and not one that Ffion knew how to handle. Numbers and computers she could normally deal with, but she had never been very good with people. Especially men.

She was used to unwanted male attention. It was something she'd had to get used to, especially in the male-dominated police environment. Her usual approach was to repel any man who came close, just in case. Certainly she'd had no trouble getting rid of Ryan Hooper when he'd asked her out.

But Jake was harder to manage because she actually liked him. He hadn't yet plucked up the courage to ask her out – mainly because she had taken care to discourage him every time he looked like he might do. But she knew that he wanted to.

The problem was that whenever she told a guy she was bisexual, they always struggled to understand. Either they ran a mile, or else they assumed she was into all kinds of kinky stuff. It was rare to find a man who could accept her as she was, and Ffion doubted whether Jake was that kind of man.

For now it was safer to keep him at a distance.

After leaving Taekwondo she went straight home to the terraced house she shared in Jericho with a couple of post-graduate students. They were both women that she'd got to know during her undergraduate days. When she'd first joined Thames Valley Police she had been assigned to Reading in Berkshire, but when she relocated back to Oxford she'd quickly found a room with her old friends.

Judy was a materials scientist studying new types of batteries for use in electric cars, and Claire was an economist specialising in developing countries in Africa. Ffion found them both in the kitchen preparing homemade falafel served with pitta bread and a beetroot salad.

'You're just in time to eat,' said Judy, taking three plates from the cupboard. 'Come and join us.'

'Thanks. I don't mind if I do.'

Claire was a vegan, and Ffion was always happy to share in a vegan meal. Optimal nutrition was very much one of her own passions. She nipped upstairs to change out of her sweaty dobok into a pair of leggings and a hoodie, and joined her house mates around the kitchen table.

As always the food was delicious. Although Claire was the vegan, her cooking skills were strictly limited and it was Judy who had prepared the meal. She brought the rigours of the scientific method to her culinary skills, experimenting and testing until she perfected each recipe. This evening's meal was no exception. Ffion chewed hungrily at her pitta bread, listening while the others talked.

She enjoyed hearing both of them speaking about their areas of research. She liked to broaden her knowledge as much as possible and was interested in everything. You never knew when a fact might come in handy. She was gaining a reputation at work as being something of a walking encyclopaedia.

'What's up Ffion?' asked Claire suddenly. 'You're very quiet.'

The trouble with living with such sharp-eyed academics was that they could always tell when something wasn't right.

'Trouble at work?' asked Judy.

They both knew she couldn't discuss the details of her work with them for reasons of confidentiality, but they also knew she was involved in the murder of Gabriel Quinn. It was understandable that they were curious about the case. But Ffion had no desire to admit that she had been defeated by a mysterious number, nor an unbreakable password. Instead she found herself telling them her concerns about Jake.

'It's quite simple,' said Judy, when Ffion had finished unburdening herself. 'You just have to be honest with him. If he's a decent bloke then he'll appreciate that. And if he isn't, then he's not worth knowing.'

'Yeah,' agreed Claire. 'For someone as bright as you, Ffion, it really ought to have been simple enough to work out.'

It really was that simple, thought Ffion. Why hadn't she

thought of that?

CHAPTER 14

The waiter at Bella Vita was young, with Mediterranean good looks and a neatly trimmed beard. He showed Bridget to a secluded corner table and held the back of the wooden chair while she took her seat. Bridget was a regular here, and the owner and staff at this family-run bistro on Walton Street all knew her by name.

'Signora Hart,' said the waiter, 'I kept the best table for you and your friend.' Somehow he managed to infuse the word "friend" with a subtle mix of intimacy and allusion. Bridget knew him well enough not to take offence.

'Thank you, Alessandro.' She smiled at him as he lit the candle in the centre of the table with a theatrical flourish.

The bistro was small and agreeable, with crisp red tablecloths on each of the tables, carefully-placed spotlighting, and specials chalked up on blackboards. The corner table certainly was the best spot for a romantic dinner, and Bridget began to relax in the familiar, cosy environment, enjoying the smell of the cooking and the gentle sound of the background music.

'Would you like to order a drink?'

'I'll wait until my friend arrives, thank you.'

'Of course.'

The waiter left two menus on the table and Bridget started to peruse the choices, her mouth already watering at the thought of creamy pasta sauces, garlic and fresh herbs. She'd been saving herself all day in preparation for this evening's dinner, having only a rather limp salad from the staff canteen at lunchtime. Hell, she'd been saving herself ever since leaving Ben. There had been no relationship with a man for over ten years now. She'd always told herself that it was for Chloe's sake, that as a single mother she had to be completely dedicated to her daughter, but perhaps the truth was that she'd been too scared. She'd thought she would never be able to trust another man again, but that was before she'd met Jonathan. The way she felt about him, perhaps she could begin to put some faith in him, to take a chance again at love.

She certainly needed something to lift her spirits. She'd left the incident room under a cloud of gloom, wondering how she was going to make headway with the case. The list of suspects on the incident room noticeboard still consisted of only two names – Hunter Reed and Lawrence Taylor – and she didn't really have anything hard on either of them, just a feeling that they were somehow involved in Gabriel's death. Todd Lee was also a person of interest, leaving a trail of guilt behind him like slime from a slug. But so far the only thing she could pin on him was a reluctance to answer police questions. The mysterious shooter had vanished without trace, and Bridget could only hope that she would learn some clue to his identity once the ballistics team had finished their analysis of the bullet. The drugs angle offered a possible lead, but was tenuous at best.

The one strand that kept drawing her back was her gut feeling that Gabriel had known someone was after him. The break-in at the boat, telling Amber that he was being followed, and then the strange need that had compelled him to repeat that mysterious string of letters and numbers over and over as he lay dying. She was sure that he'd been trying to communicate some crucial clue about the identity of his killer. Yet so far none of Ffion's searches had yielded anything useful, and she'd heard nothing back from Professor Michael Henderson, despite his promise to give the matter his full attention.

'Sorry I'm late.' She felt a hand on her shoulder as Jonathan arrived. 'My taxi got stuck in traffic.' He leaned over to give her a kiss on the cheek, and her worries about the case began to dissipate in a haze of wellbeing.

'You're not late,' she said, smiling at him. 'I was early for once.'

She'd just had time to go home, have a shower and change into a dress. The first time she'd gone out on a "date" with Jonathan, she'd had no idea what to wear. To celebrate the success of solving her previous case, and to make sure that she would be better prepared in future, she'd gone shopping with Chloe and treated herself to a few new outfits, something that she hadn't done for a good while. The dress she was wearing this evening, Chloe had confidently informed her, was suitable for a romantic dinner.

Jonathan sat down opposite. He was dressed for the warm weather in an open-necked shirt with short sleeves that showed off lightly tanned arms. He always seemed to dress with effortless, understated style, and the sea green of his shirt complemented his strawberry blond hair nicely. Close up, Bridget could see the faint lines in his skin that betrayed the fact that he was in his mid-forties, a few years older than her. Her hand drifted involuntarily to her hair and those damn grey strands. She still hadn't had a chance to do anything about them. She hoped the soft candlelight would conceal the worst.

'Shall we order some food?' Jonathan took off his tortoiseshell glasses to read the menu. 'These are for distance,' he explained. 'Close up I can see better without them. Perhaps it's time for me to start ageing gracefully and accept that I need reading glasses.' His forehead crinkled as he smiled at her. His eyes, she noted, were a warm, hazel brown.

They ordered antipasto to share, and for her main course Bridget chose linguine in a basil and almond pesto while Jonathan went for the risotto. The waiter agreed that a bottle of Pinot Grigio would be the perfect accompaniment.

'So how have you been since Saturday?' asked Jonathan.

'Busy,' said Bridget. 'I'm so sorry about missing the opera. Was it good? *La Bohème* has always been one of my favourites.'

'I gave the tickets to the couple next door,' said Jonathan. 'I didn't fancy going on my own, especially not after what happened to Gabriel.'

'Of course,' said Bridget.

'How is the investigation going?'

'It's...'

'Look, I totally understand if you can't talk about it,' he said quickly. 'I don't expect you to breach confidentiality or anything like that.'

'It's not that,' said Bridget. 'The truth is, we haven't got much to go on at the moment. Gabriel doesn't appear to have had any enemies. We've put out an appeal for people to contact us if they have any information, and of course we've interviewed everyone who knew him.'

'Who have you spoken to?'

'His girlfriend, Amber Morgan and one of the other artists exhibiting at the gallery, Hunter Reed. Dr Melissa Price and her husband Lawrence Taylor. Todd Lee who runs the art shop where Gabriel rented a studio. I've even spoken to a maths professor called Michael Henderson who knew Gabriel, and also to his neighbour on the canal, Harriet Watson. But we still don't really understand why anyone would want Gabriel dead.'

'I know most of those people,' said Jonathan nodding, 'apart from this professor and Gabriel's neighbour. It's very hard for me to imagine any of them wanting to kill

Gabriel, let alone having the wherewithal to carry out a shooting.'

'I'm inclined to agree. Anyway, enough of that. How is the exhibition going? Have you had much interest?'

Alessandro, the waiter, returned with their wine before Jonathan could reply. He opened the bottle at the table and poured a small measure for Bridget to sample. 'Signora Hart.'

Bridget felt a faint heat in her face at the title Signora. At work she was always Detective Inspector, and in her personal life she was simply Bridget. She wanted to inform Alessandro that he should call her Signorina, yet that seemed faintly ridiculous. She envied men for their uncomplicated title of "mister" and hoped that Jonathan wouldn't notice her discomfort. To cover her embarrassment she swirled the pale green liquid in her glass and took a sip. 'Very good, Alessandro. It's delicious.'

'Eccellente, Signora.' Alessandro filled their glasses and left them in peace.

'To your health,' said Jonathan, clinking his glass with hers.

'Cheers.'

Jonathan sipped his wine thoughtfully. 'Yes, the exhibition. There's certainly been a lot more interest since what happened on Saturday. I'm afraid to say that Gabriel's death has caused something of a sensation. People are coming into the gallery just to see his work.'

'And are they buying?'

'Most are coming just to look, but yes, some are buying. I hate to be profiting from such a terrible tragedy, but I'd be lying if I said I wasn't seeing a boost in sales. I dare say there will be people who buy his work now purely with a view to cashing in. Art and commerce. *C'est la vie.*' He gave a small shrug, the candle flame reflected in his glasses.

The waiter arrived with the antipasto, an artfully arranged spread of paper-thin strips of ham, garlic mushrooms, liver pâté, pickles and olives, served with warm crusty bread.

'How is Chloe?' asked Jonathan. 'She seemed like a great kid when I met her at your sister's Sunday lunch the other week.'

Bridget bit into a piece of bread topped with a slice of ham. She could almost imagine she was in Italy on the Amalfi coast. 'Chloe's just spent the weekend with her father and his new girlfriend in London.'

Jonathan looked at her with an amused expression on his face. 'Why do I get the impression that's an issue for you?'

She put her bread down and grimaced. 'Is it that obvious?'

'Just a little.'

She sighed. 'Ben was a lousy husband and not much better as a father when it came to night feeds and changing nappies, you know all the hard stuff. Now that Chloe's older he thinks he can just buy her affection with expensive iPhones and shopping trips in London. She went to Oxford Street with Ben's girlfriend, Tamsin, who sounds like a catwalk model, and spent a fortune on clothes.' She took a large mouthful of her wine. 'Sorry, I don't mean to sound so bitter, but Ben just winds me up the wrong way.'

Jonathan topped up her glass. 'It's not a problem.'

They both fell silent for a moment. It should have been Jonathan's turn now to tell her a little about his own background. She knew that he was a widower, and that his wife had died of cancer, but other than that, she knew nothing of his past. She was uncertain how to broach the issue. After a minute they both spoke together.

'What –'

'Does –'

'Sorry,' he said. 'You go first.'

'I just wanted to ask about you. Do you... I mean... did you and your wife have any children?'

A shadow passed across his face. 'Sadly not. We did try for many years. But then Angela got sick and... well, I suppose you've heard it all from Vanessa.'

'Not really,' said Bridget gently. 'She did mention that

your wife had passed away. I don't mean to pry though, if you'd rather not talk about it.'

'No,' he said. 'I don't mind at all. I'd like to tell you about Angela.'

Bridget listened with rapt attention as he told her about how they'd met at St Andrews University while he was studying Art History and she was doing Law. 'It was a classic student romance story, almost too good to be true,' he said.

'We met, we fell in love, we got married straight after graduation, and then we moved to Oxford so Angela could sit her articles. She qualified as a solicitor specialising in family law and was the main breadwinner while I was setting up my business.'

'You mean the art gallery?'

'That's right. I'd always dreamed of running my own gallery, and with Angela's financial support I was able to make my dream a reality. We were very happy together even though we never managed to have children. We were going to try IVF and then... it was a tumour in the brain. It started out with headaches, then she started to develop memory problems. All those years spent studying law... within six months she'd forgotten half of what she'd learned. She had to stop work. The tumour grew rapidly and spread through the brain. The doctors did their best. They treated it with radiotherapy, but they couldn't save her.'

He wiped his mouth with the napkin as the waiter came to clear away the starter and bring the main courses.

'I'm sorry,' said Bridget. 'You must miss her very much.'

'It's been nearly three years now,' he said. 'Time does help, but I'll always miss her.'

'I know what you mean,' said Bridget. 'You carry the dead around with you forever. It's the price you pay for being alive when they're not.'

He gave her a quizzical look.

'Vanessa isn't my only sister,' she explained. 'At least

she wasn't.'

'What happened?' he asked gently.

Bridget didn't often talk about Abigail, the memory of what happened still too painful even after all these years. But she felt Jonathan would understand in a way that other people couldn't, no matter how much they pretended to.

'There were three of us. Vanessa is the eldest and Abigail was the youngest. I'm the piggy in the middle.' She smiled. 'Anyway, Abigail was never one for following the rules. She was often in trouble at school over silly things like wearing make-up or painting her nails. She had boyfriends of course, usually exactly the kind our parents disapproved of. And then she started going to parties and staying out late. If our parents told her to be home by midnight, she'd stay out until two or three in the morning. I'm sure she experimented with drugs, a bit of cannabis, ecstasy, that sort of thing. Anyway, one day she didn't come home at all. We just assumed she was pushing the boundaries even further, staying out all night.' Bridget took a large gulp of her wine. This was the hardest part. She stared into the candle flame for a few seconds before speaking. 'A dog walker found her body three days later in Wytham Woods. She'd been strangled. She was sixteen years old.'

'I'm so sorry.' Jonathan reached across the table and held her hand in his. 'Did they catch the person who did it?'

Bridget shook her head. 'That's the worst thing of all. Her killer is still out there somewhere.'

'And would I be right in assuming that this has something to do with why you chose to join the police?'

'I think that's a fair assumption,' admitted Bridget. 'Our parents couldn't face living in the area any longer. They moved away to a small cottage in Lyme Regis. Vanessa worked hard to build the perfect family around her as a kind of barrier to protect her from the past. But I've always needed to know the truth about what happened to Abigail. And if I can't find out her truth, then I want to solve other cases so that at least some people get justice in this world.'

She realised that she was breathing hard. She had turned inward to a dark place and released passions that were normally kept locked inside. It wasn't a place she could afford to visit too often, in case it swallowed her whole.

Yet telling Jonathan about Abigail had felt cathartic, and she was glad she'd confided in him. He didn't shy away from difficult subjects the way some people did. Ben, for all his training as a police officer, had always been uncomfortable when she talked about her dead sister, so in the end she'd stopped. It was yet another barrier that had come between them.

'You have a real calling in life. I think that's very honourable,' said Jonathan, holding her gaze with his. 'I just sell squares of canvas covered in paint.'

'But you help to make the world a more beautiful place, and we all need a bit more beauty in our lives.'

Bridget realised that she had finished her main course almost without noticing it. Alessandro appeared again and refilled their glasses. 'Would you like to see the dessert menu?'

'I'm not sure,' said Jonathan. 'That was already quite a large meal. Bridget, what do you think?'

'One thing you should know about me,' she told him. 'Is that I would always like to see the dessert menu.'

It was gone midnight when they left the bistro, arm in arm. Bridget felt stuffed, and rather drunk, and strangely happy and sad at the same time. It had been a good dinner, a lovely evening, and a successful first date. Chloe would be proud of her.

'Here's a taxi,' said Jonathan, flagging it down.

He held her by the hand and pulled her close for a kiss on the mouth and Bridget felt herself melting. She'd waited ten years for this kiss, but it was worth the wait.

The taxi drew to a halt and Jonathan opened the door for her.

'Jonathan?' She wanted desperately to drag him into the taxi with her and take him home to her house in Wolvercote, but it was late and she was running a murder inquiry. Retelling Abigail's story had strengthened her determination to catch Gabriel's killer.

Jonathan seemed to understand what she was thinking. 'Thank you for a lovely evening, Bridget. I hope it's the first of many.'

'I hope so too.'

They kissed again, and then she climbed into the taxi. She watched him as she sped away, one hand in the pocket of his chinos, the other waving at her.

When she got home, the house was dark and quiet. She peeped in at Chloe and found her fast asleep in her bed. 'I did it,' she mouthed silently to her daughter. 'I went on a date at last, and I didn't mess it up.' Within seconds of her head hitting the pillow, she fell into a deep, dreamless sleep.

CHAPTER 15

Bridget stood at the bathroom sink and knocked back two paracetamol tablets with a glass of water. God, did she feel rough. Her head was thumping and pulsing like someone had taken a hammer to it. Sallow skin and puffy eyes stared back at her from the bathroom mirror. The grey strands in her hair seemed to have multiplied too. She hoped she hadn't looked this way last night. Perhaps it was time to admit that she could no longer handle a whole bottle of wine and an excess of rich food followed by only five hours' sleep.

She tried to disguise the full extent of the damage with an extra layer of make-up, but it clearly didn't do the trick because Chloe saw through it straightaway.

'Late night was it, Mum?' she asked over her breakfast cereal, an amused expression on her face.

'Just a little.' Bridget considered a slice of toast, but the thought made her feel even worse.

'So, tell me all about it.'

For once, Bridget was happy to give a full report on her date, and she was pleased to receive Chloe's qualified assent. 'Did you invite him back here afterwards?'

'No. It was late and I didn't want to wake you.'

'Really? It wouldn't have bothered me.'

'Well, it was only a first date. You shouldn't expect a man to come home with you on a first date. Should you?' For some reason, Bridget found herself craving her daughter's approval. Why was that? Because there was no one else to give it, she supposed.

'Not if he's a real gentleman. And Jonathan sounds like he is.'

Bridget basked in the warm glow of her memories of the night before. 'Yes, he's really nice.'

'I'm happy for you, Mum,' said Chloe, dumping her empty bowl in the sink and picking up her school bag. 'You deserve some happiness.' She kissed Bridget on the cheek before leaving.

Bridget smiled to herself, then donned a pair of sunglasses and headed out to her car.

Arriving at the office she grabbed herself a quick coffee, as always wishing for something stronger than the flavourless liquid the machine dispensed, and carried it to her desk. If she could just sit quietly for twenty minutes while the paracetamol worked its magic then she might be able to face the rest of the team and get on with her day.

'DI Hart, my office now.' Chief Superintendent Grayson's voice boomed even louder than usual this morning, reverberating inside her throbbing skull. She closed her eyes, took a deep breath, and crossed the floor to his office.

A manila folder lay open on Grayson's desk. 'We've received the report back from the ballistics team.'

'That was quick,' said Bridget, pulling up a chair.

'I asked them to fast-track their investigation,' said Grayson, thumbing through the pages of the report. 'Their conclusion is that the bullet used to kill Gabriel Quinn was almost certainly fired by a handgun of the type used by British armed forces.'

'A stolen weapon, then.'

'Precisely. They think it likely that the gun was fitted

with a home-made suppressor.'

'A suppressor?' Bridget's understanding of firearms was limited at best. So far in her career, she had been happy to keep it that way.

Grayson, with his military background, seemed thoroughly unimpressed by her dearth of knowledge. 'That's a silencer, in popular parlance, DI Hart.'

'Yes, sir. Of course. That certainly ties in with the witness statements, plus the video of the shooting I saw,' she added, eager to recover some standing.

'Indeed. An imperfectly-fitted suppressor will leave signature marks on the bullet, and that appears to be the case here. However' – the Chief paused for dramatic effect – 'the most interesting part of the report is the analysis of the marks left on the bullet by the rifling in the gun's barrel. As you are no doubt aware, every individual firearm leaves behind characteristic marks on any bullet fired with it. The marks are tiny and are caused by imperfections in the machining of the weapon, but under careful examination they can be used to identify a specific firearm.' The Chief paused again, turning over the pages of the report until he reached the section he was looking for. 'The team has concluded that the gun used to fire this bullet has been used in two other murders in London during the past year.'

Bridget's pulse quickened at the news. 'This could be the breakthrough we've been waiting for, sir.'

'Yes.' Grayson didn't seem to find the prospect remotely uplifting. 'In both of those other cases, the murders were drugs related and are currently under investigation by the Met.'

Bridget digested the news. 'Drugs related? The pathologist found evidence that Gabriel used cannabis and magic mushrooms, but that hardly seems to be the kind of activity people get killed over.'

'You don't think he may have been a dealer?'

'It hardly seems likely, sir. I'm building a picture of an introverted, sensitive person, dedicated to his art. We found no evidence of drugs on his boat. There's no sign that he had any criminal earnings, either. Gabriel lived in virtual poverty.'

'That may be so. Nevertheless, it's out of my hands now.'

'What do you mean, sir?'

Grayson's face was grim. 'Detectives from the Met are going to be arriving here from London later this morning. They will be taking over this investigation with immediate effect.'

'Sir?'

'I know it's not fair, but that's the way it is. This murder clearly forms part of a larger pattern. Believe me, I don't like the idea of officers from the Met tramping all over our patch any more than you do, but in this case they have good reasons for taking this line. I expect you to co-operate fully with them on this enquiry.'

Bridget felt her shoulders slump. It was true that her own investigation hadn't led far, but she was making progress. And the idea that Gabriel had been caught up in some kind of London-based drugs network was impossible for her to swallow. Still, she acknowledged that Grayson was right. The Met were entitled to take over, if this formed part of a pre-existing investigation. 'Who should I expect to be working with?'

To give him credit, even Grayson looked slightly abashed when he dropped his final bombshell. 'The officer who will head up this investigation is DCI Ben Hart.'

'What? Sir?'

Did he really expect her to work with her ex-husband on this case? Ben would pull rank and try to belittle her, she just knew it, never mind that he would be working on her home patch. On her case.

'I expect you to act professionally and to put aside any personal issues that you may have,' warned Grayson sternly. 'Is that clear?'

'Yes, sir. Perfectly clear.' Bridget rose to her feet, feeling slightly sickened by the turn of events. She strode out of the office with murderous thoughts of her own. Her headache was back with a vengeance.

CHAPTER 16

Bridget had not yet returned from her meeting with the Chief Superintendent, but the phone on her desk kept ringing. After a minute, Ffion could stand it no longer. She marched across the office and picked up. 'DI Hart's phone. DC Ffion Hughes speaking.'

The voice at the end of the line was softly spoken and a little anxious. 'Is it possible to speak to Inspector Hart?'

'I'm sorry, she's in a meeting. May I ask who's calling?'

'Ah, yes. My name is Michael Henderson. I'm a professor of mathematics at Oxford University.'

Aha, so this was Bridget's famous mathematician. Ffion was intrigued. 'Are you calling about the number?'

The professor sounded surprised. 'Yes, that's right. I am.'

'L79468235,' said Ffion.

'Indeed, yes. I've been thinking very hard about it since DI Hart left.'

Ffion nodded to herself. That made two of them. 'Any ideas?'

'Yes, actually. You may be aware that Gabriel was very interested in mathematical theories?'

Ffion thought of Gabriel's notes that were now piled high on her desk and smiled to herself. 'Yes, I was aware of that.'

'I began by working through some of the ideas that Gabriel and I had discussed,' the professor continued. 'Perfect numbers, prime numbers –'

'– the Fibonacci sequence, the Golden Ratio,' suggested Ffion.

The professor paused. 'I see that you're already well acquainted with these concepts yourself.'

'I know a little.'

'I see. I explored some of the more obvious avenues – triangular numbers, factorials, all of the well-known integer sequences –'

'But none of them match,' concluded Ffion, who had done the same herself.

'No. But then I had another idea. It might seem rather unexciting, coming from a mathematician, but have you considered the possibility that it might be something much simpler?'

'Such as?'

'A telephone number.'

Ffion felt her heart sink. Was this all that one of Oxford's greatest minds could think of? She had already had this suggestion from Ryan. 'Telephone numbers have ten or eleven digits and start with a zero,' she said to him with as much patience as she could muster.

'Ah, yes, most of them do,' said the professor. 'But what if the letter L stands for London?'

Ffion's mind took up the idea rapidly. 'London numbers have eleven digits, just like others, but the code for London is 020 instead of the usual four or five digit area code. That means that the local number following the area code is eight digits long, instead of six or seven.'

'Precisely. And so Gabriel's mysterious code might mean 020 79468235.'

Ffion was annoyed with herself for missing such an obvious possibility. 'It's certainly worth following up,' she told the professor, trying to keep the excitement from her voice. 'Thanks for your call.'

'Anything I can do to help catch Gabriel's killer,' said Henderson. 'Do you really think it might be the solution?'

'There's only one way to find out,' said Ffion, now desperate to get him off the line so she could check out the number.

'Well I hope my suggestion proves to be helpful. I don't suppose I can help you with any other matters?'

'Like what?'

'I don't know. Have you been able to guess the password to Gabriel's laptop?'

Ffion wondered what to say to that. She didn't think it would do any harm to admit that she hadn't yet managed to get into Gabriel's laptop or phone.

'Not yet.' She paused. 'You don't happen to know it, do you?'

'I'm afraid not. But if you give me your email address, I can send you some suggestions.'

Ffion hesitated. She was reluctant to admit that she needed help, but the fact was that she did. Having another mind working on the problem might make all the difference. She gave the professor her contact details.

'I assume you've already tried all the obvious ideas,' said Henderson. 'But I'll think it over and get back to you.'

'You do that,' said Ffion. She ended the call and immediately dialled the London number. She was waiting for the call to connect when the door of the Chief's office burst open and Bridget stormed out.

*

Bridget left Grayson's office in a foul mood and headed out of the office in the direction of the bathroom. She needed to grab a moment of privacy and get her head straight before briefing her team. If she spoke to anyone now, there was a very strong chance she would say something she'd regret.

Ben. When her philandering ex-husband had left Oxford and transferred to the Met, she'd thought she'd finally got him out of her life. She certainly hadn't imagined ever having to work with him again. Yet now he'd not only re-entered her personal life, seeking to reconnect with Chloe after so many years of ignoring her, but had somehow managed to worm his way back into her professional life too. The thought made her seethe with frustration and she slammed the cubicle door closed behind her.

After a minute of crying she recovered her poise. She was falling to pieces and had to get a grip. She thought she'd put these destructive emotions to bed a long time ago, but it seemed they were lurking just beneath the surface, ready to jump out and devour her self-confidence at any moment. This would never do. She was a detective inspector in charge of a murder enquiry, and she needed to act professionally, just like Grayson had said. More importantly, she must never allow Ben to see how much he rattled her. It would only make the situation ten times worse.

She emerged from the cubicle, splashed cold water on her face and began to analyse her feelings about working with Ben. It wasn't that he was a bad copper. He had a high success rate in bringing criminals to justice. And colleagues tended to like him. He was charming and charismatic, a natural extrovert with a generous nature. He was a good person to have in a group, always the centre of attention, never at a loss for small talk, making people laugh with his anecdotes. So why was she so agitated? She knew the answer and it didn't make her feel good about herself. The truth was she didn't want her team to like him more than they liked her. If that made her into a petty person, well that was just the way it was.

A thought struck her. *Did* her team like her? She honestly didn't know. She had never been naturally self-confident like Ben.

She wasn't hoping to become best friends with the

members of her team. But she did want them to respect her, and her biggest fear was that Ben would somehow belittle her in front of them. He would do it without meaning to, perhaps without realising it. Or he might even do it on purpose. She sighed. Jonathan would never behave that way.

Jonathan. She had been so happy last night in his company. She still hadn't texted him to say how much she'd enjoyed their romantic dinner. She pulled out her phone now to message him, but when she looked at the time she realised the morning briefing was due to start in two minutes. She slipped the phone back into her bag and made some hurried adjustments to her appearance, hoping that the others wouldn't notice the bags under her eyes. At least the paracetamol was starting to have an effect at last, and there was no longer the sound of a jackhammer drilling at the inside of her skull.

*

'The number you have dialled has not been recognised,' said the recorded voice at the end of the line. 'Please check and try again.'

Ffion double-checked the number she'd dialled, then replaced the telephone receiver in annoyance. She'd been certain that the professor's idea would lead her to a breakthrough. Now she felt like Jake must have done when he returned from the car-hire company, waving the driving licence of the deceased driver aloft, only to be shot down in flames by her.

She returned to her computer and entered the number into the online database. The system confirmed that the number had the correct format for a London telephone number. Unfortunately it had never been issued to a customer.

So much for that lead.

If there was a bright side to the situation, it was that she hadn't been outwitted by an Oxford professor. The game was still on, and she was determined to win it.

*

Bridget returned to her desk and gathered her papers together, including the ballistics report that Grayson had given her, and made her way to the whiteboard in the incident room. The rest of the team had already taken their places, Jake hurriedly munching on a Snickers bar, Ryan chomping his way through a doughnut, and Ffion dunking a weird-smelling herbal tea bag in her Welsh dragon mug. None of them looked very happy.

Bridget clapped her hands together. 'Okay everyone, let's make a start. I have some news to announce, but first I'd like to find out what progress has been made since yesterday.'

Ffion stood up first and half-turned to address the others in the room. 'I've been continuing to work on Gabriel's code. I've now had a response from all of the banks I requested information from, but unfortunately this seems to be a dead end. I followed up all of the individuals and businesses with account numbers matching Gabriel's number, but none has a criminal record or seems to have any connection with Gabriel. For example, one account belongs to a pensioner living in Strathclyde. Another was the bank account of a florist in Harrogate.'

'Okay,' said Bridget. 'It was worth a shot. Any other ideas on the number?'

'Nothing that's produced any results.'

Bridget turned next to Ryan. 'Anything to report?' She had tasked him with checking out Lawrence Taylor, the businessman with an eye for making a quick profit, and one of her more promising suspects.

Ryan shook his head. 'I ran the background checks like you asked. Nothing on Lawrence Taylor. He's clean as a whistle. With all respect, ma'am, I think we're wasting our time there.'

Jake had little new to report too. 'I spoke again to

Amber. She admitted that she and Gabriel smoked cannabis and that Gabriel used magic mushrooms, but denied that he was dealing. She refused to tell me who their supplier was.'

'I see,' said Bridget. 'Do you think there's any possibility that she may have been lying about Gabriel being a dealer?'

'Seriously? I just can't see it.'

Bridget nodded. 'Me neither, but it seems that the Met disagree.' She summarised her meeting with Grayson, giving them the highlights from the ballistics report and concluding with the fact that the gun used to kill Gabriel had been used in two other murders in London, both related to drugs gangs.

Ryan whistled. 'So all this art and number stuff is a red herring. Gabriel must have been more heavily involved in drugs than Amber is willing to admit.'

Andy seemed to be in agreement. 'It matches what I've been told when talking to other forces about the driver of the black Toyota. The use of a silencer, the type of bullet, the style of the murder – everything points to a contract killing.'

'Well,' said Bridget, 'whatever the reason for the murder, it would seem that the gunman was a professional, and that he, or at least the weapon he used, has been implicated in an ongoing drugs investigation. Therefore, a team from the Met will be here' – she checked her watch – 'any minute now, and we're going to have to work closely together with them. In fact, an officer from the Met will be taking over from me as senior investigating officer.'

A chorus of groans greeted her announcement. She was secretly warmed by their heartfelt response, but met it with a stern glare. 'I want full co-operation from everyone, is that clear?'

'Yes, ma'am.'

She decided not to tell them that the lead investigator from the Met was her ex-husband. No doubt they would work that out for themselves soon enough. They were detectives, after all.

CHAPTER 17

Bridget barely had time to return to her desk and collect her thoughts before the doors flew open and Chief Superintendent Grayson entered, followed by Ben and his team, a woman and two men.

She could see from the way Grayson was smiling – normally a once-a-year event reserved for the annual Christmas party – that he'd been won over by Ben's easy-going bonhomie. Making a good first impression was one of Ben's key skills. He had the knack of cracking a joke and putting people at their ease. He could captivate and beguile a room full of people in moments, and had worked his magic on her, all those years ago. Ben's problem was fidelity. Maybe he just wanted to be liked by too many people.

'DI Hart,' said Grayson, 'our friends from the Met have arrived. You already know DCI Ben Hart, of course.'

Ben was a detective chief inspector now, having risen rapidly through the ranks unencumbered by childcare and the stresses of being a single parent. His face was just as handsome and chiselled as it had ever been. He had weathered the years well, and the faint lines and grey hairs of age seemed if anything to have improved his looks. They gave him a veneer of dignity and sophistication, and of course maturity – a characteristic both he and she had sorely lacked when she had fallen head over heels and married him. The lines around his eyes were laughter lines, and there was no trace of the anxiety that had dogged Bridget all her adult life. He had stayed fit – unlike her – and carried himself well. He dressed better than the young Ben had done, in an expensive suit with a crisp white shirt and designer silk tie, and she could smell a strong scent of cologne. That was a new addition, presumably intended to please the svelte Tamsin, or perhaps a gift from her.

He smiled warmly at her and extended a hand. 'Bridget.' His voice was just as smooth and charming as when she had first met him, as if all the infidelities, accusations and heartache had never happened. 'It's so nice for us to be working together after all these years.' There was no trace of irony in his words.

She accepted his hand with a business-like shake, determined not to show any sign of how deeply he still affected her. 'Ben.'

'Let me introduce my team. This is DI Kate Macready, and these two are Sergeants Gary Smith and Derek Sutcliffe.'

'Pleased to meet you,' said DI Macready, offering her hand. She was tall – almost as tall as Ben – and enviably thin, with styled blonde hair and a tailored suit. Her face was hard, her eyes cold.

Bridget immediately felt short and dumpy next to this woman. Familiar feelings. And despite herself, she felt irrationally jealous that this stranger worked closely with Ben, even though that was the very last thing she would have wanted for herself. She forced a smile to her lips and took the hand. It felt cool, clammy and surprisingly limp.

Kate's lips curved in a smile. 'Ben told me all about you in the car on the way here.'

Bridget tried to read the other woman's face for signs of hidden meaning. She wondered what Ben might have said about her. Whatever it was, two could play at that game. 'I'm sure I could tell you a lot about Ben too,' she responded brightly.

Kate gave a throaty laugh that sounded forced. Somehow Bridget didn't think they would be sharing confidences over a bottle of Chardonnay any time soon.

Throughout the exchange of pleasantries, Sergeants Smith and Sutcliffe stood at the back, muscular and impassive like a pair of bouncers in a nightclub. Bridget was glad not to have to shake their huge hands. The men were obviously here to do the dirty work, whatever dirty work Ben had in mind.

Grayson seemed satisfied with the way the introductions had proceeded. 'Bridget, I'll leave everyone in your capable hands.' He disappeared back to his office.

'Right then, shall we make a start?' said Ben in that annoying way he had of taking charge of every situation. 'I don't suppose there's any chance of a decent coffee round here? Last time I worked here we had to put up with that cat's piss from the vending machine.' That brought another laugh from Kate, this one sounding less false.

'I'll see what I can do,' said Bridget, grateful for the coffee shop around the corner. 'Ryan, could you organise something?'

Ten minutes later, when everyone was in possession of a coffee, Bridget took the new arrivals to meet her own team. Knowing him so well, she couldn't help noticing how Ben appraised Ffion with a practised eye for anything female and sexy. But Ffion, with her usual indifference to the male gaze, shook his hand with professional detachment and failed to acknowledge his obvious interest in her. Perhaps having picked up on Ben's appreciation of Ffion, Jake seemed wary of him, greeting him with a nod and a slight frown. No doubt her sergeant's northern bullshit detector was alert to any charm offensive that Ben might try. But Ryan and Andy both greeted him with enthusiasm.

'That's her ex-,' Bridget heard Andy whisper to Ryan

as they sat back down. Of course, Andy had been around long enough to remember Ben from the old days. She could see that both Ryan and Andy had already been taken in by Ben's charm offensive.

She rounded up the team and led everyone into the incident room to report their progress to date. She was pleased to note that Ben took a seat and allowed her to stand at the noticeboard. Kate sat on one side of him, one leg crossed elegantly over the other, a faint look of amusement on her face. Smith and Sutcliffe joined Ryan and Andy at the back of the room, their expressions giving nothing away.

'So, Bridget, maybe you'd like to start by telling us how far you've got with this case?' To her ears Ben sounded patronising, as if he didn't expect the Oxford detectives to have made much progress. Perhaps he was right, but she was determined to show him what she'd done.

'Gabriel Quinn was shot and killed by a single bullet on Oxford High Street on Saturday at ten fifteen in the morning. The gunman, as you know, appears to have been a professional killer. He used a 9mm calibre firearm equipped with a homemade suppressor' – she stopped herself just in time from saying *silencer* – 'that had previously been used in two drugs-related murders in London. We've been building up a picture of Gabriel's life and contacts. He was an artist of some considerable talent, having graduated from the Ruskin School of Art five years ago. His work is currently on display at a gallery in Oxford, and in fact he'd just come from there when the attack happened. Speaking to the gallery owner, it seems that Gabriel's career was on the point of taking off. Collectors had started to recognise his potential monetary worth. In the weeks before he died Gabriel believed that his life might be in danger, and that the canal boat where he lived had been broken into. As events turned out, he wasn't just being paranoid. Before he died he was very concerned to communicate an eight-digit number which a witness managed to write down.' She pointed at the whiteboard where the number was one of the few clues they had collected. 'L79468235. We've been trying to ascertain the significance of this number, but so far without any success. However, it clearly meant something to the deceased and is therefore a key piece of evidence in our investigations.'

Ben smiled politely. 'Is that it?'

'No,' said Bridget. 'As I said, we've been speaking to everyone who was close to Gabriel, and have identified several persons of interest.' She pointed in turn to the suspects displayed on the board. 'Lawrence Taylor, managing director of Taylor Financial Technology. He's an art collector who owns a number of Gabriel's works. He stands to benefit from an increase in the value of Gabriel's work following his death. His wife, Dr Melissa Price, was Gabriel's tutor at the Ruskin School. Amber Morgan, Gabriel's girlfriend and model. Hunter Reed, another artist and a contemporary of Gabriel's, now Amber's boyfriend. Finally, Todd Lee, owner of the art shop where Gabriel rented a studio. The art shop is also where Amber works part-time.'

Ben waited to be certain that she'd finished. 'Nothing else?'

Bridget was aware how pathetic the results of her painstaking information-gathering must sound to Ben. 'We have also established that Gabriel used small amounts of recreational drugs, but have no evidence to indicate that he may have been a dealer.' That, at least, was one fact she was confident about. Whatever Gabriel had got entangled with, it had surely not been a London-based drugs gang. She stood her ground, but she could see Kate Macready covering her mouth with her hand as if trying not to laugh.

'Okay,' said Ben. 'Well, maybe we can fill in a few blanks for you. Why don't you take a seat, Bridget?'

Fuming at being relegated, Bridget sat down at the side of the room while Ben took centre stage, removing his jacket and loosening his tie, all part of the act, Bridget knew, to come across as an approachable guy.

'So, this is the way things stand,' he said, spreading his

arms wide to draw in his audience. 'For the last six months we've been monitoring the activities of a drugs network operating in and around London. The individuals behind this gang have been running a sophisticated operation, exploiting vulnerable young people to sell class A drugs both within the capital and in surrounding counties, as far afield as Berkshire, Oxfordshire and Gloucestershire. We're talking about significant quantities of heroin, crack cocaine, methamphetamine and MDMA. This gang operates ruthlessly, taking over the patches of smaller gangs, and eliminating anyone who poses a threat to their operations. We believe that they're responsible for at least four murders, and that two of these murders were carried out using the same weapon that was used to kill Gabriel Quinn. We're pretty certain we know the identity of the gunman. Kate, would you mind?'

Ben nodded to his DI, who produced several copies of a photograph from her briefcase and began to pass them around. Bridget took a copy and studied the face in the photograph. The image showed a man with grizzled beard and hair so short he was almost bald. His eyes were hooded, his cheeks hollow. A scar ran along one side of his chin. Was this the face of Gabriel's killer?

'This is Travis Brown,' continued Ben, 'a former British army sniper in the Grenadier Guards and a veteran of Afghanistan. He served two tours of duty and was awarded a Conspicuous Gallantry Cross for his bravery in action. Since retiring from the army, he's found more lucrative employment as a contract killer. So far he's escaped justice, but we're very close to running him to ground. But he's not our main man. Our key objective is to catch the people who employ him.' He pointed to one of the names on Bridget's noticeboard. 'Hunter Reed is a mid-level dealer within the gang. We've been observing him for some time now, letting things run so we can follow up the chain and catch those at the very top.'

'That's ridiculous,' interrupted Bridget. 'Hunter Reed is an artist.' She recalled the gaudy canvases she'd seen at the offices of Taylor Financial Technology.

'Hunter may dabble in paints in his spare time,' said Ben, 'but we know him as a hardened criminal dealing in crack cocaine and crystal meth. I don't know precisely how Gabriel Quinn came to be entangled in the drugs world, but I'm willing to bet it was through Hunter, and I'm also certain that's why he's dead. We haven't come all this way to talk about paintings and numbers' – there was a snort of suppressed laughter from Smith and Sutcliffe at the back of the room – 'We've come here to arrest Hunter Reed, and the sooner we get on with it, the better.'

'Now hang on a minute,' said Bridget, rising to her feet. 'What evidence have you got to support this theory?'

Ben was already pulling on his jacket and getting ready to leave. 'Oh, don't worry, we've got plenty of evidence. To be frank, Bridget, I was hoping that you might have collected some more for us. Instead of all this' – he waved his hand vaguely – 'painting by numbers.'

Kate chuckled openly at his mocking words.

'I'll show you what we have when we bring Hunter in for questioning,' continued Ben. 'But first we need to go and get the bastard. Coming?'

Bridget was fuming. She realised now that Ben hadn't been remotely interested in hearing what she had to say. He'd just been play-acting so he could dismiss her team's efforts and make his own ideas appear all the more convincing by contrast. He had already decided what this case was about. Drugs. He wasn't interested in obtaining justice for Gabriel. As far as he was concerned, Gabriel was just a low-life dealer who had got what was coming to him.

He and his team were heading towards the door like a pack of wolves preparing to go out hunting. He was no doubt hoping for further promotion on the back of such a big case. But this was her case and she was damned if she was going to let him take over. She grabbed her jacket and followed them out through the door, calling for Jake to come with her.

CHAPTER 18

Ben's team had driven down from London in two black BMWs. Smith and Sutcliffe got into one of the vehicles, and Ben and Kate took the other. Reluctantly, Bridget climbed into the back of Ben's car, and was joined by Jake. She barely had time to fasten her seat belt before Ben was reversing out of the parking space with a sharp turn of the steering wheel and then slamming the gear stick into drive. She felt the contents of her stomach lurch, and gripped the door handle to stop herself being thrown from side to side. Ben had always fancied himself as something of a racing car driver, and Bridget prayed she wasn't about to bring up the half-digested remains of last night's meal all over his leather upholstery.

With a marked police car in front and one behind, their blue lights flashing silently, the convoy of vehicles left Kidlington at speed and entered Oxford from the north, hurtling down Woodstock Road, forcing other drivers to pull over into the bus lane and barely avoiding knocking over a cyclist attempting a right-hand turn.

They executed a sharp right into Plantation Road and then headed down Walton Street, right past the Italian bistro where Bridget had dined with Jonathan only the previous evening. Ben's humiliation of her in front of her team had brought her headache back, and the aching behind her eyes only increased as the car sped down the congested street.

This part of Oxford was far too crowded to be driving in this way. The big BMW was built for cruising along the German autobahn, not careering down the cramped streets of Jericho. She watched through the side window as narrow streets flashed by, packed full of pedestrians and cyclists, and lined with rows of tightly-packed cars along each side. Jericho was a maze of one-way streets, full of parking restrictions, pedestrian crossings and other traffic-calming measures. People stopped to stare as they sped past, and Bridget hung on tightly as the car swerved right into Cranham Street.

The bells of St Barnabas were tolling midday when the cars pulled up outside the new canal-side developments. Bridget breathed a sigh of relief when they arrived. Hopefully Ben and his officers would be able to arrest Hunter without any trouble, and all this macho posturing would be entirely unnecessary.

'That's Hunter's apartment block,' said Jake, indicating a building close to the church.

Two uniformed officers emerged from the leading police car and approached the entrance of the apartment block. They pushed the buzzer and waited. Bridget watched closely, but there was no response. One of the officers pushed the buzzer again.

'Could he be out?' asked Kate.

'More likely he's still in bed,' said Jake. 'Judging from what I've seen of him.'

'I hope he hasn't received a tip-off,' growled Ben.

As they watched, Jake suddenly pointed again. A motorbike had appeared from around the rear of the apartments. A man in black leathers was driving it, with a young woman riding passenger on the back. Her long red hair streamed out from beneath her helmet.

'That's them,' said Jake excitedly. 'It's Hunter and Amber.'

The two uniformed officers turned in surprise as the motorcycle roared past them.

'Shit,' said Ben, banging the dashboard with his fist. 'They mustn't get away.'

The motorbike swerved easily around the parked cars and shot off into the heart of Jericho.

Ben spoke to the drivers of the other cars over the police radio. 'Follow that bike. He's our man.'

The second marked car sped off in hot pursuit, lights flashing and siren screaming. The black BMW driven by Smith and Sutcliffe also leapt into action, following close behind. To Bridget's alarm, Ben joined in the chase too, his foot to the floor, his hands gripping the steering wheel, and a broad grin spreading across his face.

It was like being on the very worst type of fairground ride. Ben swung the car round a corner and Bridget felt her stomach go the opposite way. Oh, if only she had known what was coming, she would never have drunk quite so much wine last night. She could hardly bear to watch as the cars chased the motorcycle around the narrow criss-crossing grid of Victorian streets.

Bridget wasn't scared of speed. She wasn't exactly the world's most careful driver herself. But the BMW was far too big to be driven so fast down these narrow roads. If she'd been in the Mini she could have nipped around easily. But Ben's car, while powerful, was hardly agile. They'd be lucky if they didn't cause an accident. An old man out walking his dog jumped back from the edge of the pavement where he'd been about to cross the road. He waved his stick at them as they shot past. At the very least, these heavy-handed tactics would give the police a bad name in an area of the city where a lot of students lived. That was no concern of Ben's, of course. It wasn't his patch. But it would only cause distrust in the police and make Bridget's job more difficult in the future.

Up ahead, the bike made a right turn and Ben spun the

wheel, heading down a side street, obviously hoping to head off the motorbike as Hunter made his bid for freedom. 'Heading down Victor Street,' he spoke calmly into the radio. 'Remain in pursuit.'

Victor Street was as narrow a street as any, not even wide enough to allow parking on both sides. The BMW shot past the colourful terraced houses, screeching around the corner with the Old Bookbinders pub and into Albert Street, which if anything was even narrower.

Another car appeared at the end of the road and came to an abrupt halt at the junction, blocking their way forward. Ben stamped his foot on the brakes, swore colourfully, and put the car into reverse, accelerating rapidly back the way they had come, just missing the wing mirrors of parked cars by inches. He was clearly loving every second of the chase.

Kate Macready, on the other hand, looked as sick as Bridget felt.

In the rear-view mirror Ben gave Bridget a wink. 'Late night last night, Bridget? You really need to watch how much you drink, at your age.' He pushed the car back into gear and took the next turn into Jericho Street. 'Don't worry. The bastard won't give us the slip that easily.'

The second police car was now close behind them, lights flashing and siren wailing in time with the throbbing in Bridget's skull. Jericho Street narrowed even further until it was just wide enough for a single car. Ben pushed the BMW faster, tearing past the playground of a primary school full of small children, and rounding a corner that brought them parallel to the main road of Walton Street.

A disembodied voice came over the radio. 'Suspect vehicle turning left onto Great Clarendon Street.'

With a squeal of tyres, Ben executed a handbrake turn, bringing the car around ninety degrees and heading up another road. 'Cut him off before he reaches Walton Street. If he gets onto the main road we'll never catch him.'

The BMW roared along the road, reaching the junction where Great Clarendon Street met Walton Street at the

Oxford University Press building. The nineteenth-century building was an Oxford landmark, its stone pillars harking back to classical antiquity. It hardly seemed like the place for a car chase.

Ben slewed to a halt, blocking half of Great Clarendon Street with the car. The following police car came to a stop right behind, sealing off the rest of the road.

Bridget turned her head. Hunter's motorbike was belting along the road, coming straight towards her. Smith and Sutcliffe and the other police car were close on its tail.

The motorbike came closer, seeking a way out, but the two cars stretched across the road offered no hope of escape.

Still the bike showed no sign of stopping. Bridget closed her eyes. At the last possible moment, Hunter swerved to a halt, bringing the bike to a shuddering stop right next to the BMW.

Ben leapt from the car and dashed towards him, dragging him from his bike and onto the ground. Sergeants Smith and Sutcliffe rushed to provide assistance, but Ben already had his man pinned down, and was cuffing his hands behind his back.

Amber climbed off the bike and stood to one side, clearly terrified by the turn of events. She removed her crash helmet and her hair blew in the wind, making her look more than ever like the subject of a Pre-Raphaelite painting. Bridget climbed out of the car and hurried over to her. The girl seemed shaken, but unharmed.

Ben read Hunter his rights before instructing the officers to take him away. 'And bring her in too,' he said, pointing at Amber.

Bridget allowed the officers to lead the frightened girl to the police car, then climbed back into Ben's BMW.

She was gratified to see that Kate Macready had turned a pale shade of green.

'Was all that really necessary?' she asked Ben when he returned to the car.

'All what?' Ben had that self-satisfied expression on his

face that he used to wear after sex. She pushed the unwelcome thought from her mind.

'All that charging about, as if you're some kind of state trooper pursuing a fugitive along the freeway.'

He grinned at her. 'All in a day's work.'

CHAPTER 19

Hunter Reed sat nonchalantly in the interview room, his chair turned sideways to the table as if unwilling to grant Bridget and Ben his full attention. Still dressed in his black leather biker's gear, with several days' worth of dark stubble on his face and neck, he looked every inch the drug dealer that Ben had accused him of being. He regarded them briefly with a look of disdain, a sneer on his lips, before turning back to stare at the wall. In profile, his arrogant Roman nose was prominently on display.

Bridget had arranged to sit in on the interview while Ben led the questioning. Hunter had declined the offer of a lawyer, and she intended to make sure that Ben followed procedures scrupulously. She wasn't going to tolerate any slapdash behaviour that could leave Thames Valley Police open to accusations of misconduct. This was still her case, whatever Ben might think.

Amber had been taken to another room for questioning by DI Kate Macready. After a terse discussion it was agreed that Jake would sit in on the interview with her. 'Hopefully Amber trusts you by now,' Bridget had told him, drawing him aside while Ben and Kate discussed their respective interview strategies.

'I'm not so sure about that, ma'am,' said Jake. 'The last time I saw her she tore a strip off me for not doing more to catch Gabriel's killer.'

'Still, do your best to win her over,' said Bridget. 'Don't let DI Macready boss you about. Amber's the best source we have for getting information about Gabriel. She must know more than she's already told us. Perhaps she'll open up now, especially without Hunter being present. Try to be sympathetic.' Bridget had every confidence in Jake, who was good at defusing tense situations and putting people at their ease. She wasn't so sure about DI Kate Macready who seemed to be preparing for the interview as if she was about to negotiate with North Korea.

The door to the interview room opened behind her and Sergeant Smith appeared. He took up position standing against the back wall, his hands clasped behind his back. The burly man seemed to communicate an unspoken threat of violence, and even Hunter turned in his seat to stare at him.

'All right,' said Ben, 'let's get started.' He switched on the interview recorder and ran through the introductory formalities, repeating the words of the caution and asking Hunter to confirm his name and address.

Hunter took his time responding, seeming to examine the innocent question for any signs of a trap. Eventually he shrugged. 'Yeah, that's right.' He leaned his elbows on the table. 'Any chance of a smoke?'

'No,' said Ben curtly. 'So, when did you first become involved in drugs?'

Hunter smiled thinly. 'I've never touched them. I don't know anything about drugs.'

'We're conducting a search of your apartment right now,' said Ben. 'We've already discovered quantities of cannabis and cocaine.'

'Maybe you planted them there.'

'Have you ever used cannabis?'

'No.'

'Cocaine?'

'No.'

'Perhaps your girlfriend, Amber, uses them?'

'I don't know anything about that.'

'How did the drugs come to be in your apartment?'

'No comment.'

'Did you know there were drugs in your apartment?'

'No comment.'

'Do they belong to you?'

'No comment.'

Ben broke off his barrage of questions to study his notes. Behind them, Smith cleared his throat. Hunter leaned back in his chair, seemingly satisfied with the way things were going so far. Bridget wondered if he had any previous experience of this type of interview.

Ben resumed his questioning. 'How often do you travel into London?'

'Now and again.'

'When were you last there?'

'I can't remember.'

'Was it last week?'

'It might have been.'

'And what was your reason for going?'

'A bit of this, a bit of that. I like to go out in the West End, visit some galleries, take in a club.'

'Where did you go this time?'

'No comment.'

'Did you travel alone?'

'No comment.'

'Who did you meet while you were there?'

'No comment.' Hunter turned to stare at the wall again.

Bridget decided to try a different tack. 'You're an artist, aren't you?' she said. Beside her, she felt Ben stiffen in annoyance.

Hunter swung back round to look at her, an amused smile playing on his lips. For the first time in the interview he seemed engaged. He turned his chair to face Bridget. 'Yeah, that's right. I'm an artist. I paint pictures.'

'I've seen some of them,' said Bridget, recalling the primary-coloured paints splashed over the canvases hanging in Lawrence Taylor's office. 'Is that how you earn your living?'

'Yeah,' drawled Hunter.

'Do you make a good living that way?'

'It's all right.'

'Enough to pay for your apartment?'

He looked away. Bridget didn't want to lose him, now that she'd got him talking. She tried another question. 'You and Gabriel Quinn were both students at the Ruskin School of Art. Tell me about him.'

Hunter appeared pleased to be asked about someone other than himself. 'Yeah, I've known Gabriel since we were both students. What do you want to know about him?'

'Did you like him?'

'He was all right, but a bit too weird to really get close to. He had these obsessions with numbers and stuff like that. He was a bit of a loner, too. I don't think he was completely right in the head, if you know what I mean.'

'No. Tell me.'

'Well, he was a bit intense. Have you seen the boat where he lived? He covered every surface with papers – diagrams, numbers, equations. I think he was searching for the meaning of the universe, you know?' Hunter chuckled. 'And he was really paranoid as well. He thought that someone was out to get him. He thought there was some huge conspiracy going on, that he was being followed.'

'Is it possible that someone really was following him?'

'No. It was all up here.' Hunter touched his forefinger to his head.

'He told Amber that someone had broken into his boat.'

'Yeah, but nothing was taken. Why would anyone do a thing like that? Trust me, Gabriel wasn't right in the head.'

'Do you know the significance of the number L79468235?'

'No.'

Beside her, Ben had been tapping his pen against his teeth in a show of impatience. Now he leaned forward with his forearms on the table. 'Did Gabriel use drugs?'

Hunter regarded him coolly for a while. 'Maybe. I think he used to smoke dope, that kind of thing. Nothing too heavy.'

'Magic mushrooms?' prompted Bridget.

'Possibly. Maybe that's what made him so paranoid.'

'Who supplied them to him?' asked Ben.

'No comment.'

'Did you supply him?'

'No.'

'Did Gabriel deal in drugs?'

Hunter laughed. 'I have absolutely no idea.'

Ben didn't join in with Hunter's laughter. 'The gun used to shoot Gabriel Quinn had previously been used in drugs-related killings in London. Who ordered the killing of Gabriel Quinn?'

'Do you think I know?'

'I'm asking you.'

'I'll tell you straight. I know nothing about who killed Gabriel.'

'I think you do. I think that you or someone closely associated with you hired a shooter to take out Gabriel Quinn.'

Hunter sighed and gritted his teeth. 'No comment.'

For the next thirty minutes Ben harangued Hunter about his alleged drug-dealing activities. To every accusation, Hunter responded with the words *No comment.* They were getting nowhere and Bridget could see Ben becoming more and more agitated. He had progressed from tapping his pen against his teeth to drumming it on the tabletop. A telltale vein started to throb in his neck. His behaviour was worryingly similar to that of Superintendent Grayson's, but Bridget knew that unlike Grayson, Ben's frustration could easily spill over into outright anger. Any minute now he would start shouting and they'd have to abandon the interview all together. She decided to jump in with another question of her own.

'Let's talk about Gabriel again. What about his paintings? Were they any good?'

The question had the effect of defusing the tension that had built up almost to explosive point. Hunter nodded. 'They weren't necessarily to my taste, but many people thought they were good. Gabriel certainly had talent, and he was original too. There was an intensity to his work that reflected his personality.'

'So why did he still live on a canal boat? Why wasn't his work earning him the kind of success that you enjoy?'

Hunter scowled. 'It's not just about talent, is it? There's more to making your way in the art world than that.'

'Such as?'

'It's as much about who you know. You need to be able to engage with people. Gallery owners, buyers, critics. Gabriel hated that side of the business. He was too busy with his numbers to spend time wooing the punters. Amber didn't really encourage him, either. She was too taken with her idea of being a muse. They weren't good for each other, those two, despite what Amber thinks. She's much better off with me.'

'So you're not sorry Gabriel's dead,' interjected Ben.

'You're putting words in my mouth. I never wished Gabriel any ill will.'

Bridget ignored Ben's interruption and ploughed on. At least she'd managed to get Hunter saying more than just *No comment* which was more than Ben had achieved.

'How is your own career going?'

'I told you. It's all right.'

'Your work was spotted early on by the collector Lawrence Taylor. Is that correct?'

'Yeah, that was my first sale. Melissa told Lawrence about my work and encouraged him to invest.'

'Who is Melissa?' asked Ben, not even trying to conceal

his irritation.

'Dr Melissa Price,' explained Bridget patiently. 'She was Hunter and Gabriel's tutor at the Ruskin School of Art. She's also the wife of Lawrence Taylor, the businessman and art collector. She turned back to Hunter. 'And has Lawrence bought more of your work recently?'

'Not so much in the past year.'

'So how would you say your career is progressing at the moment?'

Hunter looked her straight in the eye. 'It's not all sweetness and light in the art world, I can tell you. There are sharks out there waiting to rip people off.'

'Anyone in particular?'

Hunter sniffed. 'Lawrence and Melissa are two of the worst. Lawrence never pays the true value of a work of art. And Melissa is even worse. It's an open secret among the students at the Ruskin that she steals all their best ideas and reproduces them in her own work. She's always going on about the importance of originality, but she's such a hypocrite. She hasn't had an original idea in decades.'

Bridget recalled how Melissa had talked about originality in art when she'd spoken to her at the Ruskin. She'd even had the cheek to dismiss Gabriel's work as derivative. 'Did Melissa rip your ideas off, Hunter?'

'Sure she did.'

'And Gabriel's?'

'She did it to anyone who was good. She's like a succubus, draining people of their creativity.'

'Do you believe that Melissa Price might have been responsible for Gabriel's death?'

Hunter cocked his head, giving the idea some thought. 'Melissa as a cold-blooded killer? Sure, it's possible.'

'Perhaps Gabriel was planning to expose her activities?'

'I really don't know.'

'What about Lawrence Taylor? Could he have benefited from Gabriel's death?'

Hunter shrugged. 'Sure. Anyone who had a stake in Gabriel's work would stand to benefit. Take the gallery owner, Jonathan Wright, for instance. He's going to be cashing in now that Gabriel's paintings are shooting up in value.'

Bridget bristled at this outrageous slur against Jonathan. It was ridiculous to suggest that a gallery owner would hire a contract killer to murder one of his own artists. She was about to say so when Ben interrupted her.

'Interesting that you should mention the gallery owner, Jonathan Wright.'

Bridget frowned at him, surprised that he even knew Jonathan's name. He opened his file and took out a set of photographs, spreading them out across the table in front of Hunter. Bridget swivelled her head to study them.

'Is this you?' Ben pointed to a figure in a beanie hat talking to another man in dark glasses.

For the first time since the interview had begun, Hunter seemed wrong-footed. He peered at the photograph, then glanced away. 'No comment.'

'What about this one?' Hunter's face was more visible this time. There was no mistaking him.

'No comment.'

'And this?'

'No comment.'

'What these photos show,' said Ben, 'is you doing business with George Walsh, a known drug dealer, in London.'

From out of his folder, Ben produced another photo, this one a close-up of the man pictured with Hunter. In this image the man wasn't wearing dark glasses and his features were clearly visible. Do you recognise this man?'

'No comment.'

'Like I said, his name is George Walsh. These photos were taken last week by undercover officers engaged in a covert surveillance operation. We've been watching this gang for many months. We know who they are, where their supplies come from, who they use as distributors. We also know that at least two murders have been carried out in connection with the gang's operations.' He paused ominously. 'Three murders, if you include the killing of Gabriel Quinn.'

'No comment.'

'We believe that you, or a close associate, ordered Gabriel's death.' Ben dropped another photograph onto the desk. It was the one he'd shown earlier to Bridget of Travis Brown, the former Grenadier Guardsman and alleged contract killer. 'Do you know this man?'

Hunter barely looked at the image before replying. 'No comment.'

Ben reached into his file and pulled out one final photo. 'This was taken thirty minutes later on the same day as the others I showed you. It's you again, at the same location. Now you're getting into a car. Who is that behind the steering wheel?'

Bridget turned her head to get a better look at the photo herself and a chill ran down her spine. Unmistakable behind the wheel, in his tortoiseshell glasses, was Jonathan.

★

Jake wasn't warming to DI Kate Macready's interviewing technique. Her style was brusque and relentless, firing off rapid questions and making no effort to put her interviewee at ease.

Bridget would have handled things very differently, especially with someone as obviously terror-struck as Amber. *Try to be sympathetic*, she had told him. He wondered how his boss was getting on interviewing Hunter alongside Ben. It couldn't be easy for Bridget to be working with her ex-husband like this. He'd sensed a strong undercurrent of tension between them, which was hardly surprising. He'd also noticed the way Ben had been eyeing Ffion. Ben might be a senior officer, but if he tried anything on with Ffion, Jake wouldn't hesitate to intervene, although knowing Ffion she could probably look after herself, what with her doing Taekwondo and all that. He'd watched some videos of the martial art online and wouldn't want to be standing in the way of Ffion when she did one of those high kicks.

'Are you in a sexual relationship with Hunter Reed?' DI Macready's blunt question to Amber brought him rudely back to the interview. He noticed how she never framed anything with *I'm sorry to have to ask you this* or *I understand this is difficult for you.* He made a mental note never to do the same when it was his turn to lead an interview.

Sitting on the other side of the table, Amber appeared frail and lost, her emerald eyes downcast. She nervously tucked and re-tucked a strand of hair behind her ear. There was none of the confidence with which she apparently posed nude for artists to paint her. Jake gave her a reassuring nod but she failed to catch his eye. Her lawyer, a middle-aged man Jake had never met before, sat next to her. Jake had no love for lawyers, but this one seemed particularly ineffectual. Jake wondered if the man might intervene and protest at Kate's aggressive line of questioning, but the lawyer merely studied his notes through his reading glasses.

DS Sutcliffe, one of the two sergeants from London, stood near the door, as if on guard. He'd said nothing since the interview had begun and Jake had no idea what he was doing there. Amber clearly posed no danger to anyone and Sutcliffe's menacing presence wasn't helping to put anyone at ease.

'I repeat, are you in a sexual relationship with Hunter Reed?'

'Yes.' Amber's voice was barely above a whisper.

'But you were also in a sexual relationship with Gabriel Quinn, were you not?'

A faint blush covered Amber's pale cheeks. 'Yes.'

'At the same time?' Kate's harsh gaze bore down unrelentingly.

'Yes.' Amber seemed almost to be trying to curl herself into a protective ball. 'I never lied to Gabriel about it. We had an understanding.'

'I see.' A cruel smirk flashed across Kate's face. She was

clearly enjoying her power over the younger woman. Behind them, Jake heard DS Sutcliffe snigger softly. Jake wanted to stand up to defend Amber, even though his own reaction on learning of Amber's love triangle had been similarly judgemental. He hoped that he hadn't gloated in the way that Kate was so obviously doing now. She was like a cat tormenting a mouse before moving in for the kill.

'Have you ever taken drugs, Amber?'

A quick hesitation, then, 'Yes.'

'What kinds?'

'Cannabis. Cocaine. Ecstasy.'

'Who did you get them from?'

There was another brief pause, but all the defiance that Jake had seen in the girl the previous day had drained away. She was like putty in Kate's hands, and her lawyer was doing nothing to protect her. 'Hunter. He gave them to me.'

'And did he take them too?'

'He smoked joints, and he took ecstasy sometimes.'

'Did Gabriel also use drugs?'

Amber put her face in her hands and shook her head. 'Gabriel never took anything serious. He only smoked a bit of weed, and sometimes he used mushrooms. He said they helped stimulate his creative drive.'

'I bet they did. And who supplied him? Was it Hunter?'

A tear ran down Amber's already darkly-stained cheek. 'I don't want to say.'

Behind them, Sergeant Sutcliffe coughed loudly, making Amber flinch at the harsh sound. Jake had had enough of the hard-faced sergeant and his unhelpful sound effects. 'May I have a quick word with you outside, ma'am?' he asked Kate.

She shot him an unpleasant glance, but pushed her chair back and stood up. 'It had better be quick.'

Sutcliffe stood aside from the door to let them past, casting a sneer in Jake's direction.

In the corridor outside, Jake lowered his voice to speak to the DI. 'Ma'am, do you think you could ask Sergeant

Sutcliffe to leave the room? He's not assisting with the interview, and I think that the suspect would speak more freely if he wasn't present.' He wanted to say that showing some kindness might help too, but kept that thought to himself.

'All right.' He'd half expected her to shout him down, but to his surprise, she agreed without argument. They went back in and Kate dismissed Sutcliffe without giving him any explanation. He left the interview room with a ferocious look aimed at Jake.

Kate resumed the interview as if nothing had happened. 'Amber, I asked you who supplied drugs to Gabriel, and you refused to answer.' She dropped her voice to a threatening undertone. 'I would remind you that you are under arrest for a serious criminal offence. You won't be helping yourself if you refuse to co-operate.'

Again Jake looked to the lawyer, but he did nothing to come to Amber's defence.

The girl looked utterly wretched. 'It was his neighbour on the canal, Hat,' she said eventually.

'That's Harriet Watson,' said Jake.

'Yeah,' said Amber. 'Hat grows all kinds of plants on her boat.'

'Including cannabis?'

Amber nodded.

'Please speak out loud for the interview recorder.'

'Yes.'

'What about magic mushrooms?'

'Hat collects them. She goes out walking across the fields next to the canal and finds them.'

'And did Gabriel buy all his drugs from Harriet Watson?'

'Hat didn't sell them to Gabriel. She just shared them with her friends.'

'How nice.' Kate took a sip of water from a glass. When she spoke again her voice was cold. 'Tell me more about Hunter's drugs business.'

Amber seemed to crumple as if she realised that the

game was finally over. 'Hunter got involved a few years ago, just in a small way at first. He was disillusioned about the art world, said there was no money to be made there. He'd got used to living in a certain style after his initial success, but then he started to make less and less money from his paintings. He couldn't keep up the payments on his apartment, so he needed to find some cash quickly.'

'What substances did he deal in?'

'I don't know. Whatever was available. Meth, crack, ecstasy. Maybe some skunk.'

'Where did he get hold of his supplies?'

'He used to drive up to London every couple of weeks. He knew a guy there who sold him stuff.'

'And what role did you play in all this, Amber?'

Amber stared wide-eyed at the detective, clearly terrified. 'I was just his girlfriend. I admit I used some of the drugs he brought back. But I swear, I was never a dealer.'

'I see. Well that's all for now. We'll resume this interview back in London.'

'London?'

'That's right.' Kate brought the interview to an abrupt close and left the room. Her lawyer finished writing his notes and closed his book. As far as Jake could tell, he had done nothing useful to assist Amber throughout the entire process.

The young woman continued to sit across the table. She glanced nervously in Jake's direction. 'What now?'

'I'll take you back to the cells,' he said. 'Thank you very much for your co-operation.'

It didn't seem like much comfort, but he hoped he'd managed to inject some kindness into his voice. *Try to be sympathetic*, Bridget had instructed him. He didn't feel like he'd risen to the task.

CHAPTER 20

Bridget was shaking with rage after the interview with Hunter. Ben had behaved in an underhand way, keeping those photos to himself and only revealing them at the eleventh hour. He had done it to surprise her, just as much as the suspect he was supposed to be interviewing. 'You can't possibly think that Jonathan Wright has got anything to do with a drugs gang in London,' she berated him once they had left the interview room. 'Why didn't you tell me about that photo?'

Ben leaned back against the wall, completely unruffled by her fury. 'I seem to have touched a raw nerve. I don't see how we can rule out any suspect before we've thoroughly investigated them. Jonathan Wright was photographed giving a lift to Hunter Reed following the conclusion of a drugs deal. That's pretty strong grounds for believing he was involved in the transaction.'

'But there are all kinds of reasons why Jonathan might have been in a car with Hunter.'

'Such as?'

Bridget threw her hands into the air. 'I don't know. He probably just gave him a lift, that's all. He's selling

173

Hunter's paintings in his gallery. I'm sure there's a perfectly straightforward explanation.'

Ben raised an inquisitive eyebrow. 'You seem to know an awful lot about this Jonathan Wright.'

'We're friends as it happens.' Bridget could feel herself getting hot under the collar.

'Friends?' Ben was watching her closely now. 'Maybe more than friends? Chloe did mention something about you going on a date to the opera the weekend she was visiting me in London.'

'Don't you dare bring Chloe into this,' snapped Bridget, ducking Ben's question.

A smile curled the corners of his mouth. 'How was the opera by the way?' He was playing with her now, enjoying her discomfort.

'If you must know, I didn't go to the opera. I was too busy investigating the death of Gabriel Quinn.'

'But you intended to go with Jonathan?'

'Mind your own bloody business.'

Ben laughed. He'd clearly enjoyed their little spat. Then he grew serious. 'We do need to speak to him though. We need to find out why he was in the car with Hunter. If there's an innocent explanation, he can tell us himself what it is.'

Bridget shook her head. 'No. What we should be doing is following up this latest information about Dr Melissa Price stealing her students' ideas. If Gabriel was about to expose her activities, she had a motive to silence him. And her husband, Lawrence Taylor, also had a reason to want Gabriel dead. He stands to profit substantially from Gabriel's demise. If anyone's got the means to pay for a contract killing, then those two certainly have.'

Ben adopted a bored expression now. 'Bridget, I've indulged your fantasies quite enough already. Kate and I are working to take down a multi-million pound drugs ring. Hunter and his girlfriend will be returning to London with us, and I hope to use their evidence to follow this all the way to the top of the gang. I'm not interested in some petty dispute between an artist and his former tutor.' He pulled on his jacket. 'While I'm here I intend to gather all relevant information and follow up every lead. I can go on my own to pick up Jonathan, or you can come with me. I can't be fairer than that. It's your choice.'

It wasn't much of a choice, but Bridget knew that she couldn't stop Ben from bringing Jonathan in for questioning. If that was going to happen, she would be damn sure to go with him and make sure he didn't put a foot out of line. 'All right. I'm coming. And I'm warning you, I'll be watching every move you make.'

Ben ran a hand through his slicked-back hair. 'I do like it when you say things like that.'

She returned to her desk to quickly brief Jake on what Hunter had said about Melissa Price.

Her sergeant looked doubtful at the revelation. 'Melissa steals her students' ideas? Is she really that desperate?'

'That's what Hunter told me. Go into Oxford and talk to as many of her recent students as you can. Find out if there's any truth in the accusation. Oh, and take Ffion with you.' She didn't know how much Ffion knew about art, but the young constable knew about most subjects, and Bridget was willing to bet that none of the blokes in the team could tell a Rembrandt from a Renoir.

Jake's eyes lit up at the prospect. 'Will do. I'll let you know what we find. What will you be doing in the meantime, ma'am?'

'Bringing an art gallery owner in for questioning, on suspicion of dealing in drugs.'

Jake picked up on her sarcastic tone and raised an eyebrow. 'Really?'

'Yes, really. See you later.' She grabbed her bag and followed Ben out of the office. No way was he leaving without her.

★

Bridget and Ben drove to the High Street in Ben's BMW,

not speaking a word to each other. It was depressingly like the final days of their marriage, when they'd grown distant and estranged. She was furious at the way he'd probed her relationship with Jonathan. It was none of his business who she spent her time with. She'd never once quizzed him about Tamsin, although maybe she ought to, now that Tamsin was beginning to get involved in Chloe's life. Did Ben really think that Jonathan was involved in this drugs business, or was he just using that as an excuse to dig into her personal life?

They pulled up outside the gallery and Ben slapped a police parking permit on the dashboard.

'Let me do the talking,' hissed Bridget as they got out of the car.

The bell on the door chimed as they entered and Jonathan appeared from the back of the gallery. Vicky was sitting behind the counter, her legs crossed, perusing a Sotheby's auction catalogue.

'Hello, Bridget.' Jonathan's face broke into a smile as soon as he caught sight of her. 'What a lovely surprise. I did enjoy our meal last –'

Bridget put up a hand to stop him. 'Jonathan, I'm really sorry, but I'm afraid I'm here on police business.'

'Oh?' He glanced from her to Ben, who was standing a couple of feet back. 'Is it about Gabriel?'

'Jonathan, this is DCI Ben Hart from the Metropolitan Police. He's assisting us with the investigation into Gabriel Quinn's murder... and some related matters.'

Jonathan looked at Ben properly then through his tortoiseshell glasses, and Bridget could see him putting two and two together. DCI Ben Hart from the Met. Ben, her ex-husband. The man she'd been complaining about only the night before over a bottle of Pinot Grigio. Now it must look to Jonathan as if she'd been working with Ben all along. She wished she could explain to Jonathan that she'd had no idea Ben would be turning up today and trampling all over her case.

Jonathan stiffened, pushing his glasses up onto the

bridge of his nose. 'How exactly may I help you?' He addressed his question to Ben.

'I have some photographs I'd like to show you, if you don't mind.' He searched in his briefcase for the folder containing the photos of Hunter in London.

Vicky cleared some space on the counter so that Ben could lay them out. Her face held a worried look. She could obviously sense the tension between the two men, even if she had no idea what was happening.

Ben placed the photos on the white surface in a row. 'Do you recognise any of the people in these images?'

Jonathan studied the faces carefully. 'Yes. This man is Hunter Reed. He's one of the artists who's currently exhibiting in my gallery. I can show you some of his works, if you like.'

'That won't be necessary, sir.'

Jonathan returned to his examination of the photos. He peered closely at the man Hunter was pictured with. 'I've never seen this man before,' he said. He stopped abruptly as he recognised his own features in the final image. 'This is me, with Hunter. It must have been taken the day I drove Hunter into London.' He turned to face Ben, the puzzlement on his face giving way to outrage as he realised that the police had been photographing him. 'What is the meaning of this? Who took these photos?'

Ben stepped forward. 'Jonathan Wright, I am arresting you on suspicion of conspiracy to supply class A drugs. You do not have to say anything. But, it may harm your defence if you do not mention when questioned something which you later rely on in court. Anything you do say may be given in evidence.'

'Arresting me? For supplying drugs?' Jonathan laughed nervously as if he thought this was all a joke. But then he caught Bridget's eye and realised that Ben was serious.

Vicky gasped out loud, putting her hand to her mouth in horror.

Bridget could have died on the spot. Ben had misled her into thinking that they were coming here just to ask

Jonathan a couple of simple questions about his relationship with Hunter Reed in order to eliminate him from the enquiry. She'd had no idea that he was going to move in with the subtlety of an invading army. She should have realised.

'What on earth is going on?' Jonathan looked angrily between Bridget and Ben.

'That's what we intend to find out down at the station,' said Ben.

'But you can't be serious. I haven't the slightest idea what you're talking about.'

Ben pulled a pair of handcuffs from his pocket. 'I strongly suggest that you come quietly, sir. If you resist arrest I will be obliged to handcuff you.'

'Ben!' said Bridget furiously. 'Put those away. There's no need for that.'

Jonathan put up his hands in a placatory gesture. 'All right, I'll come quietly. There's no need for any force. I'm happy to help you with your enquiries if it means catching Gabriel's killer. But I resent being treated like a criminal. If you'll just let me get my jacket, I'll be with you in a moment.' He lifted a linen jacket from a hook behind the counter and pulled it on. 'Vicky, can I leave you to mind the gallery?'

Bridget looked at Vicky, who was staring at her with an expression of complete shock. 'Hopefully this won't take very long,' Bridget told her. 'Then I can bring Jonathan back to the gallery.'

Vicky nodded mutely, nervously straightening the pile of postcards that sat on the counter next to the art catalogue.

Ben returned the handcuffs to his pocket, clearly disappointed that the opportunity to use them had been taken from him. The very fact that he had brought cuffs with him was proof that he had intended to arrest Jonathan right from the start.

Bridget led the way out of the gallery and held open the rear door of the car for Jonathan. 'I'm so sorry,' she whispered to him as he climbed into the car, but there was no sign that he had heard her.

The drive back to Kidlington was excruciating for Bridget. With Ben at the wheel of the car – seemingly in buoyant mood as he tapped his fingers on the steering wheel – and her boyfriend (could she call him that?) in the back, under arrest, she felt completely helpless. She was never going to forgive Ben for this. In the space of one morning she had gone from leading a murder investigation to having her ex-husband and that bloody DI Kate Macready come in and walk all over it, mocking her theories and now destroying her personal relationships.

When they reached the station, Bridget escorted Jonathan inside while Ben went off in search of Kate Macready.

'What will happen to me now?' Jonathan asked her.

'I'm going to leave you with the sergeant, who will explain everything to you. You can make a phone call and ask to see a solicitor, which I strongly advise you to do. Then your possessions will be taken from you for safekeeping and you'll be taken to a cell until questioning.'

Jonathan's face fell. 'So I really am being treated like a criminal. Nothing like this has ever happened to me before.'

'Of course not.' She wanted to reassure him that everything would be fine, and that he would be back in the gallery in no time. But she was a police detective working on his case. She mustn't say anything that might prejudice the outcome. Instead she asked him who he wanted to phone.

'I really don't have anyone I want to speak to,' he said gloomily. 'Vicky knows and... so do you. So really, there's no one else I want to tell.'

She patted his arm helplessly and left him in the safe hands of the duty sergeant. Then, her frustration almost too much to contain, she stormed upstairs and went straight to Chief Superintendent Grayson's office. She knocked once on the door but didn't wait for him to answer before going inside.

Grayson was at his desk, annotating a report with his gold fountain pen. He looked up as Bridget burst in, frowning at the unexpected intrusion. 'DI Hart. Has there been a breakthrough on the case?'

'No, sir. Quite the opposite.' She took a deep breath. 'I simply can't work with DCI Ben Hart and his team from London. He has a completely different agenda to me. He's undermining my authority at every opportunity. He has dismissed every single one of my leads, and introduced an entirely new theory for Gabriel Quinn's murder. Our methods are incompatible. Either he goes, or I go.'

She hadn't realised precisely what she was going to say before the words were out. Now she had said them, she was struck with a sudden terror that Grayson might choose to take Ben's side over hers. What would happen then? The thought that Jonathan might be left at the mercy of Ben's interviewing made her blood run cold. Ben had no evidence to charge Jonathan, but the incriminating photograph of Jonathan with Hunter would be sufficient for him to be held and questioned for up to twenty-four hours. Ben might choose to do that, just so that he could enjoy exercising his power. She stood still, waiting to hear Grayson's judgement, praying that he would back her.

Grayson screwed the lid back on his fountain pen and regarded her with a hard stare. When he spoke his voice was level but resolute. 'DI Hart, I realise that working with your ex-husband is not easy for you, but the involvement of the Met in this case is simply out of my hands.' He placed the pen on his desk next to the open report and leaned back in his chair. 'Please don't ask me to make a ruling on whether you or Ben will lead this case. That decision has already been made, by others more senior than myself. Like it or not, DCI Hart is in charge now.' He leaned forward then and softened his voice. 'As for your position, I expect you to carry on as before. You will put aside any personal feelings and work with Ben, just as you would work with any other senior officer. The fact is that the sooner we get this wrapped up, the sooner we can get the Met off our patch. Do I make myself clear?'

Bridget nodded mutely. Grayson had overruled her request, but perhaps that was for the best. The anger and frustration that had been building in her had been released by her outburst, and she could see now that the best way for her to protect Jonathan and ensure that he was treated fairly was for her to remain on the case and monitor Ben's every move. Grayson was certainly right about one thing – the sooner the case was closed, the sooner she could get Ben off her back and out of her working life.

'All right, sir,' she told him. 'I'll do my best.'

CHAPTER 21

'What do you think of the new boss, then?' ventured Jake as he and Ffion drove through Oxford in search of Melissa Price's final year students. They'd already called in at the Ruskin School, only to be informed that the students were all to be found at a gallery called Modern Art Oxford, where they were busy taking down their exhibits after displaying their final degree work. Modern Art Oxford was located a short drive away through the busy city centre.

'DCI Ben Hart, you mean?' said Ffion in her lilting Welsh accent.

'Yeah.' The other guys in the office had taken quickly to Ben's back-slapping blokeish affability, but Jake wasn't so easily won over. If it was a matter of choosing between Ben or Bridget, he knew where his loyalty lay, and he was hoping he might find some common ground with Ffion where the boss's ex-husband was concerned.

'He's clearly the type of man who unconsciously subscribes to Freud's theory of penis envy,' said Ffion.

'Huh?' said Jake, fumbling with his gear stick and almost stalling the car. He'd thought that Ben Hart was a bit of a dick, but Ffion obviously had somewhat more elaborate theories on the subject. He pulled up at a red light, disinclined to handle the gear stick under Ffion's gaze, and instead leaving the car in gear with his foot on the clutch pedal while he waited for the light to change. 'So what did Freud have to say about... about this topic?'

'Freud believed that young girls experience anxiety when they first realise they don't have a penis.'

'Right. I see. And... um... do they?'

Ffion shook her head impatiently. 'No, of course not. That's just typical of the kind of misogynist thinking of men who believe that being white, male and heterosexual is the highest form of evolutionary development.'

'Got it.' Jake tried to picture his mates back in Leeds as being the pinnacle of evolution, but it was hard work. Perhaps that meant he wasn't the kind of man Ffion objected to. The lights turned from amber to green and he moved off in second gear, the car juddering slightly.

'Of course,' continued Ffion, oblivious to his discomfort, 'given that we live in a patriarchal society, the penis does confer a certain degree of power and privilege. If women envy anything, it's the power that derives from being male, not the genitals that go with it.'

'I guess so.' Jake hadn't expected to be discussing penises and genitals quite so early in his relations with Ffion, and was hoping that she had come to the end of her pronouncements on the matter.

He was relieved when they turned off the busy thoroughfare of St Aldate's into Pembroke Street, a narrow lane of seventeenth and eighteenth-century houses clustered together so closely that the road was barely wide enough for one car to drive along. Jake hadn't even known this street existed. That was the thing about Oxford. Even though he'd lived here for six months, he was still constantly discovering something new.

Modern Art Oxford was an unassuming establishment tucked away at the very end of the street. It wasn't the sort of place you'd stumble across unless you were actively looking for it. The building looked to be as old as its neighbours, but instead of having an attractive brick or pastel-painted facade, its brickwork had been painted an uncompromising shade of grey. It was an attempt to make the gallery look contemporary and urban, he supposed, but he wondered whether the neighbours appreciated it.

Inside, the gallery retained its edgy, minimalist feel. The walls were of white-painted brick and the flooring was all stripped wood. The roof space of the gallery had been opened up and a complicated tangle of metalwork and struts supported the ceiling. Natural light bled through from overhead skylights.

The gallery walls still held a few paintings, and several objects were arranged – or perhaps discarded – on the floor, but the exhibition was being dismantled by a number of young people, presumably the students who had created the art.

A small group of students were congregated in front of one of the pictures. Jake approached them, and saw that the work consisted of a grey circle within a black background. He peered closer and saw that the grey circle was made out of slightly manky fabric. It looked like someone had cut up a piece of old carpet and glued it onto the canvas. He couldn't quite see the appeal himself. He supposed he was old-fashioned, but he'd always thought that pictures ought to look like something.

The students turned to him and Ffion with interest. 'Hey, are you here to see the exhibition?' asked one of them, a skinny guy wearing a black fedora hat. 'It's already finished, I'm afraid. But you're welcome to take a look around while we pack up.'

'We're actually here to have a chat,' said Jake. 'Are you guys all students at the Ruskin?'

'Yeah, sure. I'm Tom. This is Kim and Sadie.' He motioned to the two girls who were with him. One of them was carefully lowering a large ceramic sculpture into a packing case. The object resembled an African fertility statue, but with bright green luminous hair sprouting out of its head. Jake smiled politely as the girl completed her task.

'Is that yours?' Ffion asked the girl, who Tom had introduced as Kim, once she'd managed to stow the artwork safely inside its box. She was a striking blonde with a pierced nose.

'Yeah. What do you think?' the girl enquired nervously.

Ffion gave the object careful consideration. 'I think it's lush,' she said eventually, and was rewarded with a broad grin. She held up her warrant card and the grin vanished immediately. The three students glanced nervously at each other. 'No need to worry,' Ffion assured them. 'No one's in any kind of trouble.'

Except for crimes against art, thought Jake, but he kept his face pleasant. 'I'm DS Jake Derwent, and my colleague and I are investigating the death last Saturday of Gabriel Quinn. I assume you've all heard about it?'

'God, yeah,' said the third student, Sadie, a redhead with frizzy hair tied up with a bright purple bow. 'At first I thought it sounded like, you know, some kind of installation art, but then it turned out it was for real and I thought, God that's sick.'

The others nodded their heads in agreement. Jake didn't see how a shooting could be interpreted as art, installation or not, but then he didn't have a degree in fine art.

'We went to see the exhibition at the gallery on the High Street,' said Tom. 'Gabriel's paintings are still on display there.'

'Yeah,' said Kim, 'that's mind-blowing. Gabriel's work is living on after his death. He's become immortal.'

The three students fell into an awestruck silence.

'So,' said Jake, 'do any of you have Dr Melissa Price as your tutor?'

'Melissa?' said Kim. 'Yeah, we all do. Everyone who works with oil on canvas has Melissa in their final year.'

'And how do you find her as a tutor?'

'Well, she's all right, I suppose. She's quite good at

teaching. She's a bit of a rampant feminist though, and she does tend to bully the boys.'

Tell me about it, thought Jake. But he was relieved to hear that Melissa picked on all guys, and hadn't singled him out for special treatment.

'Yeah,' said Tom miserably. 'She's a real bitch, actually. Sorry – am I allowed to say that? This isn't going to be used as evidence is it?'

'Not for the moment.'

'God, you don't think Melissa is involved in Gabriel's death, do you?'

'We can't comment on the investigation,' said Jake, knowing that his words would fuel speculation among the students that Melissa might indeed have killed her former student, 'but we're interested in rumours that Dr Price may have been copying some of her students' ideas and passing them off as her own. Do any of you know anything about this?'

Tom snorted with laughter. 'Worst kept secret in the Ruskin School of Art. Every year Melissa exhibits at the Royal Academy summer exhibition and it's always some idea she's nicked from one of her students. She's totally blatant about it, actually, like she thinks she's untouchable.'

'Yeah,' agreed Sadie. 'It sucks, but there's nothing anyone can do about it.'

'Hasn't anyone ever made a formal complaint?'

'Trust me, it's not worth the hassle,' said Kim.

'Why not?'

The three students exchanged anxious looks. Eventually, Tom plucked up the courage to talk. 'Melissa's too powerful.'

'In what way?'

'The art world's very small, and young artists need to quickly establish a reputation if they want to make a name for themselves.'

'They need sponsors,' said Kim.

'Yeah,' said Sadie. 'Melissa's like a gatekeeper. No one

dares to mess with her.'

'I don't really understand,' said Jake.

'When we finish our final year, we all put our work on display,' explained Tom. He waved his arms around the gallery. 'This was our final year exhibition. It's basically a launch platform for our future careers. If we attract buyers, we're in with a chance of making a career in art.'

'If not, we have to become teachers or get a proper job,' said Sadie, with a smile.

'Melissa has all the contacts. If she mentions your name to a collector, then they might buy your work. If she takes a dislike to someone, she can basically destroy their career before it even starts.'

'So no one would ever dare to challenge her,' said Kim.

'That's terrible,' said Jake.

'Right,' said Tom. 'But that's how it works.'

'For the moment, at least,' said Sadie.

'How do you mean?'

'Melissa's domestic arrangements may be about to change for the worse.'

'In what way?'

Kim grinned wickedly. 'Her husband, Lawrence Taylor is in the process of divorcing her. Without Lawrence's money behind her, Melissa's days are numbered. She'll no longer be able to make and break people's careers.'

'Yeah,' said Kim. 'And then her days of stealing other people's ideas will be over. She might have to come up with some original ideas of her own.'

CHAPTER 22

B ridget had never wanted to do an interview less than the one she was about to participate in, and yet she knew she had to be there. Ben had told her he would prefer to have Kate Macready join him, but that had only made her even more determined to see it through.

She entered the interview room to find Jonathan sitting with his hands clasped together, confusion mixed with anxiety on his face. Another man, smartly-dressed in a dark suit and sober tie – presumably his lawyer – was seated next to him. He looked familiar. The lawyer sprang to his feet as Bridget walked in. 'Andrew McAllister,' he said, offering her a firm handshake. 'I believe we've met before.'

'Yes. Nice to see you again,' said Bridget. Andrew McAllister was an experienced and dynamic lawyer from one of the established local firms. He had defended a suspect in an interview Bridget had led during a previous case, and had put up a good fight. She was relieved that Jonathan had chosen well, and wasn't relying on a police-assigned duty solicitor to look after him. Ben would make mincemeat of a junior lawyer.

She wanted desperately to reach out and take

Jonathan's hand too, to tell him that this was all a big mistake, to reassure him that he had nothing to worry about, and that Ben had acted out of order in arresting him. They could – should – have just invited him to answer a few questions and make a statement. No big deal. But Ben had never been one to pass up an opportunity for a bit of macho posturing. He was now removing his jacket and rolling up his shirt sleeves, as if relishing the prospect of a confrontation. He threw his jacket over the back of his chair and sat down, facing Jonathan. Bridget reluctantly took a seat opposite the solicitor.

McAllister wasted no time before moving to the offensive. 'I would like to know on what grounds you have arrested my client,' he began, once Ben had started the recording machine and got the preliminaries out of the way. Bridget silently cheered him on.

Ben gave him a thin smile, clearly unhappy with the solicitor's assertive stance. 'I will disclose all our evidence as it becomes relevant. For now, I'd like Mr Wright to describe his relationship with Hunter Reed.'

'My relationship with Hunter is purely professional,' said Jonathan. 'Hunter is an artist, and I exhibit his paintings in my gallery in return for a commission on sales.'

Ben consulted his notes. 'This would be Wright's art gallery on the High Street?'

'Yes.'

'And how long have you known Hunter Reed?'

'Almost exactly five years. We were introduced by Dr Melissa Price, one of the tutors at the Ruskin School of Art in Oxford. Hunter was a final year undergraduate displaying his work for his Bachelor of Fine Art degree. Melissa was very keen that we should meet. She felt that Hunter's work would be a good fit for my gallery. I agreed. I've been displaying his paintings in my gallery ever since.'

'They sell well, do they, these paintings?' asked Ben.

Jonathan pushed his glasses up the bridge of his nose. 'Moderately well. Hunter's productivity has tailed off in recent years. That happens sometimes with young artists. They begin to lose the spark that fired them. Building a career in art requires stamina and perseverance. Raw passion and talent will only take you so far.'

'Perhaps Hunter found an easier way to make money.'

'I have no idea what you might be referring to.'

'I'm referring to the sale of illegal drugs.'

'I know nothing about that,' said Jonathan firmly. 'To my knowledge, Hunter Reed is an artist making a living by selling his paintings.'

'Is that right?' said Ben. He opened the file before him and took out his stack of photographs.

Andrew McAllister leaned forward to examine them closely. 'I understand that you've already shown my client these photographs,' he said, 'and you still haven't explained who took them, or why he was under police surveillance.'

Instead of answering his question, Ben pushed the photos across the desk and spoke directly to Jonathan. 'When I first showed you these photos, you identified the first man pictured as Hunter Reed. Would you please confirm that for the record?'

Jonathan gave the image a scornful look. 'Yes, that's correct.'

'And who is the second man?'

'I told you already. I don't know. I've never seen him before.'

'Does the name George Walsh mean anything to you?'

'No.'

Ben pointed to the final photograph. 'In this photograph, Hunter is seen climbing into a car, with another person at the steering wheel. Please could you confirm that the person at the wheel is you?'

Jonathan stared at the image for a few seconds before replying. 'It's a little blurry, but yes, that's me.'

A sly smile spread across Ben's face. 'These photographs were all taken within the space of one hour, and at the same location in London. The man you claim to be unable to identify is George Walsh, a suspect in an ongoing investigation into the supply of class A drugs. Perhaps you would care to explain what you were doing, driving Hunter to his meeting with Mr Walsh on that day?'

Jonathan cleared his throat and took a sip of water. 'Yes, I remember now. I had some business to conduct at Sotheby's and I gave Hunter a lift into London. I dropped him off, then later he called me and arranged for me to pick him up.'

'That's Sotheby's, the auction house?'

'Yes.'

'And what was Hunter doing while you were at Sotheby's?'

'I don't know for certain. He just told me that he was meeting someone. He didn't mention any names.'

'And you didn't ask him?'

'I had no wish to pry into his private life.'

Ben chuckled maliciously. 'How considerate of you.' He leaned forward menacingly. 'Here's what I think happened on that day. You drove Hunter Reed into London knowing full well the nature of his business there, and also the identity of George Walsh. Having dropped Hunter off at the agreed location for their meeting, you then met with a man called Travis Brown.'

'I've absolutely no idea who you're talking about.'

'Travis Brown is an associate of George Walsh. He's wanted for questioning in connection with two murders that have taken place in London during the past year. Forensic evidence now also links him to the murder of Gabriel Quinn.'

Jonathan raised his eyebrows. 'You're telling me that this man, Travis Brown, killed Gabriel?'

'Exactly.'

'But why would he do that?'

'Because he was paid to. Travis Brown isn't a very nice man. He kills people in return for money. I believe that you became aware of him through your connection with Hunter Reed and George Walsh. On the day that you took

Hunter into London to conduct his business with George Walsh, you went to meet Travis Brown. At that meeting, you gave him Gabriel's name and you handed over the fee for the hit. Having concluded your transaction, you returned to collect Hunter, and then brought him, together with the drugs he'd just purchased, back to Oxford.'

'This is outrageous,' said McAllister. 'You have absolutely no grounds for making such accusations about my client.'

Bridget had heard enough of this charade. She leaned forward. 'Jonathan, can anyone verify that you were at Sotheby's on that day?'

If Jonathan could provide an alibi for his movements at the time the alleged meeting with the hitman took place, then Ben would have no grounds for detaining him further.

'Of course they can.' His voice held a note of indignation and Bridget flinched. Seeing her reaction, he softened his tone. 'I had a meeting with Eric Lombardi, the buyer for contemporary art.'

'What did you talk about?'

'I wanted to find out if he was interested in acquiring any of the paintings from my current exhibition.'

'Including Gabriel Quinn's paintings?'

'Amongst others, yes.'

'And would Mr Lombardi be able to verify that he met you?'

'Of course. It would be in his appointments diary. You only have to call him and he'll confirm that what I've told you is true.'

Bridget turned to Ben with satisfaction and arched her eyebrows. 'I don't think we have any further questions to ask, do we?'

'No,' said Ben, gathering his photos back into their folder. 'We'll make the call to Mr Lombardi, and assuming that he confirms your story, you'll be free to go.'

In the corridor outside, Bridget turned the full force of her fury on him. 'How could you? You didn't believe a single one of those accusations, did you?'

Ben shrugged. 'Just doing my job. You ought to be grateful to me. I've just eliminated your boyfriend from our enquiries. He seems like a decent bloke by the way. You could do worse.'

'Oh yes,' she said. 'No need to remind me. I did do worse. I married you.'

'Ha! You haven't lost your sense of humour.'

'And what about Amber? You can't seriously think she was involved in Hunter's drug dealing operation?'

'No, of course not. She's admitted to taking drugs, but I've no interest in that.'

'So you're not going to charge her?'

'I've already let her go. She's given us enough evidence to send Hunter down, and now that we have Hunter I hope to be able to follow the trail up to the next level. We've taken George Walsh into custody, and I expect to make further breakthroughs very quickly now. I had to arrest Amber, you see, Bridget. I needed to get results and it was the only way to make sure she would talk. That's why I put her in the tender loving care of Kate Mcready.'

'You really are a bastard, aren't you?'

'Sure,' he said, giving her a parting wink. 'But the most charming kind. See you around, Bridget.'

CHAPTER 23

The double decker bus lumbered slowly along the Banbury Road, lurching from side to side every time the road rose or dipped. Amber stared out of the grimy upstairs window as the bus made its way from Kidlington towards central Oxford. Every couple of minutes it stopped to take on more passengers and let others off. Amber wondered where she was going to get off herself. She'd only had enough money to buy a single ticket into town and now she was virtually broke. And homeless too.

She couldn't go back to Hunter's place. She didn't have a key, and besides, the police would be crawling all over it. Gabriel's boat was off limits too. And anyway, she never wanted to go back there. The memories were too painful. She put her head in her hands. Gabriel was dead; Hunter arrested. Her life was totally messed up. Well, that was nothing new.

At least the police had let her go. That detective from London had been a complete bitch, asking her all kinds of personal questions. She should have refused to answer any of them, but she'd ended up revealing far too much. She'd been so frightened. Still, she hadn't told the police everything.

The bus came to a halt on Magdalen Street and she got off, she didn't know why. She stood on the pavement watching it drive away. She had no idea where she was going to go next. A young girl sat on the pavement outside St John's College, begging for money. Amber reached into her pocket and pulled out a pound coin. It was the last of her money, but she tossed it to the homeless girl. They were both homeless now. What difference did it make either way?

Out of habit, she turned onto Broad Street and wandered slowly past Balliol College, skirting around a group of tourists who were blocking her path. She'd never been inside one of the colleges, and had only ever glimpsed the medieval quadrangles and manicured lawns through the entrances. The idea of all that learning intimidated her. She'd failed most of her exams at the age of sixteen, just scraping a 'C' in art. That hadn't been enough for her to stay on at school, so she'd left and taken a string of casual jobs in shops and fast-food restaurants.

Until she'd been discovered.

She remembered that day as if it was yesterday. She'd been clearing the tables in McDonald's when she noticed a guy sitting on his own with a sketchpad in his hands. He was working in pencil and was concentrating intently on whatever it was he was drawing. Intrigued, she made her way towards him, gathering discarded food wrappings and wiping the tables as she went. When she was close enough, she dared to peek over his shoulder. She must have gasped out loud because the guy shut his sketchpad with a start.

'Sorry. I didn't mean to be nosey, but you're very good.'

He offered her a shy smile. 'I come here to practise. There are so many different people in a place like this. I do their portraits quickly. The challenge is to capture their likeness before they see you or rush off. People are always rushing everywhere. They never take the time to stop and look.'

'May I see?'

He re-opened his sketchpad to the page where he'd been drawing. The faces and profiles of a dozen different people had been brought to life through his pencil. The French family with the sulky teenage kids, the loud American couple in Yankee baseball caps, Bob behind the counter dashing about taking people's orders. And then there were the pictures of her. The pictures were mostly of her. Wiping the tables, looking over her shoulder, smiling at a baby in a high chair.

He didn't seem embarrassed by them. 'You're very pretty,' he said. 'You have such a versatile face.'

'Do I?' Amber wasn't entirely sure that *versatile* was a compliment, but she liked being called *pretty*.

'Yes. I could draw you all day.'

She looked at him properly then for the first time. He was maybe a year or two older than her, with a thin, pale face and a wispy beard. But it was his eyes that captivated her. They seemed to drink her in, seeing every detail. Gazing into her very soul. She had been ignored for most of her life, but this guy saw her and had captured what he'd seen in his sketchpad. It suddenly felt as if she mattered.

'What time do you finish? I'd like to paint you.'

'Paint me?' Amber couldn't believe her ears. She looked at the clock on the wall. 'I finish in forty-five minutes.'

'I'll wait for you then, Amber.' He had read her name badge.

'I don't even know your name.'

'It's Gabriel. Gabriel Quinn.'

And that was how she'd become an artist's model. Gabriel had taken her back to *La Belle Dame* that evening and had painted her in oils. He couldn't afford to pay her but that didn't matter. All that mattered was that someone was interested in her. She'd never received any attention from her drunken father and delinquent mother. They only cared about themselves. But Gabriel adored her and within the week they were lovers. He introduced her to his artist friends and to Melissa Price, the tutor at the Ruskin School of Art. They all said she had a rare beauty, with her pale skin, large eyes and long red hair. She'd never much liked her hair before and she hated the way her skin burnt in the sun, but now she embraced her Celtic looks. She became an artist's model, something that she'd never dreamed of. And soon she'd quit her dead-end job and started work in Todd's art shop.

Passing the shop now on the other side of Broad Street, she wondered about going inside and asking Todd for help. But Todd was a creep, and a tight-fisted one at that. And Gabriel had been too tangled up with him. The less she saw of Todd the better.

Besides, there was someone else who owed her money.

She cut through Radcliffe Square, passing the domed roof of the Radcliffe Camera and the tall spire of the University Church, onto the High Street. The Ruskin School stood opposite. The grand old building was the only part of the university that Amber had ever been inside. She pushed open the heavy door and stepped into the entrance hall, feeling the chill of the stone. She hurried upstairs before she lost her nerve.

The door to Melissa's room stood open. The art tutor was inside, rearranging books on her shelves. Amber tapped nervously and walked in before Melissa could turn her away.

'Amber. What are you doing here?' The art tutor had never really liked her, despite using her as a model. Melissa was a spiteful old cow, always jealous of Amber's youth and beauty. Amber hated posing for her, but she needed the work.

'I've come for my money.' Amber's eyes flew to the easel where the half-finished nude portrait was displayed for all to see. It was a provocative pose, but Melissa paid extra when she took her clothes off. The sight of it made Amber feel exposed and vulnerable.

'I don't have any cash on me right now,' said Melissa

dismissively. 'Come back another time.'

Amber took a step closer. 'But you promised me I'd have the money a week ago.'

'Yes, well, I've been too busy.'

'Too busy?'

'Yes. It's the end of term and I have my exhibition at the Royal Academy to think about. I don't suppose someone like you would understand that.'

Someone like her? The words were a slap in the face. Melissa had always looked down on her, as if she was something Gabriel had picked up in the gutter. But it wasn't as if Melissa had any great talent to boast of.

Amber looked again at the painting. On impulse she lifted it off its easel.

'What are you doing?' said Melissa. 'Put that down at once!'

'Are you going to pay me for it?'

'You'll be lucky if you ever work here again!'

'I never want to!' Amber hurled the painting to the floor, stepping her foot through the canvas. She tugged the wooden frame and the canvas ripped down the middle. 'You're a bitch!' she cried. 'A horrible bitch and I hope I never see you again!'

★

Bridget was still in a state of fury when she arrived home in Wolvercote. As she'd anticipated, Jonathan's alibi had been quickly verified, but by the time she'd gone looking for him, he'd already been released and had been driven home by his lawyer. Bridget couldn't bear to call or text him. The way he'd looked at her during the interview, he clearly held her partly responsible for his arrest.

But there was really only one person to blame for what had happened. Ben. She would happily have thrown a punch at him, the way he'd interrogated and accused Jonathan, and the smug way he'd behaved with her after the interview. She had never been more angry at work than today.

She slammed the front door of her house behind her and threw her bag down in the corner of the living room. Then she went straight through to the kitchen, poured herself a large glass of Pinot Noir and swallowed a mouthful.

'Hey, Mum, what's up?' Chloe was sitting at the breakfast table, finishing a portion of takeaway pizza straight out of its box.

'What's up is that your father made me look like a total idiot at work today.'

Chloe looked at her in confusion. 'Dad? What was he doing at work?'

'He came charging in first thing this morning with a team from the Met, took over my investigation, almost got me killed in a ridiculous car chase, and then accused everyone involved in my case of belonging to a drugs gang.'

Chloe's eyes widened. 'A drugs gang? What, here in Oxford?'

Bridget gulped down another mouthful of red wine. 'Your father thinks that the artist who was murdered last week was tangled up in selling hard drugs.'

Chloe frowned at the news. 'That sounds strange. But Dad must have a good reason for thinking that, mustn't he?'

Bridget couldn't believe that Chloe was siding with Ben. 'Good reason?' she bellowed. 'He did it for one reason only – to get back at me. To drive a wedge between me and Jonathan and to humiliate me in front of my work colleagues.'

Chloe recoiled at the harshness of her voice. She replaced the half-eaten pizza slice back in its box. 'I think you're being unfair to Dad. He can't just go around making accusations unless he has evidence to back him up. And if he really is on the trail of drugs dealers, then I think you should be supporting him. We've been shown in school the harm that drugs do to young people, and if Dad's working to stop that, you ought to be proud of him.'

'Proud of him?' Bridget could hardly believe what she was hearing from her own daughter.

'Yes. You know, all these years I've only ever heard your version of why you and Dad split up. All that time you hardly let me talk to him at all. But now I've stayed with him and Tamsin, I can see that he's not half as bad as you make out.' Chloe sat up straighter in her chair, adopting a challenging pose. 'In fact, he doesn't seem bad at all to me. I like him a lot, and I wish that you'd allowed me to see him more often when I was growing up.'

Bridget was almost speechless. 'Allowed you to see him? The reason he never came to see you more often is because he spent all his time running away from responsibility. He was unfaithful to me, abandoned us when you were just a small child, then went off to London and never looked back. The only reason he's back in our lives now is because he wants your approval. He's never been able to take responsibility for his actions, and he'd like nothing better than to be forgiven for everything he did and to be told it wasn't his fault. And do you know how he's trying to win your approval? By taking you out to fancy restaurants, and giving you money to go shopping for clothes!' The words were out of her mouth before she could stop herself.

Chloe regarded her coldly, tears welling up in her eyes. She brushed them away fiercely. 'That's a lie! Everything you ever said to me is a lie! You're just bitter because Dad left you and now no one wants you.' She jumped to her feet and began to stride towards the door.

Bridget grabbed her sleeve as she rushed past. 'Chloe! I'm so sorry. I didn't mean to shout at you.'

'Get off me!' Chloe pulled Bridget's hand away from her. 'Don't touch me!'

When Bridget looked into her face, it was Ben's dark eyes that glared back. The tears were still there, but so was a hard defiance. Bridget dropped her hand to her side. Chloe walked out, letting the door slam shut behind her.

Bridget stared at the door in dismay, wondering how

she could have lost control of the situation so rapidly and so catastrophically. More to the point, what was she ever going to say to Chloe to make things right again?

She hated the way that Ben brought out the worst in her. She'd worked for so many years to bury her anger at his treatment of her, and had fooled herself into believing that she'd conquered it. But it had taken just a single day to bring it all bursting back to the surface, as fresh and as raw as the day she first discovered he was cheating on her.

Damn you, Ben Hart, she thought, draining her glass. Damn you to hell!

One thing she knew. Chloe was too mad to reason with now, and it would be better to leave her to calm down. She would try again in the morning.

She remained in the kitchen until the light outside had faded and the room had become as dark as her own thoughts. By then the bottle of wine was empty.

CHAPTER 24

Bridget woke after a broken night's sleep, plagued by disturbing dreams in which everyone she loved – Chloe, Jonathan, and even Vanessa – had been sentenced to life behind bars in some kind of alternative Kafkaesque version of reality. She slipped out of bed and went downstairs, only to find Chloe up early too.

Her daughter was spooning breakfast cereal into her mouth with one hand and thumbing her phone with the other. She didn't look up when Bridget entered the kitchen.

'I just wanted to apologise about last night,' said Bridget. 'I should never have lost my temper.' She swallowed nervously. 'And I shouldn't have said those things about Dad either.' It was torment for her to deny the truth of what she'd told Chloe, but she would do anything to repair the relationship with her daughter.

'It's all right,' said Chloe, still not looking up from her phone. 'No hard feelings.'

'Let me make it up to you. Why don't we go out for dinner this evening? You can pick a restaurant. Or we could go and see a film together. Perhaps even –'

'I'm going out with Olivia.'

'Oh?'

'Yes. We're going back to her place after school, and her mum's going to give us money for pizza.'

'Pizza again?' As soon as she'd said the words, she wished she could unsay them. It seemed she was constantly being goaded into criticising her own daughter. It was a feeling that every parent of a teenage girl must surely recognise.

Chloe looked up for the first time and her eyes blazed with defiance. 'Is that a problem?'

'No. Not at all.'

'Good.'

She drove to work feeling half sick with worry. She still hadn't managed to make contact with Jonathan. She'd hoped he might call her, to say that he felt no ill will about what had happened, but her phone had remained resolutely silent, no matter how often she'd checked it for messages or missed calls.

At least there was no sign of the two black BMWs in the car park when she arrived at Kidlington. Ben and his team had returned to London the previous evening, with Hunter in custody, and Bridget earnestly hoped she would never have to see any of them again. But that was wishful thinking. If Hunter's case went to court, she'd be called on to give evidence alongside Ben. Worse still, her ex-husband was well and truly back in her personal life, and the way things looked he was likely to be playing an ever greater role in the future. She parked the Mini and slapped her hands against the steering wheel in frustration. There was nothing she could do about Ben now. But there was plenty she could do to try and regain control of the investigation into Gabriel Quinn's murder. Travis Brown may have pulled the trigger of the gun that killed him, but she was still no closer to understanding who had ordered the hit, or why.

'Good morning, DI Hart.' The Chief Super seemed in an unusually genial mood when she knocked on his open office door. 'Come and take a seat. I hear that congratulations are in order.'

'I'm not sure about that, sir. If you mean the arrest of Hunter Reed –'

'Oh, come come now, there's no need for false modesty. DCI Hart tells me that the investigation is as good as finished, at least as far as the Oxford side goes. Hunter Reed has been charged and the Met made several further arrests overnight in London. Excellent work, I must say. You proved yourself to be highly professional. A successful collaboration with another force always goes down well in high places.'

Bridget sank into the chair in front of Grayson's desk, wishing he would stop talking. She preferred his normal terse manner to this effusive but misplaced praise. 'Sir, I think that DCI Hart may have been overstating the amount of progress that was made yesterday. There's no reason to think that the investigation into the murder of Gabriel Quinn is over. Travis Brown may have been the gunman who carried out the killing, but who ordered Gabriel's death?'

Grayson's buoyant mood quickly turned sour. 'I was hoping that you would be able to tell me that, DI Hart.'

'The Met were only interested in the drugs angle. They may have made progress on their own case, but apart from the identity of the gunman himself, we still have no information about why Gabriel was killed. Does anyone really think that Hunter Reed ordered his murder? He had no motive.'

'Unless Gabriel Quinn was involved in supplying drugs.'

'There's no evidence for that, sir. We know that Gabriel used recreational drugs personally, but there's no indication that he was ever a supplier.'

Grayson raised his bushy eyebrows. 'DI Hart, I take it you've heard of the principle of Occam's razor? If there are two possible explanations for something then the simplest is usually correct.'

'Yes, sir, I'm aware of that, but' – she tried to phrase her next words with care – 'that explanation just doesn't feel right. Gabriel was completely focused on his art. He loved to paint, and that was it. He was simply too innocent to have become involved in the business of supplying hard drugs.' She wasn't entirely sure how she could feel so certain about it, but she did. Call it female intuition, but she knew that the explanation for Gabriel's death lay elsewhere.

Grayson, however, was a man who dealt in facts, not feelings. 'Do you have another theory for why he was killed?'

'No, sir, but I would like to continue the investigation. We have a number of possible leads, and I believe that it's only a matter of time.'

'Do these leads include your mysterious eight-digit number?'

'It's not my number, sir. It's Gabriel's. And it was important enough for him to communicate it as he lay dying in the street.'

Grayson studied her with a stony face. 'DI Hart, in my job I don't get to hear good news very often, and I take exception when someone pours cold water all over it.'

'Yes, sir, I understand that but –'

'I do not have the resources to allow you and your team to waste time trying to solve a crime that has already been solved. Gabriel Quinn was a habitual drugs user suffering from paranoid delusions and obsessed with numbers. Quite frankly, he sounds like a crackpot to me.'

'Yes, sir, but –'

'Continue your investigation a little longer, but if you don't turn up anything by the end of the day, I'll reassign your team and move you on to something else. Is that clear?'

'Yes, sir.' Bridget rose to her feet, aware that she'd just won a small, but significant victory. 'And thank you, sir.'

He waved her from his office without another word.

★

Suddenly Bridget felt a whole lot better. Ben was gone, for the time being at least, taking Kate Macready and his two surly sergeants with him, and she was back in charge of her own case again. It was time for a briefing. She gathered her team together to assign them their next tasks.

It was fair to describe their mood as despondent. That was no surprise after the Met had invaded their turf, disrupted the investigation, and claimed all the glory for themselves. It was up to Bridget to fire them up again and get them on her side.

'So,' she told them. 'This is where we are. We now know the identity of the gunman who killed Gabriel.' She pointed to the photograph of Travis Brown, the ex-army sniper. 'The question is why? The Met are convinced that the murder was ordered by Hunter Reed, who was known to have links to the drugs ring that used Travis Brown for two previous hits, but we know of no possible reason why Hunter would want Gabriel dead.'

'I'm still pissed off that the Met knew about Hunter's activities all along,' complained Ryan. 'If Hunter does turn out to be responsible for Gabriel's death, then the Met deserve to take some of that responsibility themselves.'

Bridget was pleased to hear that Ryan's short-lived hero-worship of Ben had apparently run into the buffers. There was nothing like the discovery that another force had deliberately withheld information to make people feel resentful towards them. By acting in that way, Ben had unwittingly made himself their enemy.

Bridget was keen to find out just how far her team would back her. 'Do you think Gabriel really was involved in this drug dealing network?' she asked Ryan.

He shook his head. 'At first it seemed plausible, but I don't think it stands up. There must be something else going on.'

There was a general sound of agreement from the others.

'Then I think that our first priority must be to check out Amber's story,' said Bridget. 'Under questioning, she claimed that Gabriel obtained small amounts of cannabis and magic mushrooms from his neighbour on the canal.'

'That would be Harriet Watson,' said Ffion. 'Hat, to her friends.'

'Right. Ffion, I'd like you and Jake to visit Harriet and find out if Amber's story is true. If it is, that really does rule out the possibility that Gabriel was supplying drugs to others.' She turned again to the noticeboard and pointed at the photo of Melissa Price. 'Jake, how did you and Ffion get on interviewing Melissa's students? Is there any truth in Hunter's claim that she plagiarised their ideas?'

Jake nodded eagerly. 'Definitely. We spoke to several who were happy to confirm that. And there's more. They said that Melissa wields power over the students through her relationship with Lawrence Taylor. She decides whether or not Lawrence buys their work, so none of them are willing to challenge her, even though she rips off their work and passes it off as her own.'

'But,' said Ffion, 'that's about to change. Lawrence is divorcing her, so all her influence will soon disappear.'

'Interesting,' said Bridget. 'But I don't quite see how it explains Gabriel's murder. Ryan, I'd like you to go and talk to Amber again. Ask her about this alleged break-in at Gabriel's boat. I don't buy the story that Gabriel was simply paranoid. It's too much of a coincidence to dismiss so easily. If nothing was stolen from the boat, then the person who broke in must have been looking for something. I want to know what.'

'Okay. And what about you, ma'am? What will you be doing?'

'Oh,' said Bridget, 'I've got plenty to keep me busy. I want to pay a visit to Todd Lee and see if I can find out just what he's so desperate to hide.'

And on the way to Todd's art shop, she was going to stop off on the High Street and apologise to a certain gallery owner for the heavy-handed police tactics employed by her ex-husband.

CHAPTER 25

It was a perfect day for messing about on the river, or even on the canal. Jake and Ffion found Harriet on the deck of the *Dragonfly*, dreamily tending her plants with a hand-painted watering can, and singing softly to herself. Or maybe she was singing to the plants. To Jake's eye she looked dippy enough to be doing that. She was just as Ffion had described her, with her long silvery hair peeping out from beneath a straw sunhat, and dressed in an old embroidered cardigan, a raggedy green skirt, and purple boots on her feet. As she bent over to tend her horticultural offspring, Jake spotted red and yellow striped stockings on her legs.

'Excuse me,' he called from the towpath. 'Could we have a word, please?'

'Oh, goodness me,' said Harriet, straightening up with a start. 'You gave me quite a turn there.'

'Sorry about that,' said Jake, stepping onto the boat without waiting for an invitation. He showed his warrant card to her. 'DS Jake Derwent, Thames Valley Police. I believe you've already met my colleague.' Ffion followed him nimbly onto the deck and flashed the woman a smile.

Harriet seemed flustered by the sudden arrival of the two detectives on her narrowboat. 'Is this about Gabriel? Do you have any news?' She glanced over at Gabriel's boat, *La Belle Dame*, which bobbed gently on the water, its deck and cabin still sealed off with police crime scene tape.

'No news,' said Jake. 'Just a few more questions.'

'Of course. Anything I can do to help. Why don't you come inside?' Harriet was very clearly agitated by Ffion, who was now busy scrutinising the impressive array of foliage sprouting from Harriet's collection of flower pots.

'No, thank you,' said Ffion. She continued her inspection of the plants like a buyer at a half-price sale in a garden centre. 'I'd rather be out on deck.'

Jake smiled reassuringly at Harriet. 'It's too nice to be indoors on a sunny day like today, don't you think?'

'I suppose so,' she said distractedly, her eyes not leaving Ffion for a second. 'What was it you wanted to ask me?'

'It was something that Amber told us.'

'Yes?'

'About you supplying cannabis and magic mushrooms to Gabriel.'

Harriet's eyes left Ffion and turned to Jake with a start.

'Could you confirm that you did supply drugs to Gabriel?' asked Jake pleasantly.

'I... it was... that is...'

Ffion's voice cut sharply across Harriet's thoughts on the matter. 'This is a vigorous looking specimen,' she said, lifting up a pot containing a plant with slender, pointed leaves. 'You've brought it out on deck to make the most of the nice sunny weather, I expect. *Cannabis sativa* to give it its Latin name, if I'm not mistaken?'

'Do you have any more of those?' enquired Jake.

'A few more inside,' admitted Harriet, 'but I swear they're just for my own personal use. And my friends.'

'Did you give any to Gabriel?'

'Just as a thank you. He used to help me carry my shopping and do jobs on my boat. That's how it is on the canal. Folk help each other out, in whatever way they can.'

'In your case, by supplying illegal drugs.'

'I'm not a dealer. I've never sold any.'

'But you did supply Gabriel with cannabis for his personal use?'

'Yes.'

If Jake had been on his own, he would have left it at that, but Ffion seemed determined to apply the letter of the law. 'Possession of cannabis is a criminal offence. We'll be confiscating these plants and issuing you with a written warning.'

Harriet scowled at her.

'And what about magic mushrooms?' asked Jake.

'They grow in the meadow.' Harriet pointed to the fields on the other side of the canal. 'They're part of nature's bounty. It's not for people in power to say who's allowed to pick them. They're there for everyone.'

'That isn't what the law says,' said Jake sternly. 'Magic mushrooms are class A drugs.' He softened his voice. 'But we're not going to arrest you. We'd like to ask you about a possible break-in that may have occurred at Gabriel's boat about a week before he died.'

Harriet looked relieved. 'Yes,' she said. 'There was definitely a break-in. I saw the intruder myself.'

'You did?' Jake's notebook was in his hands in an instant.

'You can't be too careful living here on the canal. It's very easy to break into a boat. Theft isn't uncommon, even though most of us have so little to steal. And before you ask, there's no point reporting it to the police either. They never do anything.' She glared angrily at Jake.

'About the intruder?' he prompted.

'It was in broad daylight, right in the middle of the afternoon. I was in my kitchen making a cup of tea and I spotted someone coming out of the cabin of *La Belle Dame*. I knew immediately that it wasn't Gabriel. At that time of day he was always painting at his studio in town. So I came up on deck and called out to challenge the man and ask what he was doing. He told me he was looking for Gabriel, but I knew straight away he was lying. That man had a shifty look about him, if you know what I mean. He couldn't get away from me fast enough. I told Gabriel about it afterwards, but he told me nothing had been stolen.'

'Can you describe the man you saw?'

'I won't forget him. He was thin with black hair and a goatee beard. But the thing that stood out most was the octopus tattoo on his arm.'

Todd, thought Jake. It was a clear description of Todd Lee, the owner of the art supply shop on Broad Street.

*

Bridget braced herself before pushing open the door to Wright's art gallery. She was dreading this encounter with Jonathan almost as much as she'd dreaded going in to interview him. But an apology was absolutely required if she was ever going to renew her budding relationship with him. Not that there was any certainty that he would want to get back together with her. She remembered the confusion and indignation that had been written all over his face during his arrest and subsequent questioning. She was also acutely conscious of the fact that after his release from custody, he had left the police station immediately with his lawyer without waiting to speak to her. She could hardly blame him for that. After all that Jonathan had endured yesterday she wouldn't be surprised to find that she was now *persona non grata*.

The gallery was empty, apart from Vicky, who was sitting behind the counter, idly thumbing her phone. On seeing Bridget, she set the phone down and cast her a wary glance.

'It's all right,' said Bridget, giving her a placatory smile. 'I'm not here to arrest anyone today.'

The joke fell flat and Vicky looked even more anxious.

Bridget tried again. 'I'm here on my own this time. And this is a personal visit, not police business. I just wanted to speak to Jonathan and apologise for what happened yesterday.'

At that, Vicky visibly relaxed. 'He's just seeing a client in the office,' she said. 'He shouldn't be long if you want to wait. Would you like a coffee?'

'I'm fine, thanks,' said Bridget. She turned her attention to the walls of the gallery and began to peruse the paintings. Despite coming to the gallery several times, she still hadn't really had a proper chance to look at them all. 'How's the exhibition going?' she asked Vicky. 'Have you sold many paintings?'

'It's going really well, actually' said Vicky. 'We've never had so much interest. Of course it's Gabriel's paintings that are drawing the crowds. In fact we've already sold all of them.'

Bridget noticed the little red dots fixed next to many of the canvases indicating that they were sold. As Vicky said, every single one of Gabriel's paintings now had a red dot by their side. It seemed that Jonathan had, indeed, done very well out of the dead artist. It was a shame that Gabriel was no longer around to share the glory. But perhaps the paintings wouldn't have sold half as well if he hadn't died in such bizarre circumstances. She wondered who really made money in the world of art. It seemed that often the big money only changed hands after the artist was dead. Vincent van Gogh had sold just a single painting during his lifetime. The Dutch master Johannes Vermeer had died penniless, leaving his family to pay off his debts. And now Gabriel Quinn had been shot dead after spending much of his life in virtual poverty living on a dilapidated canal boat.

The door to the office opened and Jonathan emerged. 'Vicky, would you mind making us some tea? I...' His voice trailed off when he saw her. 'Bridget.'

'Jonathan.'

Vicky cleared her throat. 'I'll... just go and make the tea,' she said, scurrying nervously past Jonathan and out through the back door of the gallery.

The space seemed suddenly very large and quiet with

just Bridget and Jonathan left behind. They stood at a distance, not making eye contact. Bridget wondered how best to open what was sure to be a very difficult conversation. The awkward silence seemed to stretch out and become almost tangible.

'I just –' she began at last.

'Would you –' said Jonathan at the same time.

They stopped.

'Sorry,' said Bridget. 'After you.'

'No. You go first.'

'I just wanted to say how very sorry I am about what happened yesterday,' she said. 'When I came to the gallery I had no idea that Ben was going to arrest you. And the way he treated you in the interview room was totally unprofessional. I'm surprised your lawyer didn't do more to protect you. I might even raise an internal complaint about Ben's behaviour myself.'

'God, don't do that,' said Jonathan. 'I don't want to be the cause of any more difficulties between the two of you. He is Chloe's father after all.'

'Right.' Bridget couldn't believe he was being so reasonable about it. 'Still, I'm really sorry.'

Jonathan shrugged. 'Apology accepted.' A grin began to spread across his face. 'You know, although I was quite anxious at the time, looking back it was actually rather exciting. I got to see the inside of a police station for the first time, and found out what a police interview is like. And at least I managed to spend time with you without you running off on urgent business halfway through.'

Bridget laughed. 'So would you like me to arrest you again?'

'Perhaps not. I think once was enough.'

'Agreed. It wasn't exactly my idea of an ideal date. Is there any way I can make it up to you?'

'I guess you could always invite me out on another date. Perhaps a different venue this time, though. And without your ex-husband sitting in.'

'It's a deal,' said Bridget. 'I'll give you a call later.'

★

Bridget still felt cheered when she arrived at Todd's art shop on Broad Street. The reconciliation with Jonathan had gone better than she'd dared to hope. No matter how hard Ben had tried to break them apart, the bond that had grown between them was already too strong to be broken. She wondered where Jonathan might like to go on their next date. She still didn't have a clear idea of his tastes. He'd bought the opera tickets to please her, but what kind of music did he like most? What was his favourite kind of food? There was still so much for her to find out about him. So many new things for her to learn. She pushed open the door to the shop with a light heart, entering as the old-fashioned bell announced her arrival.

In contrast to Jonathan's light and spacious gallery, Todd's art shop felt cramped and enclosed. Stacks of shelves reaching all the way to the ceiling loomed over her, laden with sketchpads, tubes of paints, brushes and tools in all shapes and sizes.

There was no one serving behind the counter. Instead, Bridget was met by a disgruntled customer, waiting to pay for a box of pastel crayons. 'Have you been waiting long?' Bridget asked her.

The woman nodded. 'This is ridiculous,' she said. 'What sort of customer service is this? I've had enough.' She dumped the pastels on the counter and left the shop, the bell tinkling as she went.

A hush descended over the empty shop and a cold dread seized Bridget. Something wasn't right, she knew it.

Where on earth was Todd? Where, for that matter, was Amber? Surely one of them should be here. They wouldn't have just left the shop unattended, not without locking the door first. Something was clearly very wrong.

'Hello!' she called. 'Is anybody there?'

There was no response.

Bridget put one foot on the narrow staircase that

twisted up. This was the staircase that led up to Gabriel's studio that Todd had been so desperate to discourage Jake and Ffion from seeing. The wooden stairs creaked and shifted as she climbed. She called out a second time, but still no answer came. Upstairs, the shop was even more higgledy-piggledy and cluttered. The small Georgian windows threw little light into the gloom, but Bridget could see that there was no one around.

The dark wood panelling of the walls closed in on her as she ascended the final flight, and she was relieved to emerge into the open space of the top floor landing. The ceiling here was lower, but windows fixed into the roof allowed plenty of sunlight inside. She could see why Gabriel had liked to paint up here. There was a sense of space and freedom that was completely at odds with the clutter and congestion of the shop below. The bare floorboards squeaked under her feet as she crossed the landing to the studio at the back of the shop.

Just as Jake and Ffion had described, the place was a complete mess. Chunks of plaster were missing from the bare walls and ceiling. The floor was splashed with coloured paint. Half-finished canvases were stacked beneath the grubby windows. And there, messiest of all, in the very middle of the room lay the body of a man, his arms twisted underneath him, his legs spread wide. The wooden handle of a knife protruded from his back, and all around him seeped a growing stain of deep cadmium red.

*

Efficient as ever, it didn't take long for the SOCO team to seal off the crime scene and begin their investigations into the murder. Bridget led them upstairs and watched as the police photographer began taking pictures of the body from every angle. The camera flashed relentlessly, picking out the twisted body and the bright red stain that surrounded it in close-up detail. These would certainly not be works of art, thought Bridget grimly.

Dr Sarah Walker arrived promptly too and carried out an initial examination of the body. Bridget greeted her as she came back down the narrow stairs. As always the medical examiner was business-like and to the point. 'The murder victim is a man in his late thirties. Distinguishing features – black hair and a beard, with an octopus tattoo on his right arm.'

'Yes,' said Bridget. 'The description matches Todd Lee, the owner of the shop. I'd come here to question him.'

'It seems you were too late. He was killed by a single stab wound in the back. There are also signs of bruising to his face and defensive wounds on one of his hands. I'd say he put up a bit of a struggle, but was probably too surprised by his attacker to properly defend himself.'

'How long do you think he's been dead?' asked Bridget. Todd's body had still been warm to the touch when she'd found him, a little over half an hour earlier. She had checked for signs of life, but it was obvious even to her that it was too late to do anything to save him.

'My best estimate would be about one hour before you found the body. Around nine o'clock, in other words. The pathologist will probably be able to pin it down more precisely back at the lab.' Dr Walker held out an object in a plastic bag for Bridget to take. 'Vik from SOCO asked me to give you this. It's the murder weapon.'

Bridget accepted the evidence bag gingerly and peered at its contents. The weapon that had been used to kill Todd Lee looked like an antique. It had a rounded wooden knob at one end from which protruded a long, thin strip of metal ending in a wickedly sharp point. Bridget had never seen such a peculiar murder weapon before. 'What exactly is it?'

Vik, the head of the forensics team appeared at that moment from the staircase, still wearing his white hooded suit. 'Ah, yes, good question. We didn't know either, but we've done some searches online and it would appear that the murder weapon is a burin.'

Bridget was still none the wiser. 'You'll have to

enlighten me.'

Vik seemed pleased to have discovered something she didn't know. 'It's a hand-held tool used for engraving metal. The blade is made from hardened steel. The wooden knob fits comfortably into the palm of your hand, and you rest your index finger along the shaft of the blade while you engrave your design.'

Sarah Walker frowned. 'Don't they use machines for that sort of thing these days?'

'Yes, but this is the traditional way of doing it, apparently. We've taken a look around the shop, and there's nothing like this for sale on the shelves. So either the killer brought the weapon with them, or else it was lying around in the art studio upstairs. There's certainly a lot of junk up there, including other sorts of tools. All kinds of needles, knives, chisels and so on. Any one of them might have done the job just as well.'

'Any fingerprints on the handle?'

'Unfortunately not. The killer must have worn gloves.'

That wasn't what Bridget wanted to hear. But Vik did have other news for her.

'Come with me,' he said. 'There's something I want to show you.' He led Bridget outside to the tiny yard that was shoehorned between the back of the shop and the equally ancient and dilapidated building that overlooked it. A couple of white-suited forensics guys were pulling strips of blackened paper from a large oil drum that was still smouldering from the remains of a fire.

'What's this?' asked Bridget.

'It looks as if someone was burning old drawings,' said Vikram. 'It seems like a very strange thing to do. Why not just put them in the recycling if they were no longer wanted? Why go to the trouble of destroying them? We'll salvage what we can, but it might not be very much. Then it'll be your job to work out why someone set fire to them.' He grinned at her, as if delighted to have dumped yet another mystery on her.

Great, thought Bridget. A jigsaw of half-burned

drawings, the death of a key witness, and an arcane murder weapon. The Chief Super had given her until the end of the day to turn up something new, but somehow she didn't think he was going to be happy with what she'd discovered.

CHAPTER 26

Bridget returned to Kidlington with a head full of questions. Who would benefit from Todd's death? Was it the same person who had killed Gabriel Quinn? Neither man appeared to have had much money, so what was the motive? It was clear that Todd had been hiding something when Jake and Ffion had interviewed him. In particular, he had been very keen to prevent them from looking around Gabriel's studio. And now some drawings had been discovered half-burnt in the yard. Presumably either Todd or his killer had tried to destroy them. What secret did they contain? She would have to wait for the forensics team to recover as many fragments of paper as they could before trying to answer that question. In the meantime she had news to pass on.

She found Grayson in his office where she'd left him that morning, poring over a report.

'Could I have a word, sir?'

'What about?'

'There's been a development on the case. A major one.'

'You'd better come in then.' Grayson took his reading glasses off and pushed the report to one side. 'What have you got for me?'

'Sir, there's been another murder. Todd Lee. He was the owner of the art shop where Gabriel Quinn rented a studio. I found his body with a blade in his back.'

Grayson closed his eyes and rubbed the bridge of his substantial nose with the thumb and forefinger of his right hand. 'DI Hart, when I told you to come up with something by the end of the day, I didn't mean another bloody body.'

'No, sir. I realise that.'

'All right. You've made your point. Use all the resources you need. Find out what's going on and put a stop to whoever's doing this.'

'Yes, sir. Thank you, sir.'

Back in the incident room, there was a strong air of expectation. All eyes were on her as she briefed her team on the latest developments. 'So now we have two murders,' she concluded. 'One artist, one art shop owner. Hunter Reed is securely locked up in London, so that rules out his involvement in this latest death.

'Jake and Ffion, how did you get on with Harriet?' She'd sent the pair to follow up Amber's claim that Gabriel's canal boat neighbour was the source of his personal drugs supply.

Jake answered. 'Harriet admitted she gave Gabriel his drugs. In fact we found some cannabis plants growing on her boat. She told us she picks magic mushrooms from the fields nearby and shares them with her friends.'

'It would probably be better if she confined her home produce to pots of jam and chutney,' remarked Ryan.

'It looks like you were right all along, ma'am,' said Andy. 'Gabriel's murder had nothing to do with drugs.'

'It certainly looks that way to me.' Bridget was gratified to hear Andy agreeing with her.

'Yeah,' said Jake. 'But we also questioned Harriet about the break-in at Gabriel's boat. There was nothing imaginary about it. She'd actually witnessed it herself, and the intruder she described to us was almost certainly Todd

Lee.'

'And now he's dead,' concluded Bridget. 'That's not a coincidence.' She turned to the noticeboard and started writing. 'Let's list the connections between Todd Lee and Gabriel Quinn. First, they both worked in the art world. Second, Gabriel rented his studio from Todd. Third, Todd broke into Gabriel's boat, apparently searching for something, but didn't find it. Fourth...'

'Amber,' said Ffion. 'Amber worked for Todd, and she was Gabriel's girlfriend.'

'Right,' said Bridget. 'Ryan, did you manage to speak to Amber this morning?'

'No. I called her phone and left a message but she didn't get back to me. So I dropped in at the art shop, but she wasn't there either.' Ryan's gaze shifted to the floor.

'You visited the art shop this morning?' asked Bridget incredulously. 'What time was that?'

'First thing. About a quarter past nine.'

'And did you see anyone?'

'No.' Ryan shifted awkwardly in his seat. 'There was no one around. I imagined that Todd or Amber had nipped out to buy a coffee, so I waited a bit but no one came.'

'You didn't think of looking upstairs?'

'No,' said Ryan miserably. 'Oh God. I've screwed up big time, haven't I?'

She nodded. 'If you were there at nine fifteen, it's very likely that Todd was already dead, in which case you must have just missed the murderer leaving. In fact, they may even have been upstairs when you were in the shop.'

Ryan hid his face in his hands. 'I'm really sorry, boss.'

It was Andy who asked the question they were all now thinking. 'So has Amber become our prime suspect?'

'Oh, come on,' said Jake. 'Do you really think that Amber could have hired a contract killer to murder her boyfriend, and then killed her own boss?'

'I don't see why not,' said Ffion. 'Maybe she and Hunter were working together. We know that Hunter was involved with the gang that hired Travis Brown.'

'But for what reason?'

'I don't know.'

Bridget pictured the beautiful but fragile young woman she'd first seen depicted in oils in Melissa Price's office at the Ruskin. It was hard to imagine her as a scheming murderer, but it wasn't a possibility that could be ruled out, especially given her close relationship with Hunter. 'Whatever Gabriel and Todd were involved in, it's quite possible that Amber knows more than she's already told us. She might well hold the key to this mystery. And if that's the case, she may be in danger herself. I don't want her to become the next victim.'

'Where do we start looking for her?' asked Andy.

'We'll begin with door-to-door enquiries in the vicinity of the art shop,' said Bridget. 'If Amber was at the shop this morning, one of the nearby shop owners may have seen her leaving, especially if she was in a hurry to get away. Where else might she be?'

'Hunter's apartment?' suggested Jake.

'That's still sealed off,' said Bridget. 'The same with Gabriel's canal boat.'

'So we don't even know where she might have stayed last night,' said Jake. 'We don't know anything about her whereabouts since she was released from custody yesterday afternoon.'

'In that case, let's get looking,' said Bridget. 'Let's find Amber.'

★

Door-to-door enquiries were every police officer's least favourite activity. It was painstaking work, knocking on doors, waiting for responses, ringing doorbells and waiting again, before very often moving on to the next house after making a note to call back later. But in a commercial area like the corner of Broad Street where every building was either a shop of some description, or else a college, progress was much more rapid. Every door was open and there was no shortage of potential witnesses to the events at the art shop. And yet to Jake's frustration, nobody he spoke to had seen a thing. They were all too busy getting on with their own jobs. Even the smokers and vapers, who could normally be relied upon to have noticed something while clustered furtively outside in their small groups, had no memory of anyone entering or leaving the art shop that morning.

Jake was about to enter a shop selling cheesy souvenirs, or "official University of Oxford merchandise", as it advertised its wares when he heard a familiar voice behind him. 'Hey, mate, what's up?'

He turned and found Stu, the homeless *Big Issue* magazine seller, who always occupied the same spot in the middle of Broad Street. He was wearing his usual hi-viz jacket and smiling his wide grin, revealing the gap where his two front teeth were missing.

'I've been watching your boys going in and out of the art shop all morning,' said Stu. 'I reckon something big's happened.'

'It has,' said Jake. 'A murder.'

'Aye, I reckoned as much.'

'Have you been here all morning?' asked Jake.

'Aye, sure I have. This is my patch. If I want to do business I have to get here before some other bastard nicks my spot.' He held up his pile of magazines. 'Want another copy?'

'I haven't had time to read the one I already bought,' said Jake. 'But here's some money anyway.'

'Cheers, mate,' said Stu, pocketing the coin. 'So who's dead, then?' He nodded his head in the direction of the art shop.

'Todd Lee, the owner of the shop. Did you know him?'

'The skinny guy with black hair and a beard? Octopus tattoo on his arm?'

'That's the one.'

'Yeah, I've seen him around. The stingy bastard's never bought a magazine from me though. Guess he never will now.'

'So did you notice anyone entering or leaving the shop this morning?'

'You must be joking,' said Stu. 'There are hundreds of tourists passing along here all the time. I'm too busy selling to see who's going in and out of every shop.'

He made it sound as if he was doing a roaring trade, though judging from the number of unsold magazines he was carrying, Jake thought that was rather unlikely.

'Fair enough. But did you see Todd himself this morning?'

'Nah, can't say I did.'

'What about the young woman who works there? Amber. Do you know her?'

Stu's eyes lit up and he leered at Jake. 'You mean that girl with the long red hair? Aye, she's a real corker, that one. Catches your eye, if you know what I mean.'

Jake wondered what Stu would say if he saw Melissa's painting of Amber in the nude. 'So have you seen her this morning?'

'Aye, now you mention it. I think I saw her coming out of the shop. I only noticed because she usually says hello, but this morning she didn't even glance in my direction.'

'What time was this?'

Stu thought for a moment. 'Are you absolutely sure you don't want to buy another magazine?'

Jake dug deep into his pocket and fished out a note. He handed it over to Stu, who grinned broadly. 'Let me see. I'd only just arrived at my patch, so I guess it was around nine. Maybe five past. Something like that.'

'And you say you saw her leaving the shop?'

'Aye, and not just walking. She was well and truly scarpering. Like I say, she didn't even have time to look my way. Reckon she did it, then? She doesn't look strong enough to kill a man, even a skinny little rat like Todd.'

'I can't possibly say, Stu. Which direction was she heading?'

Stu pointed up the street. It was the direction Jake

himself had gone the other day when he'd walked from the Ruskin School to Hunter's apartment in Jericho.

'Thanks Stu, you've been a huge help,' said Jake. 'Buy yourself a sandwich.'

In theory, Hunter's apartment was still off limits, and all known keys to the apartment were in police custody. But it was always possible that Amber had another key, or that one of the building's other occupants may have let her inside. Considering what Stu had said and the fact that Jake had nothing better to go on, he decided to check it out.

He rounded up one of the uniformed officers who was helping with the door-to-door enquiries and asked him to drive him over to the new development in Jericho. The officer, whose name was Dave, didn't need much persuading, and took the journey at speed, using his car's flashing blue lights and siren to cut a swathe through the city traffic. 'I wish I could drive like this everywhere,' said Dave, grinning.

On arrival, the pair of them dashed up the stairs to Hunter's flat. Crime scene tape declared the apartment to be off limits, but Jake banged on the door, desperately hoping that Amber would appear. He shared Bridget's fears that something awful might have happened to her.

'Want me to break the door down?' asked Dave when there was no response. He was about twenty years older than Jake and about twenty pounds heavier and seemed to relish the opportunity.

Jake eyed him uncertainly. Breaking down the door of an empty apartment for no good reason might earn him a severe telling-off from the boss. But he didn't want to screw up like Ryan. Given that Amber was a suspect in a murder case and also potentially at risk herself, it didn't take him long to decide. He gave Dave the go-ahead and stood well back.

The big man set about his task with enthusiasm, landing a heavy kick with his boots. The door shook a little in response, but stayed fast. Dave grunted and tried again.

It took a handful of hard blows, but eventually the wood split and the door swung open.

Jake rushed inside. 'Amber!'

The apartment was deserted. The coffee table was still strewn with the detritus Jake had seen on his previous visit, the empty food cartons now growing a layer of mould and fungus. He searched the bedroom and bathroom, but there was no sign that anyone had been here since the police had searched the apartment for drugs. He tried to think where Amber might have gone.

'Let's try the canal,' he said.

*

Back at HQ, Ffion had decided not to join in with the door-to-door enquiries. She had just received an email from Professor Michael Henderson. The professor hadn't yet managed to come up with any further ideas regarding the nine-character number and letter sequence that had been Gabriel's final message to the world, but he had suggested an interesting new angle on the passwords for Gabriel's laptop and mobile phone.

The problem of cracking Gabriel's phone and laptop had been haunting Ffion since day one of the investigation. She'd tried everything she could think of. Personal names, significant dates, locations. Numbers that might have been related in some way to the mathematical sequences and relationships that Gabriel had obsessed over. And of course the tantalising nine-character code itself.

None of them had worked.

According to the professor's email, Gabriel had been obsessed with the German Renaissance artist, Albrecht Dürer. Ffion typed the name into the search box on her computer. A few clicks later she found herself staring at a black-and-white image of a winged woman surrounded by strange objects and animals, including a sleeping dog, an hourglass, a cherub, a rainbow and a magic square.

She quickly sifted through the mounds of sketches,

notes and other papers that she'd collected from Gabriel's canal boat until she found what she was looking for – the postcard that had been pinned to Gabriel's wall. She held it up to compare with the image on her screen. It was the same. *Melencolia I*. Could this finally be the key?

She tried the phone first. A four-digit passcode was required, and the professor had suggested a number of dates that might fit. She quickly entered the year of Dürer's birth, 1471. It wasn't that. Next she tried 1528, the year he'd died. It wasn't that either, but Ffion wasn't giving up that easily. Various years had held significance in Dürer's life. He had married in 1494 and made his first visit to Italy that same year. She keyed in the number quickly and was frustrated to find that this guess was also wrong. Undaunted, she ran through the other dates the professor had suggested. There was 1498, the year he'd painted his famous self-portrait, and 1507, the year he'd returned to Nuremberg and begun the most fruitful and celebrated period of his career. And then there was 1514, the year the artist had completed his enigmatic masterwork, *Melencolia I*. Ffion smiled to herself. She keyed in the date and was delighted but not the least bit surprised when it unlocked the phone.

She quickly found her way into Gabriel's messages and began to read. The bulk of them were between him and Amber and they told a sad story. Amber may have talked about an open relationship based on trust and mutual respect, but it was clear that Gabriel hadn't seen things the same way. The messages between the couple were filled with accusations of betrayal and outpourings of jealousy.

The ongoing argument had come to a head in the days just before Gabriel had been murdered. He had presented Amber with an ultimatum – 'choose me or Hunter' – and Amber, it seemed, had chosen to leave. 'I'll always love you, Gabriel,' she had written in her final message to him, 'but some things just aren't meant to be. I hope we can be together again after death.'

After death. Was that just a melodramatic turn of

phrase, or did the words convey a more sinister meaning? Could Amber really have been thinking of murdering Gabriel? Or had she contemplated taking her own life? If so, the search to find her was even more urgent than they had realised.

Ffion took the phone over to Bridget's desk. 'Ma'am,' she said. 'I've managed to unlock Gabriel's phone at last. I think you'll want to see this.'

*

The quickest route from Jericho to the canal was on foot. Jake and Dave left the car behind outside St Barnabas church and sprinted the short distance along Canal Street. A narrow footbridge took them the short distance to the other side of the canal, from where they turned and ran back in the direction they'd come, this time following the canal path towards the spot where Gabriel's narrowboat was moored.

Dave might have been built for breaking down doors, but he wasn't a long-distance runner. 'I hope you know where we're going,' he huffed.

'It's not far from here,' Jake told him.

A few minutes later a group of canal boats came into view. Jake could see Harriet's cheerfully-painted house boat and the sad, neglected form of *La Belle Dame*. Dave continued to lumber gamely along the path, but he was well behind Jake now. Jake leapt from the bank onto Gabriel's boat, making it dip in the water and sending a crest of ripples across the still surface of the canal. He shouted for Amber and began tugging on the cabin door. But the door remained fast. The boat was still padlocked, the crime scene tape undisturbed and sealing it off. It had clearly not been entered. He jumped back onto the bank and carried on to the next boat.

The *Dragonfly* looked exactly as it had when he'd last seen it that morning – with the exception of the cannabis plants that Ffion had confiscated – but there was no sign of its green-fingered owner. The doors of the boat were closed and blinds had been pulled down over all the windows.

'Harriet! Amber!' he shouted, but no reply came.

Dave staggered up to him, red-faced and out of breath. 'You want me to kick in this door too?'

'I don't think we'll need to, mate,' said Jake.

The door of the narrowboat had opened and Harriet appeared on deck, her hands on her hips, looking decidedly unwelcoming. 'What do you want this time?' she demanded.

'We're searching for Amber Morgan. Have you seen her?'

A momentary hesitation was all he needed to tell him what he wanted. Harriet stepped back in alarm as he made the short leap from the canal side onto the deck of her boat. 'What are you doing? You need a warrant to search my boat!'

'I don't think so. We believe that Amber may be in danger.'

Harriet bit her lip. 'She's inside. I'm looking after her.'

Jake pushed his way inside the cramped cabin and saw Amber lying stretched out on a full-length seat. Her eyes were closed. He rushed over to her and felt for a pulse. It was faint. Her breathing was shallow, her chest hardly moving as she slowly inhaled and exhaled.

'Dave! Call for an ambulance!' bellowed Jake. He turned angrily to face Harriet. 'What have you done to her?' he yelled.

'I haven't done a thing. She did it to herself.'

'Did what?'

'An overdose.'

'Then why didn't you phone for an ambulance?'

Harriet sniffed, as if offended. 'She asked me not to.'

CHAPTER 27

When Bridget arrived at the John Radcliffe hospital, she was met by Jake. The tall sergeant was easy to spot among the walking wounded filling up the reception area. He rose to his feet as she entered and waved her over.

'She's on ward six,' he said, leading her along the wide corridor that snaked into the depths of the hospital. 'I came with her in the ambulance.'

'How is she?'

'She's not going to die. But she's in a pretty bad state. If I hadn't found her when I did, I don't know what might have happened.'

'You did well,' she told him as she hurried to keep pace with his long strides.

They turned down a side corridor then took the lift up to the ward. Bridget was glad that Jake was with her. She was already lost.

The ward, which was divided into four bays of half a dozen beds each, was bustling with activity. Many of the patients, who were elderly, seemed to be hard of hearing, which necessitated the nurses speaking in raised voices with a forced cheerfulness that would have been better suited to a nursery class of two-year-olds. Bridget hated the thought of ending up in hospital when she was old, unable to even go to the bathroom on her own. But then she thought of her sister, Abigail, and realised that there were worse things in life than needing to use a walking frame.

Her own parents were getting on in years, but for the moment they were still in good health, thankfully. Abigail's murder had driven a wedge between her and her parents and she'd been glad when they'd sold the family home in Woodstock and moved to Lyme Regis on the south coast. Visits to their tiny bungalow were always strained, resulting in long, awkward silences. Bridget was always secretly relieved when it was time to drive back to Oxford.

The young nurse on duty at the desk stared wide-eyed at the sight of Bridget's warrant card and scurried off to fetch the doctor in charge.

'Detective Inspector Hart?'

Bridget turned to see a doctor approaching. He was younger than her, but already balding. His heavy-rimmed spectacles looked like they'd been chosen to bolster his authority.

'Hello, I'm Doctor Waring.' He held out a hand for Bridget to shake. 'I understand you're here regarding Amber Morgan.'

'That's right,' said Bridget. 'We'd like to speak to her in relation to a police enquiry.'

'I'm afraid that won't be possible at this point in time.' The polite words masked a steeliness that said the hospital was his domain and he was in charge here. He drew Bridget and Jake into a small office lined with filing cabinets. 'Miss Morgan was admitted to the department having taken a large overdose. She's had her stomach pumped and is currently under sedation to give her body time to recover from the shock. You'll have to wait until she wakes up I'm afraid.'

'How long will that be, Doctor?'

'That depends on her body's response. She could wake

up within the hour, or she could sleep for another four hours. Obviously, my primary concern is my patient's well-being.'

'I understand that,' said Bridget. She was glad that Amber seemed to be in good hands, but at the same time frustrated that it wouldn't be possible to get answers to the many questions that needed answering. 'But Amber Morgan is a key witness in a double murder enquiry. It's imperative that we speak to her as soon as possible, so I'm going to ask my sergeant here' – she indicated Jake – 'to wait until she wakes up and call me when she does.'

Bridget waited to see if Doctor Waring would protest at her decision, but he seemed willing to accept the intrusion. No doubt Jake would soon make himself at home with the help of the snack machine and the coffee dispenser.

Meanwhile she had another visit to make.

*

Strangely, one of the few people at the John Radcliffe who had the power to cheer Bridget up was Dr Roy Andrews, the pathologist, despite the fact that he spent his days slicing open dead bodies and removing their internal organs. Maybe it had something to do with his colourful collection of bow ties, one of which could always be seen protruding over the top of his surgical scrubs. Or perhaps it was his deadpan and sometimes ghoulish sense of humour. She found him in his office writing up some notes.

'DI Hart! Have you come in search of more bodies?'

She noted that today's bow tie was taken from a William Morris design of a bird pecking away at a strawberry plant. *The Strawberry Thief*, if she wasn't mistaken.

'I was passing by and wondered if you had any preliminary findings for me on Todd Lee. His body was brought in this morning.'

Roy shook his head sadly. 'I knew it. You always come to talk to me about the dead, never the living.'

Roy always enjoyed teasing her. In a younger man she might have thought it flirting, but Roy was almost at retirement age and to Bridget's knowledge had never been married.

'Perhaps you ought to have chosen a different profession if you wanted to discuss the living,' she suggested.

'You're right as always. It's all my own fault. Every man is the architect of his own misfortune.'

Bridget shifted impatiently in the doorway. She was tired and had little appetite for Roy's games today. 'I was hoping you might give me your opinion about Todd Lee?'

'The stab victim, yes.' Roy removed his half-moon reading glasses and leaned back in his chair, folding his arms over his ample stomach. 'Now that was a first for me. I've never before seen someone killed with a – what did the forensics chaps call it? – a burin? A most ingenious and elegant weapon, if you ask me. Its shaft is so long and thin. Makes for a very clean wound.' He mimed the action of sliding the blade between his own ribs. 'Tell me, are you looking for an engraver in connection with the murder?'

'Possibly,' said Bridget, humouring him. 'What I really wanted to know is the time of death, and any other relevant information you can give me. Dr Sarah Walker's best guess was around nine o'clock.'

'Ah, yes, back to mundane matters. Time of death, that's all anyone ever wants from me.' He rifled through his notes and pulled out a sheet of paper. 'Nine o'clock, you say? From the body temperature when the corpse was brought into the morgue, that sounds about right, but I'll know for sure after I've carried out the full post-mortem tomorrow.'

'Good,' said Bridget. 'Anything else?'

'Well, the unusual nature of the weapon does tell us something about the assault. Although the blade is very sharp, it would take some strength to plunge the shaft so deeply into a man's back.'

Bridget's thoughts returned to Amber, and her slender, sylph-like form. 'Could a woman have done it? A woman of slight build?'

'If she was minded to. But it would have required substantial force. The attack has the appearance of a particularly ferocious act.'

'So would it have caused a lot of blood to spray out? Would the murderer have been covered in blood following the attack?'

'No, not necessarily. The narrow blade would have made a clean cut, although the subsequent blood loss would then have been rapid. Death would have come relatively quickly. I've seen worse ways of being killed, believe me. A lot worse.'

'Thanks for your time, Roy.'

'Ah, yes, time. That's all that any of us really has, isn't it? How best to use the little that has been granted us, that's the real question.' Roy slid his glasses back on and returned to his report. He didn't look up at her again.

★

There was no news from Jake yet so Bridget went to the hospital café and, in the absence of any healthier alternative, ordered herself a coffee and a blueberry muffin. She hoped that the muffin might count as one of her five a day, but strongly suspected that it wouldn't. Really, if the NHS wanted to tackle the obesity crisis they could start with their own offerings.

She took her tray to a corner table and sat alone, regarding the muffin guiltily, and prepared herself for a long wait. What had Roy said? How best to use our time. Certainly not by staring at her food. Instead, she fished her phone out of her bag and gave Chloe a call.

They hadn't spoken since this morning, and that had been little more than a suppressed disagreement. Chloe should be on her way home from school now, although what had she said? That she was going back to Olivia's house for pizza instead. Bridget could hardly blame her. She was hardly ever there when her daughter returned home from school.

She racked her brains for a conversational gambit that would make up for the harsh words they'd exchanged the previous night, but Chloe's phone went straight through to voicemail, leaving Bridget lost for anything to say. No doubt her daughter was still mad at her for the accusations she'd levelled against Ben.

'It's Mum here,' she said. 'Just wanted to check that you were okay.'

She paused, knowing that there was no way to undo the quarrel that had taken place last night. It was just another wound that might one day heal but would always leave a scar. Parenthood left you damaged, there was no way to avoid it. All she could do was press on, forever forwards, never looking back. To rake over the past would be nothing more than an act of self-harm.

'I love you,' she concluded, and ended the call.

The muffin glared back at her, seeming to know too much. 'What do you know about anything?' said Bridget crossly. 'You're nothing more than a sugary snack.' She took a large spongy bite out of it.

She was still chewing when her phone rang. It was Jake. 'Yes?' she said, through a mouthful of crumbs.

'Ma'am? Just wanted to let you know that Amber has woken up.'

'I'll be right there.' She took one last bite of the muffin and hurried back to the lift, her coffee untouched.

*

Amber looked small and frail in the hospital bed, almost like a broken doll. Her skin was pale and ashen like a wraith's. Only her green eyes seemed to hold any signs of life. She lay beneath the crisp white sheets, her long red hair fanned out against the pillow.

Like a drowning Ophelia plucked from the water seconds before death, thought Bridget. Had she wanted to kill herself? Or had the overdose been accidental? The girl's unsettling resemblance to Lizzie Siddal was stronger than ever. Amber must have been very familiar with the tragic fate of the Pre-Raphaelite model and muse she had styled herself on. It was tempting to assume that she had consciously decided to follow her heroine's footsteps to the grave.

Amber didn't react when Jake asked her how she was feeling. For several seconds she seemed not to have heard him. 'Okay,' came the reply eventually.

It was the first time Bridget had heard Amber's voice. She had seen her when Ben and his team arrested her and Hunter in Jericho, but had never actually spoken to her. The girl's words were barely audible. Her lips hardly moved.

'This is my boss, DI Bridget Hart,' continued Jake. Amber's eyes flicked to Bridget, who smiled and did her best to appear reassuring. 'Is it all right if we ask you a few questions about what happened this morning?'

Amber shrugged her narrow shoulders beneath the sheets.

Looking at her now, it was almost impossible to imagine that this fragile girl could have wielded the blade that killed Todd Lee. It was even harder to believe that she could have somehow been responsible for the gangland-style murder of her ex-boyfriend, Gabriel Quinn. Yet Amber had been very close to both men, and to Hunter Reed too. Hunter certainly might have arranged for Gabriel to be killed, and Bridget couldn't afford to dismiss the fact that in Roy's professional opinion, even a woman of slight build might have driven the engraving knife into Todd's back if she'd been minded to.

She pulled up a plastic chair and sat down, her face level with the patient in the hospital bed. 'Hello, Amber. You can call me Bridget. I'm so sorry this has happened to you. You were fortunate that Jake brought you into hospital when he did. Doctor Waring tells me you should make a full recovery.'

Amber gave no reaction. Bridget wondered what she was thinking. In cases like this, it was often hard to tell whether the person whose life had been saved was glad, or if they were disappointed to wake up and find themselves still breathing. Hopefully, in time, with the right care and support, Amber would come to see that she had much to live for. She was still so young. And beautiful too. Even after her near-death experience, there was a magical allure to her face that made it hard to look away.

'So,' said Bridget, 'can you tell me what happened today? Let's start at the beginning. Where did you stay last night?'

Amber's lips moved silently for a moment, and then she began to speak. 'Harriet. I stayed on Harriet's boat. I had nowhere else to go.'

'And where did you go after you left the boat?'

'To work. It was a work day, and I needed the money.'

'Okay. You're doing very well. What time did you arrive at work?'

'I always try to get there by ten to nine. The shop opens at nine.'

'What about this morning? What time did you arrive today?'

'I was a little later than usual, maybe just after nine.'

'And was Todd already there when you arrived?'

Amber closed her eyes.

'Amber, was Todd in the shop?'

The girl dragged her eyes open as if the effort was huge. 'The door wasn't locked. That wasn't unusual. Todd likes to get in early. He's often there when I arrive.'

'Was he there when you arrived this morning?'

Amber shook her head.

'Did you look upstairs?'

'Todd doesn't like me going upstairs.'

Bridget noted that Amber was speaking about Todd in the present tense. She wondered if she even knew that

Todd was dead. 'Why is that, Amber? Why doesn't Todd like you to go upstairs? What is he hiding there?'

'Not hiding. Working.'

'Working on what?'

'He and Gabriel. They started working together on a new project.'

'What new project, Amber?'

'Todd wouldn't tell me. He said to keep my nose out of it.'

'But what about Gabriel? Did he tell you anything?'

Amber said nothing.

Behind her, Bridget heard the door to the room quietly open and close. Doctor Waring had entered. 'Inspector Hart, you've had long enough. My patient needs to rest now.'

'Just a few more questions,' said Bridget. She turned back to Amber, whose eyes had closed again. 'Amber, What did Gabriel tell you? What was he working on with Todd?'

Amber forced her eyes open once more. 'It was art,' she muttered, her words almost too quiet to hear.

Bridget frowned. 'What kind of art?'

'I don't know. Gabriel did all the work. Todd just gave him the things he needed.'

Bridget knew she would only be able to ask one or two more questions before Doctor Waring brought the interview to a halt. 'Amber, did you see Todd this morning? Did you go upstairs?'

Amber nodded.

Bridget waited for her to elaborate. When she didn't, she pressed for more. 'Was Todd alive when you saw him?'

A tear began to roll down Amber's cheek. 'Todd's dead,' she whispered. 'I saw him in the studio. I tried to push open the door but it was stuck. I couldn't push it open all the way... because of Todd. He was lying on the floor.'

'Did you see anyone else?'

'I took some pills,' said Amber, 'and I drank a bottle of

vodka.' She shook her head from side to side, her eyes now wide and staring. 'He's dead. Todd's dead. And Gabriel's dead. And Hunter's gone. It's just me now. I wish I was dead too.' She started to sob.

The doctor pushed forward and administered an injection into her arm. 'That's enough!' he told Bridget. 'No more questions. Please leave now. My patient needs rest.'

★

Bridget drove Jake back to Kidlington in a subdued frame of mind. It was sobering to see a young person like Amber so close to the edge.

Bridget understood all too clearly what the young woman must have been going through as she fled from the discovery of Todd's body. Her actions may have seemed irrational, but Bridget remembered a time in her own life when she had also run from the truth, trying desperately to blot out the thought of her sister's body lying strangled in Wytham Woods. Bridget hadn't considered taking her own life after Abigail was murdered, but she'd certainly sought oblivion, first in alcohol, then by throwing herself into police work, and perhaps ultimately by giving herself to Ben. She had been consumed by the desire simply to forget everything that had happened. Looking back, perhaps the demise of her marriage had been inevitable from the start. Maybe the whole sad episode had been nothing more than an attempt to escape the memory of tragedy. Was it possible that in some way Ben wasn't even to blame for the infidelities that had brought the marriage to such a bitter end? Had she subconsciously driven him away in an effort to bring about her own destruction?

One thing she knew from bitter experience – the events of the past would never go away, no matter how much you tried to shut them out. Sooner or later you had to deal with your demons, or else they would deal with you.

'What are you thinking ma'am?' Jake's words roused

her from her introspection.

'I was thinking that I'm inclined to believe what Amber told us. I don't think she could have murdered Todd. What do you think?'

'I agree with you. I know we only have her word for it, but unless she's the world's best actor, I don't think she was lying to us just now.'

'No, I'm certain that Amber is another victim, just like Gabriel and Todd. It was lucky that you found her and called an ambulance. What made you go to the canal?'

'Just a hunch,' said Jake.

A hunch. Sometimes that's all there was to go on. Sometimes it could make the difference between life and death.

Bridget had a hunch now. 'What do you think Gabriel and Todd were working on?' she asked Jake.

Jake shrugged. 'I've no idea. Do you think it's significant?'

'Oh yes,' said Bridget. 'In fact, I think it's the key to everything.' And if she was right about that, it was essential to find the killer before anyone else died.

When they arrived back at Kidlington, Ffion was waiting anxiously for them. 'I heard what happened,' she said. 'Is Amber okay?'

'She's going to be all right. Let's gather the team in the incident room. I have a theory I want to talk about. And then I want to hear if you've managed to get into Gabriel's laptop yet.'

By the time she'd grabbed herself a much-needed coffee, the team had assembled.

She waited while Jake briefed them on the day's events, noting the modesty with which he described his own life-saving heroics. She noted also the brief flicker of admiration that passed across Ffion's face. She couldn't quite work those two out. There was a story there, but not a simple one.

Andy was next to bring them up to speed. 'Vik from SOCO dropped these off this afternoon,' he announced, holding up a cork board with about a dozen fragments of yellowed paper fixed to it. The edges of the paper fragments had been blackened from fire damage. They had clearly once formed a single sheet of paper, but more than half of it was now missing. 'This is all they managed to salvage from the fire in Todd's back yard. Most of it disintegrated when they tried to pull it out. Vik reckons that if they'd got there half an hour sooner, they'd have been able to save the whole lot.' He cast a quick glance at Ryan, who squirmed in his seat and turned away.

Bridget stared at the damaged pieces of paper that had been carefully arranged on the board, imagining a half-completed jigsaw and trying to picture what the missing parts of the image might have looked like. She wasn't able to form any clear ideas. 'Anyone got any suggestions?'

Jake squinted at the various images. 'Is that the branch of a tree at the top?'

Ryan turned his head on one side. 'Yeah, and there's a bird in the top left corner.'

'I reckon that's someone's foot at the bottom,' said Andy.

Harry, the junior constable, had blushed crimson. 'Is that a woman's boob?'

They were all correct, but still Bridget couldn't guess what the overall image represented.

Ffion knew, however. 'It's Adam and Eve in the Garden of Eden. The tree is the Tree of Knowledge, the bird sitting on its branch represents wisdom. There are four other animals missing from the picture: a cat, an elk, a rabbit, and an ox, representing the four humours: cruelty, melancholy, sensuality, and lethargy.'

'How can you be so sure?' asked Jake.

Ffion smiled. 'Because I finally managed to break into Gabriel's laptop.'

That was the news Bridget had been most hoping to hear. After Ffion's earlier success in cracking the password to Gabriel's phone, she'd been pinning her hopes on the Welsh DC having two lucky breaks in a row. After all the bad luck that had dogged the case so far, she didn't think it was too much to ask for.

'So,' continued Ffion. There was triumph in her voice, and her face appeared happier than it had been in days. Her Welsh accent was also more pronounced than ever. 'Once I'd discovered that the passcode to Gabriel's phone was 1514, it was totally obvious what the password to his laptop would be.'

The others stared at her blankly.

'I think it might be less obvious than you think,' said Bridget.

Ffion sighed. 'Professor Henderson suggested that the key might be the German Renaissance artist, Albrecht Dürer. Gabriel was obsessed with Dürer and had a print of the artist's most famous engraving pinned to the wall of his narrowboat. I knew that the phone required a 4-digit number, and so it was most likely going to be a year. After a few attempts, I hit on 1514, the year Dürer completed the engraving. Then it was obvious that the password to his laptop would be the name of that engraving.'

'*Melencolia*,' said Bridget. 'Of course.'

'Exactly. So when I looked through Gabriel's laptop, a lot of what I found was information about Dürer. He had folders and sub-folders filled with images of all Dürer's works. Woodcuts, engravings and paintings – all sorted by year of production. As well as the pictures themselves, Gabriel had written long essays on each one, often thousands of words long. He was interested in what the art meant, how it related to his own theories of numbers, but most especially the techniques that Dürer used to create his work. He was studying how Dürer produced his woodcuts and copperplates, the type of paper used for printing, the kind of ink used. He wanted to understand all the practical details. Dürer himself wrote quite extensively about his techniques and methods, and Gabriel had copies of these texts on his laptop.'

'That's what I suspected,' said Bridget. 'So tell us more about the pictures Todd was burning.'

'Well, the drawings that I found earlier in the sketchbook I took from Gabriel's studio were details copied from Dürer's *Apocalypse* series of woodcuts. Todd was desperate to try and stop us from seeing them, even though they appeared to be perfectly innocuous.'

Ffion pointed excitedly to the fragments on the noticeboard. 'And this print is a copy of *Adam and Eve*. It's one of Dürer's most famous engravings.'

The rest of the team seemed decidedly unimpressed by Ffion's breathless announcement.

'So they're just copies of old prints?' said Ryan.

'Then why did Todd try so hard to hide them from us?' asked Jake.

'Because they're not just copies,' said Bridget. 'They're recreations. Gabriel was studying Dürer's work in order to produce prints in the same style. That's what he and Todd were secretly working on in the studio. Todd supplied all the specialist equipment needed to make engravings –'

'Such as the burin,' said Ffion.

'Right,' said Bridget. There was an irony there, she supposed, in that the tool that Todd had himself provided had been used to kill him. 'And Gabriel carried out the work.'

'So were they producing forgeries?' asked Jake, his brow slowly wrinkling in thought.

Bridget hesitated. So far it was just a theory. Speculation. But it felt right to her. 'That's what I think they were doing together. It explains why Todd wouldn't allow Amber to visit the art studio. It explains why he was so reluctant to let Jake and Ffion look there, and why he was burning the evidence of what they'd done. That might also have been why he broke into Gabriel's narrowboat – to search for incriminating evidence.'

'So had Todd fallen out with Gabriel for some reason?' asked Ryan. 'Is that why Gabriel was murdered?'

'It's possible,' said Bridget. 'At this point we just don't know. But if both Gabriel and Todd were murdered because of this, then there must have been at least one other person involved in the forgeries.'

Bridget's attention drifted to the noticeboard beside her, and the photos that were pinned to the board. Dr Melissa Price. And her husband, Lawrence Taylor. One an art expert, known to be an unscrupulous cheat. One a wealthy investor with a keen eye for profit. Either of them might have masterminded the forgeries. Or they might have done it together. And Dr Roy Andrews was confident that Todd's killer could have been a man or a woman.

'What about the gallery owner, Jonathan Wright?' said Jake.

Bridget's head snapped round to face him. 'Jonathan? What about him?'

'He's not on our list of suspects, but perhaps he ought to be. He knew both men, he's knowledgeable about art, he buys and sells artwork for a living. He could easily have been the third member of the ring.'

'No,' said Bridget firmly. 'It couldn't possibly have been Jonathan.'

She could feel herself growing hot and angry at the suggestion, but told herself to calm down. Jake was just being a good detective, coming up with ideas, making connections. She hoped he couldn't see from her face just how much the suggestion had upset her.

Of course, none of the team knew about her developing relationship with Jonathan. They didn't know that she had gone out to dinner with him earlier that week, nor that she was hoping that their friendship might develop into something more intimate.

'I don't think we can dismiss the suggestion so easily,' said Andy. 'Gabriel's murder took place immediately outside Wright's gallery, which suggests that the gunman was tipped off that he was going to be there at that time. Remember that the gunman had connections with the drugs gang, and the Met photographed Jonathan Wright driving Hunter into London, just a few days before Gabriel's murder.'

'And Todd's art shop is just around the corner from the

gallery,' added Jake. 'It only takes a few minutes to walk from one to the other.'

'Ah,' said Bridget. 'I can stop you there. Jonathan couldn't possibly have murdered Todd, because his alibi for the time of Todd's death is cast-iron. You see, I was with him at the gallery myself.'

CHAPTER 28

When Bridget came downstairs for breakfast the next morning, Chloe was already in the kitchen buttering a slice of toast.

'Did you have a nice time at Olivia's house yesterday?' Bridget asked her.

'Yeah, good.'

Bridget had been hoping that the tension between them over the last couple of days would have worn off by now, but it seemed that Chloe wouldn't be so quick to forgive her. Chloe hadn't got back until late last night, but Bridget had said nothing about that. She had been too exhausted, and in any case, the last thing she needed was to start a fresh argument.

She lingered by the kitchen worktop, not knowing what to say. Every possible topic of conversation that suggested itself sounded to her like nagging.

'What?' asked Chloe.

'I didn't say anything.'

'No, but you have that look.'

It seemed that Bridget couldn't win. She took a deep breath. 'Listen, I realise things have been difficult between

247

us. I shouldn't have said those things about your father. I'm sorry.'

There, she'd said it. The magic word. When Chloe had been little, Bridget had always told her that saying you're sorry made everything all right. She waited for Chloe to respond.

'Yeah, we're good, Mum.' Chloe dumped her plate in the sink and grabbed her school bag. 'Sorry, but I've gotta go.' She gave Bridget a quick peck on the cheek as she left.

Bridget watched her go. They had reached some kind of truce, it seemed, but things would never be quite the same again. Chloe was growing up and growing away from her. That's what teenagers did, but it didn't make Bridget feel any easier. She had thought that the eyes staring back at her so defiantly the other evening were Ben's, but now she saw they were the eyes of her dead sister, Abigail.

Abi had been about the same age as Chloe when she had entered her rebellious phase, staying out late and refusing to tell their parents who she was with. Chloe's behaviour was nothing like that of course. Not yet. And Bridget would do anything, absolutely anything, to stop Chloe following in Abigail's path.

*

'Inspector, what brings you back here?' Dr Melissa Price opened her door to Bridget in a less than welcoming manner. She stood in the doorway, blocking the entrance to her room at the Ruskin. Her fingers were adorned with rings, and her nails were painted black. Today her long grey hair was coiled up on her head like a sleeping serpent.

'May I come in?' asked Bridget. 'I have some more questions to ask you.' When Melissa hesitated, she added, 'I'm sure that you'd prefer to answer them in private, rather than out here where everyone can hear them.'

Melissa shot a glance into the corridor and reluctantly allowed Bridget to enter. 'I don't have long. I was just about to go out.' She took up position on a couch, but neglected to offer her guest a seat.

Bridget was happy to remain standing. It wasn't often that she had the chance to look down on someone she was about to interview. She looked around the office and noticed that the painting of Amber had disappeared.

'I suppose this is about the death of that art shop owner,' muttered Melissa, affecting boredom. Glossy fingernails, as dark as midnight, brushed silver hairs from her face.

'Todd Lee,' confirmed Bridget. 'Did you know him?'

Melissa seemed to consider her answer carefully before replying. 'I sometimes bought supplies from his shop, that's all. I know that Amber worked at the shop part-time and that Gabriel rented studio space there. I have to tell you that I didn't like the man.'

'Why was that?'

'Did you ever meet him yourself?'

'No.'

'If you had, you wouldn't have liked him either. He reminded me of a weasel. I can't say I'm sorry he's dead.'

'Have you heard that Amber tried to take her own life?'

At that, Melissa looked genuinely shocked. 'What? No. What happened? Is she all right?'

'The doctor tells me that she should make a full recovery in time.'

'Why did she do it?' asked Melissa.

'Why would anyone want to take their own life?' asked Bridget.

A hint of emotion – guilt? sadness? – flickered across Melissa's face, but she soon hid it away. She said nothing, but Bridget had her full attention now.

'I'd like to talk more to you about Gabriel,' said Bridget.

'What about him?'

'When he was a student here, would he have studied the work of other artists?'

'Of course. The Ruskin School pursues a broad curriculum. We teach the history and theory of art, as well as practical courses in a range of media.'

'Would Gabriel have learned about any artists in particular?'

'He would have studied a range of different artists. You know, we strongly believe in allowing our students to follow their own interests. Gabriel would have been free to learn about many different artists and art movements.'

'When I last spoke to you, you told me that Gabriel had talent. Did that talent include the ability to reproduce work in the style of other artists?'

'Yes, that was a skill Gabriel had. He was a big fan of the old masters. You know, anything before around 1800. He had the ability not only to see how a painting looked, but to understand how it had been created. He was fascinated by the techniques of the old masters and had the patience to apply those techniques himself. He could probably have painted in any style he put his mind to.'

'Could he have produced work good enough to fool an expert?'

'Maybe. He was very meticulous with his research, and would sometimes reproduce the same piece of work over and over again until he got it just right. I tried to get him to move on and broaden his portfolio, but it was like he was stuck in a groove.' Melissa stopped and regarded Bridget with an appraising look. 'What kind of work are you talking about?'

'In the period before his death, he was studying Renaissance engravings, in particular the work of Albrecht Dürer.'

Melissa shook her head dismissively. 'That's not my area of interest. Gloomy German stuff. It sounds just like Gabriel. It's not an easy style of work to reproduce, however. It would be very time-consuming, and it would require specialist tools and equipment.'

'Gabriel had those tools. We believe that Todd supplied him with everything he needed to produce forgeries of Dürer's prints.'

'Forgeries?' Melissa laughed. 'Oh, Inspector, you can't

possibly think that Gabriel would ever have got involved in any kind of art fraud. If you'd known him, you'd have understood that he wasn't remotely motivated by financial considerations.'

Bridget nodded. That certainly matched the impression she'd formulated of Gabriel during the course of the investigation. 'Then perhaps he saw it as a challenge.'

'No, Gabriel was too honest. He was an innocent, really. Still childlike in many ways. He would never have wanted to perpetrate some kind of deception against the art world. It was against everything he stood for.'

'Then perhaps someone else might have misled him and tricked him into using his skills?'

'That sounds more likely,' said Melissa. 'It wouldn't have been difficult for an unscrupulous person to have taken advantage of Gabriel.' She glanced away from Bridget and studied her own fingernails.

'Might Todd Lee have been that person?'

At that, Melissa snorted with laughter. 'Todd never struck me as a very intelligent person, Inspector.'

'Then what about you, Dr Price?'

Melissa's face blanched. 'Me?'

'It wouldn't be the first time you've exploited others for your own financial gain, would it?'

'I have absolutely no idea what you're talking about,' said Melissa, but her eyes were unable to meet Bridget's. She shifted uncomfortably in her seat, like a trapped animal searching for a way to escape.

'We've taken statements from several of your present and past students who accuse you of plagiarising their ideas and passing them off as your own.'

'Plagiarism?' Melissa seemed to sink into the sofa under the weight of the accusations. 'I may have borrowed some ideas as inspiration for my own work. It's easily done. I may not even have been conscious of what I was doing.'

'That remains to be seen. I can tell you that we'll be passing on our information to the Ruskin School.'

'Please don't do that.' Melissa seemed to be unravelling

before her. 'I didn't mean any harm, but it's so difficult coming up with original ideas year after year. There's so much pressure to always be creating something new. You can't imagine how exhausting it is.'

Bridget felt no sympathy for the woman. 'But that's what artists do, isn't it? It's your job to create. And it's your job to help your students, not to steal their ideas.'

The woman on the sofa was now a mere shadow of the arrogant tutor who had opened the door to Bridget just ten minutes earlier. 'Are you finished now,' she asked, 'or do you have any more questions?'

'I do have one more. Where were you yesterday morning, between eight thirty and nine?'

'Was that when Todd was murdered?'

'Please just answer the question.'

Melissa's shattered expression visibly relaxed as she considered her response. She breathed a long breath out before answering. 'Actually, Inspector, I can tell you exactly where I was and who I was with. From nine o'clock I was in a faculty meeting to discuss next year's teaching. You can speak to the head of my department and the other tutors who were present. They'll all confirm I was there.'

'And before nine o'clock?'

'Well, I was on my way to the meeting.'

'Thank you, Dr Price. I have no more questions for now.'

CHAPTER 29

Only three days had passed since Bridget had last visited the offices of Taylor Financial Technology, yet in that time something seemed to have changed. Some subliminal alteration had taken place, either in the building or in the people who worked there. It took her a moment to put her finger on it. The car park, which had previously been full of shiny, executive cars, was now almost entirely empty. Were all the staff away on a training course, or had some less fortunate fate affected the previously dynamic company?

As she entered the building through the revolving doors, the gleaming surfaces and sleek reception desk were just as solid as before, yet somehow their shine seemed to have worn off. Where Gabriel's painting had once hung was now bare wall, darker than its surroundings and outlined by a thin line of dirt. The orchid on the coffee table was also looking the worse for wear and had shed some of its petals as if it had not been watered.

'May I help you?' Even Kerry, the receptionist, had lost some of her sparkle, and was looking tired and fed up.

'I'd like to see Lawrence Taylor, please,' said Bridget.

'I'm afraid that Mr Taylor is in an important meeting and has given strict instructions not to be disturbed.'

'It's in connection with a murder enquiry.'

That made Kerry sit up straighter. 'I'll see if he's available for you. One moment.'

She picked up the phone, but just then the lift doors pinged open and Lawrence Taylor appeared, followed by another man who Bridget recognised instantly. It was her brother-in-law, James. She watched in astonishment as the two men crossed the floor towards her.

They walked apart, keeping a respectful distance from each other, and their stiff body language and unsmiling faces suggested that their meeting had not been a success. Bridget wondered if this was the big deal that Vanessa had hinted at over Sunday lunch. If so, it looked as if it had fallen through.

James stopped in surprise when he saw Bridget standing by the desk. 'Bridget, what are you doing here?'

'I could ask you the same thing.'

James glanced awkwardly in Lawrence's direction. 'We had a meeting, but it's finished now. I was just leaving.'

Lawrence stood to one side, observing them, but he said nothing. In contrast to the unbridled confidence he had exhibited during her last visit, he gave the distinct impression that he was no longer in charge of events. Behind the desk, Kerry watched the gathering with undisguised curiosity.

James coughed. 'I assume you're here on official business,' he said to Bridget, 'so I'll leave you to it.' He looked keen to make his exit. He turned to his host and held out a hand. 'Lawrence, I'm sorry things haven't worked out as we'd hoped. All the best.'

Lawrence shook James's hand grudgingly and James left the building.

'Inspector,' said Lawrence, with a sardonic smile. 'I assume that you're here to speak to me. How can I be of help?'

'I'd like to speak to you in relation to the murder of

Todd Lee.'

Lawrence barely batted an eyelid. 'In that case, you'd better come up to my office.'

They took the lift up, Lawrence saying nothing and avoiding Bridget's gaze. She studied him, noting the dark rings beneath his eyes, and the way his head leaned forward. The last time she'd seen him, his posture had been upright; he'd given the impression of a man much younger than his fifty-odd years. Now he looked his age. A lot could change in just three days, it seemed.

The lift arrived on the third floor and the doors opened. Lawrence gestured for her to go on ahead, and she stepped into the open-plan office. On her first visit, the area had been busy with employees sitting at desks in front of hi-tech computer monitors. Now it was largely deserted, save for a number of people packing equipment into boxes. Lawrence Taylor walked with the air of a man who had been defeated. There were more bare patches on the walls of his office where previously Hunter's paintings had hung.

'They're all gone,' said Lawrence, noticing the direction of her gaze. 'Sold for cash. But they didn't raise anything like enough. Anyway, it's all over now.' He closed the office door behind him and leaned back against it. Then he loosened his tie and undid the top button of his shirt. 'Drink?'

Bridget expected him to offer a tea or coffee but he strolled around to the other side of his desk and retrieved a bottle of whisky from a drawer. He set it on the desk and pulled out two shot glasses.

'Not while I'm on duty.'

'Of course. Very laudable.' He poured a large measure for himself and sank into his leather chair. 'It looks like I'm permanently off duty.' He chuckled to himself and swallowed a mouthful of the whisky.

Bridget sat on the arm of the sofa to one side of the desk. Once again she found herself looking down on the person she was interviewing. For all his faults, she couldn't help but feel a little sympathy for Lawrence. He certainly presented a much more charming front than his wife. 'Business not going well?'

Taylor slid the whisky to one side and leaned his elbows on the desk. He put his head in his hands. For a moment Bridget worried he was about to break down. She hated to see grown men cry.

'I'm ruined,' said Taylor, shaking his head. 'Absolutely bloody ruined. I built this company up from nothing, and now I've lost everything. I've already had to make people redundant. Good people. I hated doing that to them.' He took another large swig of his drink and ran a hand through his hair, causing it to stick up at odd angles.

'Perhaps you should go easy with that,' said Bridget. She needed Lawrence to stay sober if she was going to get any sense out of him.

'Oh, I don't think so. I think that staying sober at this moment would be a very bad idea.' He drank the rest of the whisky and refilled his glass. 'Today's meeting with James was my last chance,' he continued, 'but he walked out on me. I can't say I really blame him. I'd walk out on me too.'

'I hear that you've walked out on Melissa. Or did she walk out on you?'

'Ha. Melissa only married me for my money. As soon as the business started to struggle she began to get itchy feet. I told her I could turn things around, in fact I very nearly did. But now she's going to end up with nothing. Let's see how she gets on without me. She's never been able to make a success of being an artist. She doesn't have the talent,' he added bitterly.

'Is that why you turned to art fraud?' asked Bridget. 'To try and save your business?'

Taylor raised his eyebrows. 'Art fraud?' He laughed. 'Now there's an idea, a bloody good one. God, I wish I'd thought of that. I could have got Melissa to make the forgeries – she was never any good at coming up with any original ideas.' He chuckled at his own joke.

'So you aren't aware that Gabriel Quinn and Todd Lee

were involved in producing art forgeries?'

'What on earth are you talking about? I've been too busy trying to turn around a struggling business, and look where that's got me.' He waved a hand in the general direction of the building. 'People say that running a business is easy and that the boss just sits around all day while the employees do the hard work. They should try it themselves some time. Then they'd know the truth.'

He was beginning to ramble, and Bridget spoke to him carefully. 'Mr Taylor, we believe that Gabriel Quinn and Todd Lee were murdered in connection with an art fraud. Someone was hoping to make a lot of money exploiting Gabriel's talents. But somewhere along the way things went wrong. First Gabriel was shot dead, and now Todd has been killed.'

'God, and I thought my problems were bad.' He finished his whisky and poured himself another. 'Sorry, I can't help you. I don't even know who this Todd Lee was.'

'Mr Taylor, I have to ask you where you were yesterday morning between the hours of eight and nine o'clock?'

'You're asking me to provide an alibi?'

'That's exactly what I'm doing.'

'Well I can tell you.' He was starting to sound belligerent, but it was perhaps just the drink talking. 'I was in a meeting with James Ellwood. Seems that you two know each other. Is that good enough for you?'

'Thank you,' said Bridget, rising to her feet. It would be easy enough to check whether Taylor was telling the truth. A quick call to her brother-in-law was all it would take. 'I'll see myself out.'

*

The post-mortem report on Todd Lee's death was waiting for Bridget when she returned to Kidlington. Efficient as always, Roy must have carried out the autopsy while she was visiting Melissa and Lawrence. She opened the document and quickly scanned the summary.

There was little in the report that she didn't already know. The cause of death and the murder weapon were already clear. Unlike Gabriel, Todd's body showed no traces of illegal drugs, although the state of his lungs revealed the damage that twenty cigarettes a day could do.

There was only one surprise – the time of death. Although Roy had initially agreed with Dr Sarah Walker's provisional estimate of nine o'clock, the subsequent detailed autopsy now suggested an earlier time of between eight and nine. Eight thirty was Roy's best guess.

It was a difference of just half an hour, but the new information cast a new light on Melissa and Lawrence's alibis. A quick phone call to the faculty head at the Ruskin confirmed that Melissa's meeting hadn't begun until nine o'clock. And the Ruskin was only a five-minute walk away from Todd's art shop.

Bridget made a second phone call, this time to her brother-in-law. It took her a moment to establish that James's meeting with Lawrence hadn't begun until nine o'clock on the dot.

'His company has been struggling for years,' James told her. 'He took on too much debt when he was expanding the business. The banks were all too happy to lend him money before, but now they've cut off his credit and are demanding repayment of the outstanding loan. No one will invest in him now, so his company is doomed. I feel rather sorry for him, actually. He didn't deserve what happened. Will we be seeing you on Sunday for lunch?'

'I'm not sure. It depends how this case goes.'

'Good luck, then.'

'I need it.'

She decided to gather her team to bring them up to speed on her latest interviews with the businessman and his wife.

'So, both Lawrence and Melissa had the opportunity to murder Todd,' concluded Ffion.

'And with Lawrence's business going down the pan, both of them had an obvious financial motive to get involved in art forgery,' said Jake. 'Either might have done it, or they could have done it together.'

'There's also some news from the Met in London,' said Andy. 'Travis Brown has been arrested. Armed officers picked him up in a dawn raid. They're questioning him but so far he's saying nothing about who hired him. They don't sound optimistic that he's going to talk.'

'What about Hunter?'

'Hunter has admitted to various drug offences, but still denies hiring Travis to carry out the hit on Gabriel.'

'That doesn't prove he didn't,' said Ryan. 'What if the Met are right after all? Just because we've ruled out Gabriel's involvement in the drugs network, it doesn't mean Hunter's telling the truth. What if he arranged for Gabriel to be killed because of some personal grudge, perhaps to do with Amber? Maybe this art fraud theory is just plain wrong.'

'Then who killed Todd Lee?' demanded Bridget. 'And why?'

Ryan shrugged. 'I don't know, ma'am, but I think we're missing something.'

Bridget said nothing, but privately she was inclined to agree with Ryan. They were certainly still missing some vital clue. She asked herself if she was barking up the wrong tree with her art forgery theory. There was no hard evidence to prove that she was right, and no proof that either Melissa or Lawrence had anything to do with it.

She imagined what Ben would say if he were here now. He would probably laugh her all the way to the moon if she told him what she thought. He had already dismissed her investigation as painting by numbers.

Ben's view was crystal clear. Hunter Reed had ordered Gabriel's murder. He wouldn't bother looking for something more complicated. And yet Ben's theory did nothing to explain the murder of Todd Lee. It seemed wildly improbable that the death of Gabriel Quinn and Todd Lee were unrelated. They must be linked, and Bridget was confident that the person responsible for the murder of both men was someone she had interviewed in the past few days.

She felt sure that Todd had been involved in some criminal activity, and had been murdered because of it. Todd himself had tried to destroy evidence of what Gabriel had been doing in his studio. He had broken into Gabriel's boat, searching for something, but had left empty-handed. It seemed likely that he had been killed because of what he knew.

Hunter had been in custody since his arrest. He couldn't have killed Todd Lee. Someone else must be involved.

Melissa Price had no alibi for the time of Todd's murder. She'd had plenty of time to call in at Todd's shop on her way to the Ruskin. Melissa certainly had the knowledge and connections to have run an art fraud. And she had shown herself to be a greedy, unscrupulous individual, hungry for wealth and power.

Lawrence Taylor desperately needed money to bail out his failing company, and he had connections in London and with art investors. He also had no firm alibi for the time of Todd's death. And together Lawrence and his wife might have made the perfect team.

Amber Morgan remained a strong suspect, despite having tried to take her own life. She was the person most strongly connected to Gabriel, Todd and Hunter. By her own admission she had been the one to discover Todd's body and they only had her word for it that she'd arrived at the art shop after nine o'clock. She could easily have got there earlier and killed Todd herself. She might even have taken the overdose to divert attention away from herself.

There was even Harriet Watson, Gabriel's neighbour on the canal, who had supplied him with drugs. She was the only person who had witnessed the break-in at *La Belle Dame*, and for all Bridget knew she might have invented the whole story to frame Todd and deflect suspicion from herself. And despite telling Bridget of her dislike for Amber, it was Harriet who Amber had turned to for help when she had nowhere else to stay. Perhaps Harriet was still hiding something from the investigation.

Bridget paced back and forth in frustration. This investigation had been a riddle from the start. Although she had suspects, she had no clear evidence to incriminate any of them. And she was still no nearer to understanding the meaning of the cryptic sequence of letters and numbers that were Gabriel's last words. Perhaps the mystery of the number would remain unsolved forever. Perhaps, as Ben had implied, there was no mystery to solve, merely the meaningless ramblings of a troubled and paranoid young man as he lay dying.

'Well, there is another possibility,' said Jake.

'What?'

Jake shuffled his feet and rubbed his nose in the way he did when he was unsure about something.

'For God's sake, spit it out,' said Bridget, a little too sharply. 'I'm all ears.'

'Well, I don't think there's anything wrong with the art fraud theory. It's the only one that really does tie everything together, but we still haven't yet considered the most obvious suspect.'

'And who is that?'

'Well, ma'am, you rejected this idea yesterday, but I still think we have to consider Jonathan Wright, the gallery owner. Jonathan knew both Gabriel and Todd. The Met photographed him in London with Hunter, so that links him to Travis Brown too. He's ideally placed to sell forged works of art. And he doesn't have a watertight alibi for the time of Todd's murder.'

Bridget narrowed her eyes. 'Yes he does. I was with him.'

Jake shuffled his feet again. 'What time was that exactly, ma'am?'

'It was half past nine.' As soon as she had said it, Bridget realised the implications. The post-mortem had placed the time of death at least half an hour earlier than that. The art gallery was just a street away from the art shop. Jonathan would easily have had time to leave the shop and return to the gallery, or perhaps to call in at the shop before he opened the gallery at nine.

'Ma'am, is there any reason we shouldn't consider him a suspect?'

Bridget's blood ran cold. Had she been blind all along? The notion that Jonathan could have masterminded a criminal operation and been responsible for not one, but two murders, was absurd. And yet...

She took a deep breath and met Jake's gaze. It was obvious he knew there was more to her relationship with Jonathan than she had admitted.

'All right,' she said. 'We should talk to him.' She hated to think what this new suspicion would do to her budding relationship with Jonathan. But then again, what relationship? They'd had dinner together once, that was all. It was hardly the romance of the century.

'Jake, you come with me.' She had to stay objective and keep an open mind. Jake would help her to do that. She wasn't sure she could trust herself.

*

A young couple holding hands and eating ice-creams were browsing the paintings in the window of Wright's art gallery, trying to decide which one they liked best. A pleasant way to spend your time, thought Bridget, as her car pulled up next to the gallery. After this case she didn't think she'd ever be able to look at art in quite the same way again.

A hundred questions were racing through her mind as she stepped out of the Mini and onto the High Street. Was Jonathan really involved in a conspiracy to forge works of art, or would he be able to provide a robust alibi that would exclude him from their enquiries? Even if he could, Jake's suspicions had placed doubts in her own mind. Had Jonathan's visit to London with Hunter really been entirely innocent? How could he not have known that Hunter was going there to buy drugs? Had he been foolish, or merely naive? Or worse still – culpable. She had misjudged a man's character very badly once before, when she had married Ben. She dreaded making the same mistake again.

The bell above the door tinkled as she pushed the door open and went inside, Jake right behind her. Vicky, sitting behind the counter, looked up to greet them. Her smile slipped slightly when she saw who had entered the shop. Not a potential customer, but the police. Again. She looked warily from Bridget to Jake and back to Bridget. 'Hello?' she ventured in a wavering voice.

'Hi,' said Bridget. 'Sorry to bother you again, but is Jonathan here?'

'Not today. He's gone to London on business.'

Bridget's heart sank at the news. What kind of business might Jonathan be involved with in London, today of all days?

'There's an auction at Sotheby's,' explained Vicky. She picked up the auction catalogue that lay on the counter and held it out for Bridget to see.

Bridget took the heavy catalogue and flicked it open, flipping through the glossy pages of paintings, prints and drawings, each accompanied by a detailed description and an eye-watering reserve price. 'Is this today's auction?'

'Yes. Jonathan was very excited about it.'

'Any particular reason?'

'He's hoping to buy some works for the gallery, I expect. But he also mentioned that a rare old master was up for sale. It's not the kind of thing Jonathan sells. He deals in contemporary art. But he was interested in seeing it. It's on page –'

'I think I've found it,' said Bridget slowly. She couldn't quite believe what she was seeing. A feeling of dread was creeping over her. Jake leaned over her shoulder to take a look. The picture in the catalogue was very clearly a print in the style of Albrecht Dürer. Coincidence? She had long since given up believing in coincidences.

The description in the catalogue read: *Adam and Eve,*

Albrecht Dürer, 1504. Engraving. Reserve price, £250,000.

The black and white print showed Adam and Eve in the Garden of Eden. The Tree of Knowledge stood between them, the duplicitous serpent coiled around its trunk. Eve held out the forbidden fruit for Adam to taste, and fig leaves protected their modesty. The image depicted the momentous moment of mankind's fall from grace. Had Gabriel Quinn forged this print in imitation of his hero, Dürer? And in doing so, had he unwittingly brought about his own downfall? And what, precisely, was Jonathan's part in all of this?

'There's something else, ma'am,' said Jake. 'Look.' He pointed at a reference code below the illustration: L79468/235.

Bridget stared at the number. It confirmed her worst fears. 'This is what Gabriel was trying to communicate just before he died.' She showed it to Vicky. 'What does it mean?'

'It's Sotheby's lot number for the item. The "L" refers to London, as opposed to New York or Paris. The next five digits are the reference code for today's auction. The last three digits refer to this particular item.'

'Was this catalogue here the last time Gabriel was in the gallery? The morning he was shot?'

Vicky's brows knitted together tightly in concentration. She began to nod. 'Yes, it was. You know, now you mention it, I remember him looking at it. He'd been here to speak to Jonathan about the exhibition, and afterwards he picked up the catalogue and began browsing. Gabriel was always interested in all kinds of art. Then suddenly he slammed the catalogue down on the counter and rushed out of the gallery. Well, you know what happened next. At the time I didn't think much of it. Artists can be a bit temperamental, and Gabriel often behaved strangely. I'm sorry, if I'd realised it was relevant I'd have told you this before.'

'Not your fault, Vicky. We've been chasing our tails on

this investigation, but now I think we're getting somewhere. What time does the auction start?' she asked with a heavy heart.

'Two o'clock.'

Bridget looked at her watch. It was almost midday. 'Come on,' she said to Jake. 'We need to get back to the station right away.'

CHAPTER 30

Clutching his copy of the Sotheby's catalogue, Jonathan entered the surprisingly modest building on New Bond Street in the heart of London's West End that housed one of the world's greatest auction houses. The auctioneers had been founded in 1744, originally selling books. At the end of the nineteenth century it had expanded to include fine art, jewellery, watches and wine. It was now one of the world's largest brokers, with over eighty locations including London, New York, Paris and Hong Kong.

Inside the building, the look was of understated opulence. Jonathan joined the crowds of well-dressed guests, ready for the pre-sales socialising that always went on at these events. In the old days, Angela had accompanied him whenever she was free. She'd enjoyed the social aspect and was better at it than he was. He'd had to get used to doing it on his own, but maybe one day Bridget would come with him. He hoped so.

The auctions sometimes became major social occasions, attracting celebrity guests including stars from the world of film and music. He'd been present in the

London salesroom when Jenny Saville's self-portrait *Propped* had made history by selling for £9.5 million, becoming the most expensive artwork ever sold by a living female artist. And he still remembered vividly the dramatic evening when Banksy's *Girl with Balloon* sold for a million pounds, only to spontaneously self-destruct immediately afterwards, by means of a hidden paper shredder that the artist had built into the frame.

He hadn't been looking to buy either of those works, of course. They were well beyond his price range. Nor was he planning to bid for today's highlight, the rare Dürer print that was being sold by a private collector. It was expected to sell for several hundred thousand pounds. Still, he was interested to see how much it would fetch.

He approached a couple of London gallery owners that he knew fairly well who were in conversation with the art critic from *The Guardian*. 'Hello there, Simon, Greg,' he said, shaking hands vigorously. 'Joanna, how are you?'

As industries went, the world of art dealers and gallery owners was a rather select crowd. Most people knew each other and, if not exactly friends, were at least reasonably well acquainted. But every conversation, no matter how cordial on the surface, was always laced with an undertone of curiosity and competitiveness. This was business after all. Everyone wanted to know what a given artist was really worth. What was the next big trend going to be? Who was up and coming? Who was on the way out? Who was most likely to win the Turner Prize this year? Knowing the answers to these questions could be the difference between making a fortune or going out of business. It paid to keep yourself informed.

The trio greeted Jonathan with undisguised interest. They had been discussing a recent exhibition at the Guggenheim in New York before he had joined the conversation. It was years since he had been to America, and he was interested to hear what they had to say. But now that he had arrived, the discussion moved to a much juicier topic.

'Tell us,' said Joanna, the *Guardian* journalist, 'what's the latest on the Oxford murders?'

The other two, Greg and Simon, who owned a gallery in a converted warehouse in trendy Shoreditch, studied him with a look of lurid interest on their faces. Joanna had her phone in her hand and Jonathan wouldn't have put it past her to record the conversation so that she could rush off and write an article. *Oxford Gallery Owner Reveals Truth Behind Murdered Artist.* Was there no end to the money to be made from death?

'I'm afraid I don't know any more than has been on the news,' he said. He hated telling an untruth, but he wasn't going to feed the rumour mill. He certainly wasn't going to reveal that he'd been arrested and questioned about one of the murders. Or that he'd had dinner earlier that week with the Senior Investigating Officer. He mumbled an excuse about needing to speak to someone on the other side of the room and moved away.

He had been hoping that today's auction would take his mind off the terrible events of the past week but it seemed that whoever he spoke to sooner or later steered the conversation round to the murder. One of the more brazen dealers even went so far as to ask him how much he had personally profited from Gabriel's death. The question made him feel soiled, as if he were an accomplice of some kind. The fact that the dealer's assumption was correct, and profits had soared in the wake of the shooting only made the matter worse. It was blood money, and he wasn't at all sure that he wanted it. Perhaps he would make a charitable donation in Gabriel's name.

'Jonathan.' A woman's arm looped itself through his and drew him away to a quiet corner of the room. It was Nadia, who owned a shop in South London specialising in art from Africa and the Indian sub-continent. 'I see that you're the centre of attention today, and for all the wrong reasons. Come and talk to me instead.'

'Nadia, how nice to see you.' It was a relief to meet a sympathetic listener at last.

She patted his shoulder. 'Don't worry, all this fuss will soon blow over. In a month from now, everyone will have forgotten all about it. Sooner than that. Some of these people have the attention span of a goldfish.'

Jonathan hoped she was right. Vicky had been nervous about minding the gallery on her own today. With both of the murder victims being people he'd known, he'd begun to wonder if anyone else close to him might be in danger. He'd considered asking Bridget for police protection but didn't want to appear ridiculous and besides, the police had better things to do than guard an art gallery.

'Are you here today for anything in particular?' asked Nadia, waving her own copy of the auction catalogue at him.

'Always on the lookout for a bargain,' said Jonathan with a grin. 'But I suppose like most people I'm interested to see what price the Dürer will fetch.' There was certainly an air of excitement and anticipation in the room usually only felt when a Van Gogh or one of the French Impressionists was up for sale.

'Me too,' said Nadia. 'He's not the sort of artist I sell, but I've always admired the intricacy of his work, carving such detailed images onto wood or copper. I simply can't imagine anyone having that much skill and dexterity.' She noticed someone on the other side of the room. 'Sorry to be rude, but if you'll excuse me, I must go and speak to Siobhan about a set of Indian prints. It was lovely talking to you.'

As she drifted away, Jonathan flicked through the catalogue again. He didn't want to be drawn into any more conversations about the Oxford murders. He checked his watch. The auction would be starting in ten minutes. He wondered if there was enough time to grab a quick coffee beforehand. Then he felt a tap on his shoulder and turned around.

'Hello, Jonathan. How nice to see you here. If I'd known you were coming up to London today I could have offered you a lift.'

'Oh,' said Jonathan. 'What a surprise.'

And not an entirely pleasant one. For some reason he couldn't quite put his finger on, the unexpected appearance of the new arrival made Jonathan feel distinctly ill at ease.

CHAPTER 31

The Subaru's engine started with a roar and grew louder still as Jake drove off, wheels spinning on the tarmac. Bridget just had time to strap herself in and brush the empty KitKat wrappers from the front seat. 'Try not to break the law too much,' she told him, 'and can we please turn this dreadful music off?'

'Oh yeah. Sorry, ma'am.'

It had taken a while before she had been able to speak to someone at Sotheby's who had both the authority and the knowledge to tell her who was selling the Dürer print, but eventually she had been given a name. She had breathed a sigh of relief, then nodded grimly to herself. Of course.

On telling Jake and Ffion that they were going to the auction in London, Ffion had raised a concern.

'Ma'am?' she had queried. 'Should we inform the Met about what we're doing?'

It had taken Bridget no time to consider her response. 'No way. This is our case and I'm not handing it over to the Met on a plate so they can take all the glory. This time we're getting in on the action, and I'll deal with any consequences.'

They quickly joined the M40, and then powered down the motorway towards London, in the fast lane the whole way. Jake was a good driver, Bridget had to give him that. As the miles passed without incident, she felt herself begin to relax.

In the back seat, Ffion seemed subdued. Bridget wondered if it was because she had been unable to crack the mysterious code that had dogged the inquiry right from the very beginning. But Ffion couldn't blame herself for that. In the end, it had turned out to be nothing to do with mathematics, but all about the world of art.

Meanwhile, Jake was in his element in the driving seat. He'd always been into cars, he explained, ever since he was a young boy. When questioned he admitted, somewhat modestly, that he'd passed his advanced driving test with flying colours. Maybe when the time came for Chloe to have driving lessons Bridget would ask him to take her out for some practice sessions. She could only imagine the strain it would put on the mother-daughter relationship if she tried to do it herself.

They made excellent progress until they hit the Westway flyover coming into Paddington on the approach to central London. Here, shiny new offices were springing up either side of the dual carriageway, dwarfing the older, Victorian terraces and pubs which stubbornly refused to give way to their bigger and flashier counterparts. That was London for you, mused Bridget. A melting pot of old and new, rich and poor, all jostling for space.

Traffic slowed to a crawl and they found themselves stuck behind the Oxford Tube coach. Perhaps they ought to have informed the local police after all. Bridget would never forgive herself if they missed this chance to make an arrest. She checked her watch nervously, wondering whether to make the call to the Met. 'Is there any way we can avoid this traffic?' she asked.

'I don't know,' said Jake. 'I've never driven in London before.'

'Take the next turn-off,' said Ffion from the back seat.

Jake followed her instructions and left the dual carriageway at the next junction, leaving the bus passengers from Oxford stuck on the main road. Soon they were crossing the tracks of the Great Western Railway and heading down grand terraces of identical white houses, three or four storeys tall, each one worth an unimaginable sum of money. Around Hyde Park they found themselves held up by the ubiquitous red London buses which lumbered around the city much like their counterparts in Oxford. Bridget checked the time again. The auction was due to start.

Ffion continued to direct Jake from the back of the car. Without her instructions they would have been completely lost, but with her help they deftly negotiated the obstacle course of roadworks, motorcycle couriers and one-way streets. Eventually Jake turned the car into New Bond Street.

'Nearly there,' said Ffion.

Bridget peered out of the window at the designer boutiques and fashion houses that lined this exclusive area of real estate. This was Mayfair, London's most expensive district, and one of the world's most desirable locations. A place of glamorous apartment buildings, bustling restaurants and theatres, and the chicest retail outlets.

Right here, among the rich and the famous, walked a ruthless killer.

*

For someone who Jonathan had first met just two days earlier, when he'd brought Gabriel's painting into the gallery to be valued, Professor Henderson was acting in an all too familiar manner.

Jonathan cast surreptitious glances around the room, looking for an opportunity to make his excuses and move away from the maths professor from Oxford. Even talking to the art critic from *The Guardian* with her intrusive questions about the Oxford murders might be preferable to being buttonholed by Professor Henderson. But all his other acquaintances seemed to have dispersed and he found himself stuck in a corner of the room at the mercy of the professor and his overweening manner.

Jonathan didn't normally take against people, it wasn't in his nature. But something about the maths professor put him on his guard. The man exuded a sense of self-satisfaction that was almost distasteful. He'd first sensed it when the professor had turned up at his gallery, clutching his Gabriel Quinn painting. He'd been in a state of high excitement, breathless even, as if he'd run all the way from the mathematical institute, desperate to get his picture valued. It had been the morning Bridget had popped in to the gallery to apologise for his arrest of the day before.

He had made it clear to Jonathan that he was eager to sell the painting as quickly as possible, and had even offered it for sale at their meeting. Jonathan had declined to make him an offer. It felt wrong for someone to be so keen to make a profit so soon after the artist's tragic death. Instead, he had advised the professor to hold onto his painting for a while longer.

He wondered what interest the man could possibly have in an auction of fine art.

'There's quite a crowd here today, isn't there?' said Henderson, looking around the room and licking his lips.

'There certainly is.'

'Some of these bidders look as if they have money to spare, wouldn't you say?'

'No doubt they do.'

An elegantly dressed woman walked past, her face partially obscured by designer sunglasses and leaving a cloud of perfume in her wake. 'Gosh,' said Henderson, recognising her as a well-known actress. 'Isn't that –'

'Yes, I think it is,' said Jonathan, cutting him off. Sotheby's was a good place to bump into millionaires; billionaires even, but he had never been interested in celebrity-watching.

Killing by Numbers

'They're all here for the Dürer, no doubt. Is that why you're here?'

Jonathan frowned. Perhaps Henderson knew more about art than he had assumed. The conversation they'd had on Wednesday morning had shown the professor's appreciation of the subject to be superficial at best. 'It'll be interesting to see how much it goes for. Do you have any particular interest in Dürer?'

The professor held up his copy of the glossy sales catalogue, patting the front cover reverentially, as if it were a sacred text. 'I lecture on him,' he said proudly.

'Really?'

'Oh yes. Of course, I'm no *art critic*,' – he spoke the words disdainfully – 'but I do know a thing or two about mathematical symbolism.'

'I see.' Jonathan glanced at his wristwatch, but the professor ploughed on regardless.

'You know, I used to think that artists were idealists in pursuit of truth and beauty. Like monks, perhaps – or mathematicians! But I've come to see that they're just like everyone else. Out for what they can get and keen to make a quick buck.' He rubbed the thumb and forefinger of his right hand together.

'That's a rather cynical view, don't you think?' said Jonathan.

'Not at all.' The professor's voice had taken on a hard edge. 'I used to be married to an artist, so I should know.'

Despite himself, Jonathan found his curiosity piqued. 'Really? Who was that?' He found it hard to imagine any of the women he knew married to this rather unpleasant man.

'Dr Melissa Price. She teaches at the Ruskin School of Art. You probably know her.'

'I do,' said Jonathan, unable to keep the surprise out of his voice. 'You were married to Melissa?' It seemed an extraordinary claim. Melissa had been married to Lawrence for as long as Jonathan had known her. He wondered if Henderson was inventing the story, or was

275

actually deluded.

'Oh, yes. Melissa and I were at university together. She was studying Fine Art at the Ruskin School; my subject was Mathematics. She always had ambitions to be a famous artist, but deep down all she really wanted was to be rich. She struggled to make it as an artist and my salary as a mere academic was never going to be enough for her. The marriage ended very quickly.' There was no hiding the bitterness in his voice. 'But there are easier ways to make money than slapping paint onto canvas. She left me to marry that businessman, Lawrence Taylor.'

'I see. I'm sorry.'

Henderson laid his hand on Jonathan's shoulder. 'Don't be sorry. Shall I tell you why?' He leaned closer and Jonathan recoiled from his sour breath. 'I'm going to have the last laugh. When this auction is over I'll be richer than either of them, and then she'll be sorry she left me.' There was a gleam in the professor's eyes that Jonathan found disturbing.

'What can you mean?'

The professor gave a hearty laugh. 'My dear man, I'm here to sell. In fact, it looks as if the auction is about to start. Shall we take our seats?'

The room was already emptying as the buyers, sellers and interested onlookers made their way into the auction room itself. By the time Jonathan entered the room, most of the seats had already been taken, save for a couple of free places on the front row. Against his better judgement, he followed Professor Henderson to the front of the room, immediately below the auctioneer's lectern, and took his seat.

★

'There it is,' said Ffion. She pointed at a large blue flag that was waving in the breeze above a white porticoed doorway. 'That's Sotheby's right there.'

Jake pulled up outside the building. Bridget's door was

open even before they had fully stopped. She jumped out and ran towards the entrance.

A liveried doorman appeared from out of nowhere and blocked her way. He examined the orange Subaru with obvious distaste. 'I'm afraid you can't park here, madam. There are double yellow lines.'

Maybe if they'd arrived in a Rolls or a Bentley, the parking wouldn't have been a problem, thought Bridget.

She thrust her warrant card into his face. 'Police. Where's the auction taking place?'

Stunned into compliance, the doorman pointed them in the right direction. 'But the auction's already started,' he said. 'You can't go in now.'

Bridget pushed past him into the entrance hall, flashing her warrant card to forestall any further attempts by the staff to stop her. Jake and Ffion followed close behind. When they reached the doors leading to the auction room, she paused for a second. She was confident that the murderer would be in this room, but even if he wasn't, she would at least be able to put a stop to the sale of the fake Dürer – a work of art that wasn't genuine, and which two people had died for.

She pushed open the doors of the auction room.

CHAPTER 32

The excitement in the room was palpable. Jonathan could feel it running through the audience like electricity. The international agents at the side of the room stood poised, ready to whisper frantically into their telephone receivers as soon as the bidding began. This was the moment everyone had come for.

In the seat next to him, Professor Henderson could barely keep still. He had developed an annoying tic, tapping his thigh with his fingertips and bouncing his foot up and down.

The auctioneer took a sip of water as the white-gloved auction assistants turned the moving dais beside him and the Albrecht Dürer print appeared to murmurs of appreciation from the audience.

'This is it,' said Henderson, leaning in towards Jonathan.

'And now, ladies and gentleman,' announced the auctioneer, 'we move on to our final lot. Lot number 235, Dürer's print of *Adam and Eve*, dating from 1504, and which is now showing behind me. I will start the bidding at two hundred and fifty thousand pounds. Do I have two hundred and fifty thousand pounds? Yes! Two hundred and sixty thousand pounds? Yes! Two hundred and seventy thousand?'

Bidders around the room were quickly raising their hands in a quest to outdo each other. A Japanese woman with a phone clamped against one ear kept thrusting her hand into the air, outbidding the others around the hall who were also showing a great deal of interest.

'Do I hear seven hundred thousand pounds?' called the auctioneer.

Henderson was practically jumping out of his seat, craning his neck to see who was bidding. He kept muttering, 'Yes! Yes!' every time the auctioneer raised the asking price. Jonathan stared at the maths professor in disbelief. Could Henderson really be the owner of this Albrecht Dürer print? It seemed impossible, but from the way he was behaving, he was either the genuine owner or was suffering from some kind of psychotic delusion. How could the man have come into possession of such a rare and valuable item?

The exuberant voice of the auctioneer cut across his thoughts. 'Nine hundred and ninety thousand pounds! Any advance on nine hundred and ninety thousand?'

Jonathan could scarcely believe that the bidding had reached such a high value. It was certain to set a new record for the German artist's work.

The Japanese agent was jabbering frantically into her phone. Suddenly she raised her hand again.

'One million pounds!' cried the auctioneer.

Then the doors at the back of the room burst open and a voice shouted, 'Stop!'

★

'Stop! Police!' Bridget strode into the packed room and a hundred stunned faces turned towards her in outrage. The auctioneer stared at her, his hammer held aloft, his mouth open like a gasping fish.

Jake and Ffion took the side aisles while Bridget strode down the middle of the room, holding her warrant card high and searching to left and right. The man she was looking for must be here somewhere. She had telephoned the maths department in Oxford before setting off and had been told that Professor Michael Henderson was taking the day off to attend to important personal business in London. Henderson had fooled them all, but not for any longer. She was going to expose him for what he was – a fraudster and a murderer. But where was he?

'What... what on earth is going on?' spluttered the auctioneer. 'This is outrageous. You can't just barge in here and... We're in the middle of an auction.'

An eerie silence fell over the room so that when Bridget spoke, her words carried loud and clear. 'This is a murder enquiry. And that' – she pointed to the Dürer print on the wall behind the auctioneer – 'is a fake.'

The allegation of art fraud caused the room to erupt in an outburst of fury, in a way that the word "murder" had barely aroused a ripple of interest. The well-mannered gathering of art aficionados became an angry mob. Bidders leapt to their feet, shouting and gesticulating. Several left their seats and rushed towards the Dürer for a closer look at the offending object. Yet others whipped out their phones and began filming the uproar.

Bridget needed everyone to calm down or Henderson, if he was here, would get away. 'Please remain in your seats!' she shouted, but it was no use.

A movement on the front row caught her eye. There was Jonathan, waving her over, and sitting right next to him was the maths professor. As she began to move in his direction, Henderson sprang to his feet, jumped onto the stage and disappeared behind the revolving dais, knocking one of the white-gloved assistants out of the way.

'Get him!' shouted Bridget to Jake and Ffion.

★

In all his years as a gallery owner, Jonathan had never attended an auction that had been raided by the police. The Sotheby's staff, normally so calm and professional, were flapping around, not knowing what to do. The auctioneer was appealing fruitlessly over his microphone for calm. Agents were screaming down the phone to their buyers, trying to explain what was going on. The art critic from *The Guardian* must surely have been beside herself. First a record-setting price for a Dürer print, now its dramatic exposure as a forgery – this was the art scoop of the decade.

Jonathan turned to see Professor Henderson punch one of the Sotheby's staff in the face and disappear behind the stage. Could that man really be the person behind Gabriel's murder? The killer who had stabbed Todd Lee with a burin? The criminal who had masterminded the sale of a fake work of art?

Jonathan had inspected the print earlier in the day at close quarters and had never suspected it might be a forgery. But if, as he now realised, it was Gabriel's work, he wasn't surprised that everyone had been fooled. Gabriel had always been a perfectionist, and meticulous in his approach to his craft. But Gabriel would never have knowingly produced a forgery in order to fool the art market and make a fortune. Despite what Henderson had said about artists being in it for the money, Gabriel had been a man of the utmost integrity. He'd often told Jonathan that he didn't paint for the money. If he had created a work in the style of another artist, it must be because he'd been tricked. And no doubt he'd been killed to keep him quiet.

Jonathan felt the anger growing inside him.

He climbed onto the stage and slipped behind the revolving dais where first Henderson, and then Bridget and the other police officers had gone.

★

Bridget stepped behind the scenes of Sotheby's and found herself in a tangle of corridors located behind the auction room. It was like being backstage at a theatre. This was the part of Sotheby's that buyers and sellers didn't normally get to see; where men in overalls carted priceless objects from one place to another. Doors opened up into rooms stacked full of paintings, sculptures, pottery, porcelain, jewellery and bottles of fine wine. Was that a genuine Ming vase on that stand? And was that a Van Gogh propped against the wall as if it had just been picked up at a car boot sale? It was like finding yourself suddenly in the middle of a treasure trove. But amongst all these priceless artifacts, the object of their search was nowhere to be seen. Professor Henderson had vanished.

'Where did he go?' asked Jake, looking around in bewilderment. 'He can't have just disappeared.'

'I don't know.' Bridget was starting to regret her decision not to call for back-up from the Met. What had she been trying to prove? That she was a better cop than Ben? If she lost Henderson now – and accidentally knocked over a piece of Ming dynasty china at the same time – there'd be hell to pay back at Kidlington. Grayson wouldn't hesitate to demote her back into uniform. She'd end her days as a traffic cop on the Blackbird Leys estate in East Oxford.

'We need to split up,' she said. 'But be careful. He might be dangerous.' She thought of the burin that Henderson had used to kill Todd Lee, and of the cold-blooded and ruthless way that he had ordered the death of Gabriel Quinn.

'No worries,' said Ffion. The young constable sprinted nimbly up a flight of stairs, taking them two at a time.

Jake set off purposely down a corridor, his long legs carrying him at a rapid pace.

Left alone, Bridget began to work her way through the rooms packed with auction lots.

*

The top floor seemed to consist of nothing more than offices full of administrative staff sitting behind computer screens or on the telephone. Shocked faces turned towards Ffion when she barged in, demanding to know if anyone had seen a middle-aged maths professor on the run. No one had.

She checked both male and female toilets, kicking open the door to one of the cubicles when its occupant failed to respond. A young woman stared back at her in horror, but there was no sign of the missing professor. She broke into a stationery cupboard stuffed with paper, pens and paper clips, then doubled back the way she had come, satisfied that Henderson wasn't on the top floor of the building.

As she started to descend the stairs she had previously climbed, she heard a scream from below. She broke into a run.

★

On his previous murder case, Jake had turned out to be the hero at the final hour, and he was keen to repeat his success. He strode along the corridor, pushing open doors and searching inside each room. Nothing.

If he could just find Henderson, overpower him and make the arrest, then he'd be the golden boy of the station once again. Then Ryan might start to show him a bit more respect. Grayson might offer him a pay rise. And maybe even Ffion would agree to go out for a drink with him. So what if she had funny ideas about patriarchal society and Sigmund Freud? Jake believed in equality for women too. Did that make him a feminist? He thought it probably did. He was sure that Ffion didn't actively dislike him. Sometimes she even laughed at his jokes. She was probably just shy, underneath all that cool bravado.

The sound of a woman screaming brought him back to the present. It sounded like the boss. He ran from the room and back down the corridor.

★

It truly was like being in Aladdin's cave. Jonathan had never seen so many *objets d'art* in one place, and from all four corners of the world. Before setting up his own gallery, he had considered working in an auction house himself. He'd imagined handling paintings by Monet or Van Gogh as if they were everyday objects. Now here, it seemed, they were.

He stopped at the doorway to one room where an imperial Ming vase stood on a stand. He found himself drawn to it like iron filings to a magnet. He had never seen a vase that was quite so beautiful. He put out a hand to touch it, aware that he really shouldn't, but knowing too that he'd never get another opportunity in his life to touch such a precious object. His fingertips were millimetres from the exquisitely patterned porcelain when he heard a scream. He snatched his fingers away from the vase as if an alarm had gone off, and ran from the room towards the sound.

★

Bridget thought that the basement storeroom was empty, apart from the vast collection of ceramic bowls, vases, plates and pots that were arranged on shelves around the walls. She screamed in fright when Henderson appeared suddenly from behind the door where he had been hiding, taking her completely by surprise.

He advanced towards her, a mad gleam in his eyes. 'You!' he said. 'You did this!'

Bridget stumbled backwards, bumping against the wall shelving and setting its collection of bowls and vases rattling noisily.

Henderson was dressed in the only outfit she'd ever seen him wearing – corduroy trousers and tweed jacket – but he was no longer the kindly professor she had spoken to before, and who had helped them unlock Gabriel's phone and laptop. Now his face was contorted into an ugly scowl and he raised his fist as if to strike her. 'Don't scream again,' he warned her, 'or I'll break your nose.'

Bridget did as she was told. With any luck, her scream had been loud enough for the others to hear. Even if not, Jake and Ffion were searching the building and would no doubt discover her here.

Her thoughts drifted to Chloe. Their reconciliation had been tenuous at best. Bridget was filled with dread at the prospect that something might happen to her in this basement room before she'd had a chance to fully restore her relationship with her daughter. If she could just keep Henderson talking, help would arrive soon. She looked for a way out of the room, but he had her cornered for now. He backed steadily away from her, and pushed the door closed with his foot. 'This is all your fault,' he accused.

'I didn't do this, Professor,' she said calmly. 'You did it yourself, when you tricked Gabriel Quinn into forging art for you.'

He didn't try to deny it, in fact he seemed quite pleased with himself. 'Gabriel was easy to trick. He was a fool.'

'I thought you admired him. You said he had an affinity for mathematics.'

'Gabriel liked to think he was some kind of mathematical prodigy, but he was just tinkering with numbers. I saw that he had artistic talent though – a talent that could be put to good use. He could make more money copying the works of a great artist than by messing around with his own silly ideas.'

'But Gabriel would never have agreed to make forgeries for you if he'd known you planned to pass them off as genuine works and sell them.'

'Of course not. He was an idealist. That's why he died penniless.'

'He died because you arranged for him to be murdered, Professor.'

A thin smile crept across Henderson's lips. 'True. But

you have to admit that it was an elegant solution to the problem. Gabriel had guessed too much. He refused to produce any more work for me. I sent Todd round to his boat to remove any incriminating evidence that might be there, but still I knew that eventually he was going to go to the police. That naive honesty of his just wouldn't allow him to stay silent. That's what got him killed.'

'And Todd?'

The professor snarled. 'That oaf! I wish I'd never got involved with him. I only met him through Gabriel. I told him to destroy all the evidence, but he couldn't manage even that. Then he started demanding money from me. I had no choice, he had to go.'

'I see.' Except Bridget still didn't really understand why the professor had gone down this road in the first place. 'Tell me why you decided to make the forgeries.'

'Why? Why do you think? To sell them!'

'But you must earn a good salary as a university professor.'

'You'd think so, wouldn't you? I was always content with what I had. But my wife thought otherwise.'

'Your wife?'

'Dr Melissa Price.' He smiled when she showed surprise. 'Oh yes, Melissa and I were once married. But she told me I'd never amount to anything. That's why she left me. She was wrong! Do you know how much money I made today? A million pounds! I've made more out of art in one day than Melissa has made in her entire career. So tell me who never amounted to anything!'

'I see. So you tricked Gabriel into forging a copy of *Adam and Eve* so you could become rich. You know that Adam and Eve were tempted by the promise of knowledge. You were tempted by greed.'

'Greed? You think I did all this for the money?'

Now Bridget was nonplussed. Isn't that what the professor had just told her himself? 'What then?'

'I did it to prove that I could! I did it for Melissa!'

Henderson had become deranged, and Bridget

cowered away from him, but he came on relentlessly. 'Art is a scam,' he declared. 'There are no right or wrong answers in art, it's just a matter of personal opinion. What use is that? In mathematics, I deal with numbers and universal truths. That's where real beauty lies, not in splashes of paint.'

Bridget should have tried to calm him down, but the professor's hubris rankled her. 'And yet you decided to deceive people by selling a forgery.'

'Who cares? People who have that much money to throw away on pictures deserve to be deceived.' He reached out and picked up a vase from a wall shelf. He held it up, turning it to reveal the intricate patterns on its slender neck and curved body. 'Who cares whether this was created five hundred years ago or yesterday? A vase is a vase!' He threw it at the floor.

Bridget cringed as the ancient ceramic shattered into pieces.

Henderson reached for another. 'And this?' The second vase smashed against the wall, bringing bowls and pots crashing down.

The door behind him burst open and Bridget looked up. Jonathan stood in the open doorway, panting for breath. 'No!' she cried. 'Don't come any closer!'

Henderson whirled to face him, but Jonathan stood his ground. 'Don't you dare hurt her,' he commanded.

'Or what?' The professor reached down and grabbed a ceramic shard from the broken pieces of pottery.

Bridget lunged forward to grab his arm, but he was too strong for her. With a great roar he shrugged her off and threw himself across the room, slashing with the sharp weapon.

Jonathan dodged to one side, but the professor spun and lunged again.

At that moment, Ffion and Jake appeared in the doorway. But they were too late.

The professor's hand swung through the air. Bridget shrieked as the razor-sharp ceramic edge pierced

Jonathan's abdomen.

Jonathan crumpled to his knees, blood spraying from the gash.

Then suddenly Ffion was flying through the air. She spun gracefully, with one leg outstretched, her foot connecting squarely with Henderson's jaw and sending him sprawling back against the wall. More priceless ceramics crashed to their ruin.

Jake was on him in seconds, pushing his face against the floor and cuffing his hands behind his back. 'You're under arrest, mate.'

But Bridget was only vaguely aware of his actions. She kneeled on the floor, pressing her hands to Jonathan's stomach, trying to stem the flow of blood. 'Call an ambulance!' she shouted. 'Someone call an ambulance!'

CHAPTER 33

A hospital corridor was never a relaxing place to wait. Bridget sat on the edge of her chair, desperate for news, her eyes following the progress of doctors, nurses, admin staff and patients up and down. She jerked in her seat every time a door crashed open or closed, or a distraught relative called out. Nothing in the hospital's emergency department ever happened quietly. In her hands she cradled a plastic cup of tea. The brown murky liquid was even less palatable than the disgusting gloop they served at the Kidlington canteen. She set it on the floor, cold and barely touched.

It had been hours since she'd last seen Jonathan. By the time the paramedics had arrived at Sotheby's, he'd lost so much blood he was starting to lose consciousness. Bridget had tried to bind the wound with her own jacket, but it had been too little to completely stop the bleeding. They'd loaded him onto a stretcher, hooked him up to an IV drip and, on arriving at the hospital, had whisked him straight into emergency surgery. Another stab victim to add to London's growing list of knife crime. Except this wound had been administered not in a knife attack between rival street gangs, but by a deranged mathematician wielding a splinter of antique Chinese porcelain.

Ben had been wrong about Gabriel's killing being drugs-related. But she took no comfort from being right. She would have given anything to have been wrong, and for Jonathan to be safe. Instead, he had been drawn right into the centre of events, and had paid the price with his own blood. A priceless vase had been transformed in an instant from an object of exquisite beauty to a deadly weapon.

Art and death, she mused. They seemed always to be so closely entwined.

She had phoned Chloe to let her know she was unharmed, knowing that the incident was certain to be reported on the news that evening. An Oxford professor wanted in a double murder enquiry had been arrested after disrupting an art auction, which had led to the destruction of millions of pounds of rare Ming dynasty china. It would be the main headline in all the news broadcasts, and front page in tomorrow's papers too. She dreaded to think what Grayson would have to say.

But at least Chloe had been relieved to hear from her, although shocked to learn about Jonathan.

'He'll be all right,' Bridget promised. 'I'm sure he will.'

She held herself responsible for the fact that Jonathan had been injured. If only she had called for back-up, or delegated the arrest to the Met, instead of trying to track down the killer single-handedly. It had been an unforgivable error of judgement. Jonathan had only tried to stop the professor because he cared about her. Her own stupid pride had led to him being stabbed.

She looked up as fresh footsteps approached. A young doctor stopped in the corridor before her. 'DI Hart?'

She leapt to her feet. 'How is he?'

'He's out of surgery and he's going to be fine. The wound was deep but it didn't damage any internal organs.'

'Oh, thank God for that.' Bridget felt almost faint with relief. 'Can I see him?'

'He's just coming round from the anaesthetic, but I can let you see him for a few minutes. After that he'll need to get some rest.'

'Thank you,' said Bridget. 'Thank you for everything you've done.'

'No problem.' The doctor remained a moment longer, still looking anxious. 'I must warn you though, he's still very weak. It may be some time before he'll be fit enough to be discharged.'

★

There was no need to break the speed limit on the drive back to Oxford. Jake drove carefully, still a little shaken after the violence that had unfolded. He only had Ffion with him in the car now. The boss had gone with Jonathan in the ambulance to the hospital. Officers from the Met had arrived to take Henderson away. The auction had been called off amid all the furore. They'd be on the national news this evening for sure.

The mood in the car was subdued after the high drama. Jake tried to break the ice. 'I hadn't realised that Bridget and Jonathan were an item,' he ventured.

'Hadn't you?'

'Well, I had my suspicions when she refused to consider him as a suspect. But...'

'I think they make a good couple.'

'Yeah. They do.'

The M40 motorway was busy with evening commuters returning home from work and Jake kept his eyes fixed on the road ahead. 'That was some kick-ass move you did there, knocking the professor over,' he said. 'I reckon you're the hero of this case, for sure.'

'Thanks.'

'Did you learn to do that in Taekwondo?'

'It's called a roundhouse kick,' said Ffion. A mile or two passed before she added, 'I can show you how it's done if you like.'

'Yeah, sure, why not?' said Jake. 'When?'

'I'm not doing anything tonight.'

Jake swallowed. Was Ffion asking him out on a date? He'd been waiting for an opportunity to ask her out for ages, but hadn't found the moment, or the courage. Now, it seemed, she had beaten him to it. A martial arts lesson wasn't exactly what he'd had in mind, but he was cool with that. 'I'd like that,' he said. 'Then maybe we could go for a drink after? Or grab a bite to eat?'

For a moment she stared out of the side window, her face turned away from him.

He wondered if he'd said the wrong thing. 'Of course, if you don't want to, that would be cool, I mean –'

'It's not that,' she said, turning back to face him. 'I would like to go out for a drink with you. But there's something you should know about me first.'

★

It seemed to Bridget that Vanessa had gone to even greater lengths than she normally did to produce the perfect Sunday lunch. The smell of roast beef emanating from the kitchen was delicious.

'She's killed the fatted calf for you,' joked James, unscrewing the top off a bottle of Shiraz and pouring her a generous glass. 'When she heard about the attack at Sotheby's she was beside herself with worry.'

'It wasn't me she should have been concerned about,' said Bridget. 'It was Jonathan. But I visited him last night and he's making a good recovery.'

'When do they think he'll be able to leave the hospital?'

'Probably in a few days. The gash to his abdomen was quite deep, and he lost a lot of blood. I was really worried about him at first.'

'I was worried about you too, Mum,' said Chloe.

'I know, I'm sorry, sweetheart,' said Bridget, putting her arm around her daughter. The dramatic events in London had produced a miraculous reconciliation in their relationship.

'You were right all along, Mum,' Chloe had told her after Bridget had explained everything that happened. 'Dad was wrong.'

It wasn't as simple as that, Bridget knew. Ben was determined to be involved in Chloe's life now, and Bridget would have to learn to share her daughter. But they would find an amicable way to do it – one that didn't involve angry words and slammed doors.

'The important thing,' said James, 'is that you and Jonathan are safe, the criminals are all behind bars, and justice has been done.'

If only it was that straightforward, mused Bridget. It was true that she'd solved the case and caught the killer, but she had made mistakes along the way that would haunt her for a long time. Grayson had been quick to bring them to her attention.

'You should never have gone to London yourself,' he had reprimanded her. 'The Met were far better placed to make the arrest, and they would no doubt have carried out their duty with a lot less fuss.' He held up a newspaper that carried a particularly lurid article, including a photograph of a Chinese vase with a red line crossed through it. *Smashing Arrest!* read the headline above. 'I hope that Sotheby's have good insurance. More to the point, you might have been killed. Then I'd have been without one of my best detectives.'

That was as much praise as she was ever going to get from the Chief Super. She had mumbled an apology and been dismissed from his office.

'Moreover,' continued James, 'the bad guys got their due. I heard that Taylor Financial Technology has gone into administration, and that Lawrence Taylor has applied for bankruptcy. There's also a rumour that he's left his wife.'

'Yes, that's true,' said Bridget. Melissa Price hadn't chosen her husbands well. The first was now in custody, charged with murder; the second was ruined. And Melissa herself was likely to lose her job and her reputation too. Bridget had heard better news about Amber Morgan. The young woman had been discharged from hospital and was living with Harriet Watson on the *Dragonfly* while she got herself back together. Bridget hoped she would keep herself clean from drugs in future.

Vanessa appeared then from the kitchen and instructed everyone that lunch was ready to be served. As they made their way through to the dining room, she pulled Bridget aside and threw a sisterly arm around her shoulder.

'Jonathan must really care about you,' she said in a low voice, 'if he's prepared to forgive you after all the trouble you've caused him.'

Yes, thought Bridget. Maybe he does. But she wasn't going to let Vanessa get away with this half-disguised rebuke. 'Jonathan doesn't have anything to forgive,' she said. 'I didn't ask him to come searching for me backstage at the auction house. He did it because he wanted to, because he was worried about me.'

Vanessa sighed. 'Well, yes, I suppose so.'

'And you should have seen him. He was fearless. A real hero.'

Vanessa always had to have the final word. 'That's what I thought myself. You're so lucky I introduced you to him. In fact – have I mentioned this before? – you're incredibly fortunate to have me as your sister.'

They were still laughing together when they took their seats at the dining table.

DO NO EVIL (BRIDGET HART #3)

Old friendships. Dark secrets. Deadly lies.

When Detective Inspector Bridget Hart returns to her old Oxford college for a reunion dinner, she's hoping for a fun weekend catching up with old friends. But the reunion takes a macabre turn when body parts are served up at the college feast, and one of her friends is found murdered.

With Bridget's arch rival Inspector Baxter leading the murder enquiry, and herself a potential suspect, Bridget is forbidden from taking part in the investigation. But that doesn't stop her from carrying out her own private enquiries.

Bridget soon realises that the murderer is someone known to her. And as the weekend continues and more bodies are found, it becomes clear that they will stop at nothing to get what they want. Can Bridget uncover the dark secrets of the past in time to halt the killing, or will she be next on the murderer's list?

Set amongst the dreaming spires of Oxford University, the Bridget Hart series is perfect for fans of Elly Griffiths, JR Ellis, Faith Martin and classic British murder mysteries.

 Scan the QR code to see a list of retailers.

THANK YOU FOR READING

We hope you enjoyed this book. If you did, then we would be very grateful if you would please take a moment to leave a review online. Thank you.

BOOKS IN THE
BRIDGET HART SERIES:

Aspire to Die (978-1-914537-00-4)
Killing by Numbers (978-1-914537-02-8)
Do No Evil (978-1-914537-04-2)
In Love and Murder (978-1-914537-06-6)
A Darkly Shining Star (978-1-914537-08-0)
Preface to Murder (978-1-914537-10-3)
Toll for the Dead - Due Oct 2021

PSYCHOLOGICAL THRILLERS

The Red Room

ABOUT THE AUTHOR

M S Morris is the pseudonym for the writing partnership of Margarita and Steve Morris. They both studied at Oxford University, where they first met in 1990. Together they write psychological thrillers and crime novels. They are married and live in Oxfordshire.

Find out more at msmorrisbooks.com where you can join our mailing list.

Made in the USA
Las Vegas, NV
29 June 2023

74020240R00177